MARSHAL OF MEDICINE LODGE

OTHER NOVELS BY STAN LYNDE*

The Bodacious Kid
Careless Creek
Vigilante Moon
Saving Miss Julie

*Also available as audiobooks, from
Books In Motion
9922 E. Montgomery Suite 31
Spokane, WA 99206
Tel: 1-800-752-3199
www.booksinmotion.com

MARSHAL OF MEDICINE LODGE

A Merlin Fanshaw Western

Stan Lynde

iUniverse, Inc.
New York Lincoln Shanghai

MARSHAL OF MEDICINE LODGE
A Merlin Fanshaw Western

Copyright © 2005 by Stan Lynde

iUniverse books may be ordered through booksellers or by contacting:

iUniverse
2021 Pine Lake Road, Suite 100
Lincoln, NE 68512
www.iuniverse.com
1-800-Authors (1-800-288-4677)

Cover painting, *A Portrait of a Young Cowboy*, by Carolyn Anderson
Image courtesy of Bill and Bobby Spilker and the Montana Historical Society

ISBN: 0-595-33666-3 (pbk)
ISBN: 0-595-66987-5 (cloth)

Printed in the United States of America

To the Crow Indian people—

Past, Present, and Future

CHAPTER 1

───────── ▼ ─────────

By the time the big thaw hit Dry Creek, Montana, in April of 1886, I had enjoyed about all the peace and quiet I could stand. U.S. Marshal Chance Ridgeway had made me one of his deputies the previous summer, but he'd asked me to spend the winter helping Glenn Murdoch, the county undersheriff, keep the peace in my hometown. We must have done a good job. Dry Creek was so peaceful that winter, it was all a man could do to keep from falling asleep on the job.

Glenn and me played cribbage a good deal, and I swept the office and cleaned up the jail. I split wood for the stove, fetched meals for the infrequent prisoner, and helped Glenn make his rounds at night. We would rattle door handles on the shops along Main Street and check the alleys for lurking desperadoes, but all we ever turned up was an occasional drunk or alley cat. It was nobody's fault, but my time with Glenn that winter was about as exciting as watching paint dry.

Most of the winter was open and mild. Too mild, the cattlemen said, for the range was seriously overstocked and the plains were as dry as a Methodist picnic. Then, along about the middle of March, the snow commenced to fall and the bottom dropped out of the thermometer. Now I said the snow began to fall, but that's not entirely accurate. What it did was blow in horizontal-like out of the north, piling up against the sides of buildings and drifting to ten feet or so in the coulees.

Water holes froze and snowed over. Cattle moved out ahead of the storms, and cowpunchers took to living in their saddles as they tried to turn the critters back toward their home range. Freight wagons bogged down. Merchandise bound for the shops and stores didn't arrive. People worried about running out of wood for their stoves. Folks turned cranky and stopped talking to each other. Everybody was tired of winter.

The night before the big thaw came, I helped Glenn make his rounds as usual, even though we expected neither solid citizens nor evildoers to be out in such weather. We floundered around, stumbling through the drifts, while the wind lashed at our faces and the cold put a hurt on fingers, ears, and toes. I could almost always make Glenn laugh, but when I faced into the storm and hollered, "That's enough, durn you! Where was your cold wind last August?" he never even smiled.

Afterward, I warmed up some at the potbellied stove in the office before heading back to my room at the boarding house. When I stepped outside, I was surprised to find the wind had quit. For a second there, I almost thought Old Man Winter had knuckled under to my scolding. Even so, the night was plenty cold. The muddy ruts of Main Street were froze hard as iron where the wind had blown them clear. Stars spangled the sky, and the night was so still I could hear Johnson's dog barking two miles west of town.

When I reached the boarding house, I swept the snow off my clothes and pulled off my boots. The house was quiet and dark, with only the parlor lamp burning low. I cat-footed down the hall to my room, closed the door behind me, and slid between the soogans. I was asleep almost as soon as my head hit the pillow.

Next morning, when I woke up and looked out the window it was a whole different world. Water dripped off the roofs and spattered onto the boardwalks. The street was bare and muddy where snow had lain the night before. Puddles reflected the red skies of sunrise. Sometime after midnight, a chinook wind had blown in and thawed out the valley. It had sighed down the eastern slopes of the Rockies, melting the crusted snow, and it had broke Dad Winter's grip on the land.

When I sat down at the boarding house table that morning, there was conversation and laughter aplenty in the dining room. The widow Blair had cooked up a platter of griddlecakes, eggs, and deer sausage, and her boarders were doing their best to show their appreciation. Bucky Peterson, printer's devil at the *Dry Creek Democrat*, was flirting with Miss Ames, the new schoolmarm, forking in grub all the while.

Doc Taggart was recovering from a mild case of snow-blindness, and he looked like a nearsighted gopher as he squinted against the morning light and sipped his coffee. Old man Jackson had his napkin tied around his scrawny neck and was wolfing down griddlecakes. And Lucy McNabb, who clerked at the dry goods store, giggled like a schoolgirl at the jokes of Ben Feeney, express man for the stage line. We sure were one big happy family that morning, and all because of a change in the weather.

Ben Feeney grinned at me as I sat down next to Doc. "Look who's here, folks," he said. "It's Merlin Fanshaw, deputy U.S. marshal and Progress County's champion eater. If he didn't oversleep once in a while, we'd all starve."

I considered taking offense, but Ben was just feeling frisky. Besides, he handed me the platter of griddlecakes as he made his remark and I was too hungry at the moment to argue.

"My stars, ain't that the truth," said Lucy. "I never seen anybody eat so much or show it so little. I swan, you're thin as a rail, Merlin!"

Doc Taggart put down his coffee and squinted at me. "Merlin has the metabolism of a hummingbird," he said. "He doesn't stand still long enough to gain weight."

I grinned back. "It's Miz Blair's fault," I said, "I don't expect I'd eat so much if she wasn't such a fine cook."

It was the widow's turn to enter the jesting. "I'm glad you appreciate me," she said, "but there isn't much profit in cooking for you. Perhaps I should raise my rates."

I swallowed a mouthful of griddlecake. "You'd just drive me to bankruptcy," I told her. "I couldn't resist your cooking at any price."

I can't deny it. I have always liked to eat. And it is true that I never seem to put on weight. I don't know if what Doc Taggart said about metabolism is true or not, but it is a fact that I have weighed an even one-thirty since I was sixteen and nothing I do seems to change it.

Doc was watching me eat like I was some kind of medical exhibit. "How do you stay so slim, Merlin?" he asked.

I didn't answer him right away. My ma taught me it wasn't polite to talk with my mouth full. I took a sip of coffee, and shrugged. "Durned if I know," I told him. "I've always been snipe-gutted and lean. I never hankered to be otherwise. I'm five foot ten, though I wish I was taller, my hair is brown, and my eyes are blue. I've got freckles on my nose and cheekbones, and the more I go out in the sun the more of them I get. I'm not a female, I'm not a fat man, and I'm not a bull elk, nor a lizard. I'm just me, Merlin Fanshaw, like the Lord God made me, and I try not to worry about it. Besides, you're the medical man. You tell me."

Doc Taggart finished his coffee and placed the cup carefully in its saucer. "*Cogito, ergo sum,*" he said soberly. "I think, therefore I am."

Leave it to a durn doctor to get in the last word.

A person could sense a whole new attitude around Dry Creek that week. Folks who had been close-mouthed and surly began to talk to each other again. Neighbors greeted one another with a smile. People told jokes. Some people even laughed. It wasn't so much that winter was over. This was Montana, after all, and everybody knew there could still be snow and cold weather aplenty, no matter what the calendar might say. But they also knew Dad Winter's time was nearly up. He might fuss and grumble some, but his days were numbered. Spring was coming, and everybody knew it.

Lukas Bierstadt announced that his daughter, Betty Lou, was getting married to George Fielding's youngest son, Jack. He said Betty Lou had asked him for a formal wedding, but he had told her no; he didn't have a white shotgun. Instead, he said she could have a sooner-the-better wedding, and he would host a dance for her over at the schoolhouse a week from Friday. Lukas hired a three-piece band—fiddle, guitar, and banjo—and put an ad in the *Democrat* inviting the entire community.

I asked my sometime lady friend, Pandora Pretty Hawk, if she'd like to trip the light fantastic with me, but she said she'd rather go to the dance. I told her that would be fine, and seeing as the dance was free and I was making good money as a full-time deputy I would also spring for a steak dinner that evening over at Ignacio's Café. Pandora kissed me on the mouth and scampered off to make herself a dress or something.

During the week that followed I gave the jail and marshal's office a thorough cleaning. I scrubbed the floors and cleaned the windows. I even whitewashed the inside walls of the cells. The front door had got out of true during the winter, so Glenn and me oiled its hinges and rehung it. Then Glenn decided nothing would do but that he paint the door a sort of cucumber green, so while he was doing that I looked in on my horses over at the livery.

Rutherford had wintered well. He nickered when I approached the corral, and when he came over to me I gave him a handful of oats from my coat pocket. The little buckskin was shaggy with winter hair, and he had cockleburs in his mane and tail. I slipped a halter on him and tied him to a corral pole. "You look a fright," I told him. "I reckon you need a beauty treatment." Then I spent the next hour with currycomb and brush, grooming him until he shone like a new penny. I combed the burrs out of his mane and trimmed his tail back even with his hocks. Then it was time to look to his feet.

I took my time shoeing the buckskin, talking to him all the while. I had not had much chance to ride him during the past few months, and I told him I was sorry I hadn't looked in on him more often. Horses are sociable; they like it when a feller talks to them. They're good listeners, and they seldom interrupt. I told him I'd come back the next day to ride him. I said we would go out and look the country over. Come the next day, that's just what we did.

The following Thursday, the day before the dance, I was sitting in Glenn's swivel chair at the office with my feet propped up on the desk. I was reading an old copy of *The Police Gazette* when Percy Purcell, the telegraph operator, came in.

"Are you still reading that magazine?" he asked. "I saw that issue in this office a year ago."

"Ain't still reading it," I said. "Reading it again. Some of these stories get better over time."

Percy handed me a folded telegram. "Well, here's something new for you to read," he said. "I don't mean to spoil the suspense, but it's from your boss."

My feet hit the floor. "From Marshal Ridgeway?"

Percy took the pot from the stove and poured himself a cup of coffee. "Last I looked," he said.

Ridgeway's message was short and to the point. "Have assignment for you. Meet me my office three P.M. Friday."

Percy sipped his coffee and tried to read my expression. "Well?" he said. "Good news or bad?"

"You already know what it says. As to whether it's good news or not, I guess that all depends on how a feller looks at it."

"Well, how do you look at it?"

I stood up and read the telegram again. "Getting an assignment is good news. Having to tell Pandora I can't take her to the dance tomorrow night is the bad news."

Ridgeway's office was in Silver City, some twenty-odd miles from Dry Creek. I figured I could ride Rutherford and be there with time to spare if I left town by eight-thirty in the morning. The little buckskin had not been hardened to the trail after the winter, but I had been feeding him oats over the past several days and I knew he could make the trip all right. I would set an easy pace and graze him some as we traveled.

Ridgeway hadn't said so in his telegram, but I figured there was a good chance I'd be sent out on whatever assignment he had for me directly from Silver City.

My bay horse was an older animal, but he, too, had wintered well. I would pack my bed on him and lead him. I still didn't know what Ridgeway had in mind, but I wanted to be ready for anything.

Pandora took the news pretty well, considering. She was helping the widow Blair with her spring-cleaning when I rode up to the boarding house, and her face lit up like Sunday morning when she saw me. I never have known how to tell a woman bad news, so I just reined up at the gate and set there on Rutherford. Somehow, doing that seemed to tip my hand. Pandora came to the gate and looked up at me; her eyes lost their shine and went flat. Her smile faded and her expression turned serious.

"What is it, Merlin?" she asked.

"Well, Pandora," I said, "I sure do hate to disappoint you, but something has come up."

Her voice went as flat as her eyes. "You aren't going to take me to the dance," she said. It was not a question.

"Well, it's not that I don't want to," I said. "There's nothing I'd rather do. But I got a telegram from Marshal Ridgeway this morning. He wants me in Silver City tomorrow."

Pandora pulled her shawl more tightly about her shoulders and sort of hugged herself like she was cold. "I am disappointed," she said, "but I do understand. It's all right."

I wanted to get down and take her in my arms, but I didn't. I just set there on Rutherford and felt awkward. "I really do feel bad, honey," I said. "I know you were lookin' forward to the dance."

"Oh," she said, "I'll still be going. I just won't be going with you."

"Uh—you're going?"

"Yes. Johnny Peters asked yesterday if he could take me. I told him I was going with you. But now—"

"Johnny Peters! Little Johnny Peters? The kid that used to pick his nose when we were in school?"

"He doesn't do that anymore. And he's not 'little' anymore, either. He's a bit taller than you, actually."

"Well—I reckon we all grow up, but Johnny Peters! I mean—"

"Merlin!" she said. "You're jealous!"

"No, I'm not either," I lied. "It's just that—well, it sure didn't take you long to find somebody else to go with, did it?"

Pandora's voice was soft. "Let's not misunderstand each other on purpose," she said. "I'll see you when you get back from Silver City." Then she turned and walked away, toward the back stairs of the rooming house.

When Pandora went inside, the sun went behind a cloud and the day turned cold and gloomy. It stayed like that for quite awhile.

Friday morning broke clear and bright, with just enough bite to the air so you knew the season of spring was not yet a cinch bet. Ice had formed on the pools and puddles, and I could see my breath as I walked on down to Walt's Livery.

Twenty minutes later I had packed my bedroll on the bay and had saddled Rutherford. The buckskin must have been half asleep as I led him out onto the street. He spooked when he stepped on an icy patch, breaking through with a sound like a pistol shot. He did a nervous little quickstep, rolled his eyes, and looked so embarrassed I had to laugh aloud. I slid my Winchester into its scabbard, swung up into the saddle, and struck out on the road to Silver City. It was twenty minutes past two in the afternoon when I reached the outskirts of town. Minutes later, I left my horses with the hostler at the Blue Dog Livery and walked west up Plata Street to the old part of town. Silver City had begun its life as a hell-for-leather mining camp. Like most such places, it had started out haphazard and careless.

In the beginning, tents and cabins were scattered every which way along the winding gulch that was to become its main street, but as the town grew, the settlement had taken on a more orderly air. Developers surveyed the camp, laid out streets and city blocks, and replaced the ramshackle with the solid and pretentious.

Town lots of that day tended to be narrow but deep, no more than 20 or 30 feet wide in some cases but extending back at right angles to the street for 120 feet or more. Buildings stood cheek by jowl with one another, facing the street with highfalutin' facades and sharing walls with their neighbors.

Before the ore played out and the boom at Silver City ended, mining men had built some grand buildings there. In one of these, above the post office, U.S. Marshal Chance Ridgeway had his headquarters. When I came to the doorway that led to his office, I turned in off the street, climbed the creaky stairs to the second floor, and opened the door.

The big room at the top of the stairs was as just as I remembered it, and yet somehow not quite. Against the north wall, U.S. Marshal Chance Ridgeway sat behind his cluttered desk, his silver hair shining in the light. I took out my pa's old pocket watch and snapped open its cover. I looked at the marshal and grinned.

"Sorry I'm early, Marshal," I said. "According to my timepiece I'm not due here for another minute and a half."

Ridgeway ignored my jest. I heard his swivel chair creak as he stood up to greet me. "I admire a man who's timely," he said. "It's good to see you, son." He offered his hand and I took it. His faded blue eyes met my own. "Pull up a chair," he said, "and set yourself."

An old barrel-back saloon chair stood nearby, and I pulled it over to the desk and eased into it. As I glanced about the room, it seemed at first little changed since my last visit. The rusted old stove still stood at its center, squat and solid on stubby iron legs. Navajo rugs in black, red, and white designs lay atop the oiled wood of the floor. High on the south wall a dusty mounted pronghorn head looked down its nose through glassy eyes. Bookshelves and file cabinets stood against the wall behind Ridgeway, beneath a flyspecked map of Montana Territory and a furled American flag. Even so, there was something about the room that seemed different to me.

As my eyes grew accustomed to the light, I began to notice the changes. A second desk and chair that had once occupied the far side of the room were missing. I noticed unfaded squares on the walls where pictures had hung. All at once, in the shadows, I saw packing crates and boxes filled with papers, files, and law books.

Before I could ask it, Ridgeway answered my question. "Moving," he said. "I'll be shifting my headquarters to the capital at Helena this month. I've taken offices on the second floor of the Goodkind block." He took in the room and its contents with a sweep of his hand. "Freighters will be in to pack all this plunder later this week."

From a coat pocket, Ridgeway produced the curved briar he favored and filled it from a leather pouch. He took his time tamping the bowl, glancing at me now and then from beneath his eyebrows. I waited, knowing the old lawman would not be hurried and that he would get around to the point of our meeting when he chose. Finally satisfied with all his preparations, he popped a match alight with his thumbnail, held the flame over the briar's bowl, and puffed away like a locomotive building up steam.

Finally, when he had the pipe burning to his satisfaction, Ridgeway leaned back in his chair and studied me again. Blue smoke hung in layers above us, swirling in the afternoon light. The marshal picked up a folded paper from his desktop, unfolded it, and studied it for a moment. Then he folded it again and put it aside.

He looked at me and asked, "How much do you know about the Crow Indians?"

His question caught me off guard. I guess I had expected him to ask about Glenn Murdoch or how things were in Dry Creek, or even how I'd been since I saw him last, but he had not.

"Well," said I, "I know your deputy, Luther Little Wolf, although I haven't seen him for awhile. My lady friend at Dry Creek, Pandora Pretty Hawk, is Crow Indian on her mama's side. And I met that Crow medicine man, Bear Singer, and his missus last year. I guess that's about the size of it, Marshal."

"Meaning no offense, son," Ridgeway drawled, "but that ain't a whole hell of a lot, is it?"

"No, sir."

"Well, then, allow me to enlighten you some. The Crow tribe live in what they believe is the best place on earth. They believe their country was given to them by First Maker, who created the world and then divided it up between all the people. The Crow say their land is neither too hot in summer nor too cold in winter, but is always pretty much perfect when it comes to climate. It has high mountains, including all or parts of the Bighorn, Pryor, and Beartooth ranges.

"The Crow brag on their clean, clear rivers and lakes, abundant wildlife, and rich grasslands. They say First Maker gave them their country so he could test their courage, and that he surrounded them with powerful enemies to make them strong.

"The Crow sided early with the white man, welcoming the fur trappers and serving as scouts and allies against their old foes, the Sioux and Cheyenne, right up to and beyond the Battle of the Little Bighorn. Guess they figured the enemy of their enemies was their friend.

"Anyway, they held on to their traditional land pretty well—at least until their paleface friends decided they wanted it. Ranchers, farmers, and drifters have moved onto Crow land by hook or by crook, and the Indians ain't all that happy about it, to say the least.

"Their traditional country has become a reservation now, and even though it has been whittled down some over the years, it still takes in a good deal of the southeast corner of Montana right down to the Wyoming line.

"There's a few white settlements there, including Fort Custer on the Bighorn River, a trading post or two, a couple of missionaries, and the town of Medicine Lodge some twenty miles south of the new Crow Agency. There are two big cow outfits in the area and a couple of small ranches, all trespassing on tribal land. There are a dozen or so farmers along Medicine Lodge Creek, and they're trespassing, too. The Crow are on short rations, and hungry. Every now and then, they steal a steer or two from the cowmen. The cowmen strike back, and steal the Crows' horses. Once in a while, somebody gets shot. Even so, it is a marvel to me the situation ain't a whole lot worse. Considering that red men and white don't understand each other at all, they have mostly got along well down on the Crow. Until just lately."

Ridgeway's pipe had gone out. He broke off his account to stir up the tobacco in its bowl and relight it. When he had the briar burning well again, he seemed to be trying to recall where he'd left off in his story, but I wasn't fooled. Chance Ridgeway may have been pushing sixty, but there was nothing wrong with his memory. I figured he was testing me.

He looked confused. He scratched his head. "Let's see now," he said. "Where was I?"

"'Until just lately.'"

"Oh, yes. Well, sir—Medicine Lodge fancies itself a real up-to-date town. It has a bank, a mayor, a town council, and everything. The council hired an old-time lawman name of Dan Wingate as city marshal. Dan was nearly eighty years old and half blind, but he'd been a good officer in his younger days. Like I said, the reservation was fairly peaceable at the time, and nobody saw much need for a town tamer—or the money they'd have to pay one. They gave old Dan a stipend and a warm place by the stove, and he took on the job of keeping the peace.

"Then about a month ago, things changed. A young renegade name of Archie Young Bull embarked on a career of outlawry and general mischief in and around Medicine Lodge. Archie heads up a gang of ne'er-do-wells like himself, and they began to accost citizens, break into houses and stores, and steal pretty much whatever they could lay their hands on. Old Dan tried to arrest them, but Archie's boys jumped him in an alley and nearly beat him to death. Broke his nose and his jaw, and fractured three of his ribs. One of the ribs punctured his lung. Doc Westby, of Medicine Lodge, worked most of the night to save his life."

"What happened to Archie and his gang?"

"Nothing. After seeing what befell their marshal, none of the town's upstanding citizens wanted to be next. Archie took Dan's gun and badge, and set the marshal's office ablaze. The building is made of stone, so it didn't burn, but the fire made quite a mess of the interior."

For a moment, Ridgeway was silent. He seemed lost in thought as he looked off into the distance. At length, he turned back to me.

"One of the councilmen said he'd heard about a deputy from down in Cheyenne—a former soldier name of Jefferson Brown—who was looking for work. The town council still didn't want to pay much, but the beating of old Dan, and the fire, spooked them. The city fathers held a powwow, put a little more money in the pot, and sent Brown a telegram. Jeff accepted their offer. He rode north and took over a month ago as marshal of Medicine Lodge."

Ridgeway's pipe had gone cold again. This time he tapped the ashes out in the palm of his hand, dumped them into the wastebasket, and put the briar in his pocket. When next he spoke, his voice had a determined ring to it.

"Now it is my hope that City Marshal Brown will put an end to Archie Young Bull's mischief and restore peace and order to Medicine Lodge. The last thing this territory needs is Indian trouble, or a bunch of nervous settlers demanding protection by the Army. As United States Marshal for the territory, I figure to send Jeff a little help."

Ridgeway fell silent again. I could hear the ticking of the Regulator clock on the wall behind me. The steady buzz of a housefly seemed loud in the stillness. Ridgeway swung his chair about and looked at me.

"I figure to send him you," he said.

CHAPTER 2

▼

Ridgeway leaned back in his swivel chair, his fingers laced across his vest. He was waiting for my answer, but of course he already knew what it would be. "I'm curious, Marshal," I said. "Why didn't you give this job to Luther Little Wolf? He's been your deputy longer than I have, he's a full-blooded Crow Indian, and he speaks the language."

The marshal straightened. "Luther is on assignment over in the Missouri Breaks country, tracking rustlers and whiskey runners out of Canada. You have my full confidence, son."

"One more question. I thought the Indian police enforced the law on the reservation."

"They do, mostly. But the town of Medicine Lodge is a special case. The Crows don't want towns, or settlers, on their land. But some of those big cowmen I told you about have friends in high places. In spite of the Crows' objections—and the treaties and agreements our government has made with the tribe—they managed to get the township approved.

"Medicine Lodge has been set aside from tribal authority by special decree. The town makes its own laws. Indian police have no jurisdiction inside the city limits."

Ridgeway looked thoughtful. "There is one more thing," he said. "On the reservation, the Indian agent is pretty much absolute ruler. He answers only to the commissioner of Indian Affairs in Washington, who answers only to the secretary of the Interior, who answers only to the president.

"The agent oversees the Indian Police Force, the Court of Indian Offenses, and the Tribal Council. That means one man makes the laws, enforces the laws, and judges the lawbreakers. Sometimes he even arrests and punishes Indians without holding trials.

"Some Indian agents are good men," Ridgeway continued, "honest, and dedicated to helping the Indian people. Others are damned scoundrels who have finagled the appointment so they can enrich themselves at the Indians' expense. Most, I suspect, are bureaucrats who fall somewhere between those two extremes. For some reason, they all seem to take the title of 'major,' whether they've been anywhere near an army post or not.

"The agent at the Crow Agency is 'Major' Malachi Weede. I've let him know you're being assigned to Medicine Lodge on my orders. I expect you should pay him a courtesy call on your way through, but don't let him buffalo you. You answer only to me."

I shoved my chair back and got to my feet. "All right," I said. "When do I leave?"

Ridgeway stood up and came around from behind his desk. He grinned, and his face became a riot of wrinkles. "Why, I suppose right after I buy you dinner down at the Early Bird Café," he said. "You do still eat dinner, don't you?"

My own grin matched Ridgeway's, but without the wrinkles. "Oh, yes," I told him. "I still eat dinner."

Over chicken and dumplings and apple pie, Ridgeway filled in the details of my travel. I was to put my horses on the evening train out of Silver City and ride the rails as far as Junction, where the Bighorn River meets the Yellowstone. From there, I was to ride south, ford the river at Fort Custer, and continue up the Little Bighorn valley to the new agency, and then to Medicine Lodge.

"You can telegraph me when you get there," Ridgeway said. "Marshal Brown is expecting you."

"How will I know him?"

My question seemed to strike Ridgeway as humorous. The marshal chuckled, and there was a twinkle in his faded blue eyes. "Oh, I wouldn't worry about that," he drawled. "I expect you'll know him, all right."

At the depot, the flagman helped me load Rutherford and the packhorse into a stock car and invited me to ride the caboose with the crew.

"There ain't but me, a couple of snipes, and a pusher ridin' this evenin'," he said. "There was a snake, but he got bumped by the pusher's whiskers."

I told him I was much obliged, but I had no idea what he was talking about. "I mostly speak English," I said, "but it seems you mostly speak railroad."

The flagman laughed. "Sorry, Deputy," he said. "What I said was there was only me, a couple of section hands, and a team leader in the caboose. I said a switchman was going to ride with us, but he got displaced on account of the team leader's seniority."

I grinned. "Much obliged, pardner," I said. "That makes it a little more clear. Any of you boys play cribbage?"

The flagman introduced me to the others and we shook hands all around. Then he dug up a crib board and a dog-eared deck of cards, and we commenced to pass the time at a penny a point. Those pasteboards had seen better days. They had been used so much they were hard to read, and so limp they were durn near impossible to shuffle. A feller might better have tossed those cards with a salad fork, but we didn't have one of those. Anyway, we played as we traveled. I still lost more games than I won, but I didn't do near as bad as I had with Glenn back in Dry Creek.

The train pulled into Junction City right at sundown. Cottonwood trees stood black against the last light as I unloaded Rutherford and the bay. I had grown used to skimpy towns with grand names by that time, but Junction City took the cake. There were two or three weathered buildings still standing, and some jumbled piles of burned timbers and planks here and there, but little else. The late light reflected off the river, and a pair of sandhill cranes took flight from the muddy bank, but that was about all there was to see at Junction.

"There used to be quite a town here," the flagman said. "A merchant name of Basinki opened a general store over there near the ferry landing back in seventy-seven. River steamers were still coming up the Yellowstone then, bringing supplies from down river. Within a year or two, there was a fair-sized settlement here.

"But sometime in eighty-three a fire broke out in a saloon and burned up most of the town. Riverboats stopped coming when the Northern Pacific came through. There are a few freight haulers that still pick up supplies here, and North Western Express runs a stage line from across the river at Custer station some ninety miles south to Rock Creek, Wyoming. But I don't figure the town's ever coming back."

"I won't be here long, anyway," I said. "I'm heading south come morning." Just then the train whistle's hollow snort broke up our powwow.

"No rest for the weary," the flagman said. "Time to go back to work."

"I'm obliged for your help," I said, "and for the card game. Why don't you take that money I lost and buy yourself a new deck?"

The flagman laughed, turning away toward the train. "Couldn't do that, Deputy," he said. "I don't have time to mark a new deck."

I still don't know if he was joking or not.

The light was nearly gone by the time I led the horses to a grassy knoll away from the river and staked them out. Below, in one of Junction City's few remaining buildings, lamplight glowed yellow in a window. From somewhere down there, a dog barked. Far away, down the track, I could hear the lonesome wail of the train's whistle.

I made myself a meal of beef jerky and water before I unrolled my bed and slipped into it. I lay on my back and looked at the stars for a while, thinking about all that Ridgeway had told me. I wondered what kind of man Marshal Jeff Brown might be, and I hoped he was up to the job of keeping the peace in Medicine Lodge. More to the point, I hoped I was up to the job.

And then I thought of Pandora. I recalled her face, the cheekbones high and touched with color, her large, dark eyes shining and warm when she looked at me. Then I remembered how she had looked when I told her I couldn't take her to the dance. She would go then, she said, with Johnny Peters. With Johnny Peters! Well, if that's the way she was going to be, she could just go with that durn nose picker! I surely didn't care.

I was still telling myself that when I finally drifted off to sleep.

Dawn came gray and overcast. A cold wind blew in across the river, making it hard to get up and face the day. I allowed myself five more minutes in the warmth of my blankets, but wound up taking nearly ten. Finally, I stood up, put my hat on, and pulled on my britches. I couldn't keep my teeth from chattering. My boots were stiff, and cold as ice. Just getting up and dressed that morning was the hardest thing I would do all day.

By the time I saddled Rutherford and packed my roll, I was feeling some better. However, the wind had picked up and building a cook fire was out of the question. I'd have given five dollars for a cup of hot coffee, but I was shaking so bad I would probably have spilled it.

The ferryman came out of one of the buildings as I walked down to the landing. I told him "howdy" and paid him to take me, and my horses, across. He ignored my greeting but took my money. Minutes later, I was on the other side and headed south. The wind had risen, blowing cold and even harder than before. I pulled up the collar of my coat and set out on the stage road. I was glad the wind was at my back.

I rode out at a rapid clip, holding Rutherford and the packhorse to a trot. An hour later, sunlight broke through the overcast and lit up the Pine Ridge Mountains to the west. The road followed the Bighorn River south, its waters muddy and its banks marked here and there by stands of willow, ash, and cottonwood. I gave the horses a twenty-minute break at noon, ate the last of my jerky, and pushed on.

There were no other travelers on the road that day. Deep ruts in the gumbo testified to the recent passage of freight wagons and a stagecoach, but I saw neither. At about three o'clock I spied a band of more than forty pronghorns, grazing on good grass beyond the river. They watched my approach for a time, and then, as if at some common signal, they all moved out at an easy lope.

I reached Fort Custer just after sundown. The fort stood upon a windswept plain atop steep bluffs overlooking the junction of the Bighorn and Little Bighorn rivers. It had been built the year after Custer's Seventh Cavalry got whipped just twelve miles away by the Sioux and Cheyenne. I don't know why the government chose that place to build a fort. Shortly after the battle, all the Indians went to reservations. There wasn't a whole lot for the army to do except drill and hold parades.

I showed my papers to the duty officer, and he allowed I could spend the night, if I was so inclined. I put up my horses at the stables, spread my blankets with the troopers at their barracks, and accepted an invite to supper. I had heard many a tale of poor and even dangerous army food, but on that night, I was pleasantly surprised. The grub was roast beef with potatoes and gravy, and no man could have asked for better. I went back for seconds—just to be polite, you understand—but drew the line at thirds. I figured I should set an example and try to show at least a little self-restraint.

Afterward, the troopers asked me about life as a deputy U.S. marshal, and I told them some tales, a few of them true. Then the bugler blew taps, the duty sergeant put out the lamps, and I fell asleep like a milk-fed pup.

The next morning I was back on the road before noon, moving up the valley of the Little Bighorn. By two o'clock I had reached the Crow Agency. The settlement turned out to be a scatter of government buildings, cabins, frame houses, and tents accommodating everything from offices and shops to barns and stores. Tepees stood farther out, stark white in the sunshine. A pair of Indian boys, maybe ten or twelve years old, rode herd on a score of pinto horses down near the river as I passed. I greeted the youngsters with a smile and a "good mornin'," but they only watched me, their dark eyes serious and guarded.

I found the Indian agent not at his office, but at his residence. The house was a substantial, two-story dwelling that boasted two stone fireplaces, fresh white paint, and a broad, roomy porch. A heavyset Indian man, wearing a badge and a belted Colt's revolver, walked out to meet me as I rode up.

"Merlin Fanshaw, deputy U.S. marshal," I said, pointing at my own badge. "I'm here to see Major Weede."

The Indian policeman studied me a moment, and then turned and went inside. A moment later, the agent appeared. Major Malachi Weede turned out to be an albino, or mighty close to it. He was dough-faced and clean-shaven, fat as a boar hog, with milky skin and strange pink eyes like a rabbit's. He invited me inside and offered me a chair near the fireplace.

Weede's sitting room was heavily furnished in the Victorian manner, with overstuffed parlor chairs and a sofa, a mirrored hall tree, bookshelves, tapestries and plant stands, and various Indian-made decorations.

"Marshal Ridgeway wrote me a week ago," the agent said. "He told me he'd be sending a deputy. I understand you'll be assisting City Marshal Brown at Medicine Lodge."

I had to smile. Weede had known I was coming a week before I did. "Yes, sir," I replied. "Those are my orders."

Weede studied me, his pink eyes intense. After a moment, he said, "As you can see, I have a skin condition—can't be outdoors as much as I'd like. As agent here, you might say I'm the chief paleface." His laugh was a thin chuckle.

Weede took a gold watch from his vest and snapped open the case. "I'm afraid we'll have to cut our meeting short, Deputy," he said. "I have an appointment over at my office with some contractors." He closed the case and returned the watch to his pocket. Standing, he extended his hand. "Thank you for stopping in," he said. "If there's anything I can do to help you, please let me know. Medicine Lodge is only twenty miles away, and you can always reach me by telegraph." Then he took a wide-brimmed straw hat and a lady's parasol from the hall tree and ushered me out onto the porch.

"I need to get on the road anyway," I said. "Thanks for your time."

I swung back into the saddle and turned Rutherford away, toward the road. The last I saw of Major Weede that day, he was walking toward the agency buildings, shaded by a parasol in the hands of the big Indian.

Beyond the agency, the land rose above cottonwood groves to the hills and bluffs where Custer's men had died. As I moved on up the valley, a low range of mountains, timbered and green began to take shape to the east. I recalled what

Ridgeway had said about the Crows believing their country was the best place on earth. Riding along that afternoon in the sunshine, the sky blue as paint, through the high grass and wildflowers that covered the valley floor, it was easy to see why they thought so.

The sun had set by the time I reached Medicine Lodge. The town was an orderly handful of buildings, set upon a broad and treeless flat. Most of the business places had closed for the evening, but the saloons were open, and thriving. The Legal Tender seemed to be the principal drinking place. Cow ponies crowded the hitch rail out front, and the sound of a piano—played with more enthusiasm than skill—drifted out onto the street.

I turned my horses onto a broad thoroughfare that paralleled the stage road and drew rein at the town's livery stable. The big barn doors were open to the street. A smoky lantern hung from a wire inside and filled the interior with yellow light and dark shadows. I stepped down off the buckskin and stood at his side for a moment until I got my land legs.

"Evenin'," said a voice. "Somethin' I can do for you?"

The speaker stepped into the light. He was a wiry man in his forties, with a weathered face and an open smile. He wore knee-high gumboots, and he carried a manure fork.

"Arnie Moss is my name," he said. "Moss, like what a rollin' stone don't gather. You need to put your horses up?"

"Depends. How much?"

"Two bits a day, each. Forty cents, if you want me to grain 'em."

"I expect to be around for a while. How much by the week?"

"Make it a dollar and a half. Two and a half with oats."

I handed the man five dollars in silver. "That's for two weeks, with grain. Like I said, I expect to be around for a while."

"I take you for a cowhand," Moss said. "You lookin' for work?"

"No. I've got a job. With the new town marshal, Jeff Brown."

Moss's glance was sharp. He looked at me as if he hadn't really seen me before. "I heard you were comin'. You a friend of his?"

"Never met the man. You wouldn't know where I could find him, would you?"

"He'll be in his office this time of night, or makin' his rounds. Just walk up the street, past the bank. You'll pass a saddle shop and a cabin on your right. Next building is the marshal's office and jail."

"Much obliged. By the way, my name's Fanshaw. Merlin Fanshaw."

We shook hands.

"I'll be back for my bedroll when I know where I'll be camped."

Moss nodded. He grinned, as if he knew some special secret I wasn't in on. "No hurry," he said. "Welcome to Medicine Lodge."

I walked west, past a blacksmith shop, the express office, and the hotel. Lamplight glowed soft through the lobby windows, and a streetlight on the corner cast an inky shadow before me as I went by. I crossed the street, strode past the bank, the saddle shop, and the cabin Moss had mentioned. Just beyond lay the square bulk of the marshal's office and jail. I caught the sour smell of charred wood as I approached the door. Through the window I saw a man seated behind a desk, his face hidden in the deep shadow cast by his hat. A coal-oil lamp, turned low, lit the room.

I knocked on the door. "Marshal Brown?" I said. "It's Merlin Fanshaw, from Dry Creek. Chance Ridgeway sent me."

The voice that answered was a deep rumble. "Come in," it said.

The man stood as I entered. He turned the lamp up and light flooded the room. Then he raised his head and smiled.

Marshal Jeff Brown was a stocky man, big-shouldered and solid. He wore a double-breasted flannel shirt beneath his suspenders, and his badge caught lamplight and reflected it back. All this I took in at a glance, but it was his face that caught me off-guard. It was a strong face, clean-shaven and firm of jaw. His eyes were dark, his nose wide and flat, and his teeth were white as fresh snow. But it was the color of the man's skin that took me by surprise—Marshal Jeff Brown was a Negro, and black as midnight!

Now it ain't that I had never seen a black man before—I had encountered porters on the railroad, a black barber one time in Silver City, a shoeshine boy over at Maiden, Montana—but I hadn't known any of them personally, and I surely had never met a black marshal before. I have no excuse for what happened next, but I'm afraid I stared, then stammered, and generally lost my composure.

I said, "Why—you're a ni—"

Marshal Brown's laugh was like music. "I'm a ni—? You callin' me a ninny? A nincompoop? Or maybe a Nimrod? Or do you only mean to say I'm a fine-looking Negro gentleman of African persuasion?"

Right then, I wished more than anything that the earth would open up and swallow me whole. "Damn, Marshal," I said, "I'm sorry—I—I never meant—"

"I know that, Deputy," the marshal said. "You ain't the first, and you won't be the last, to be put off some by my color. Some of the big cowmen around here are died-in-the-wool Southerners, and they just about can't stand seein' a black man walkin' around with a badge and a gun. I'm black, all right, but that ain't who I am. I expect a man is somethin' more than the color of his hide."

From the heat in my cheeks and ears, I knew I was blushing. I shook my head. "I sure hope so," I said. "I have a feeling my color just went to red."

The marshal offered his hand and I took it. "I'm glad you're here," he said. "I suppose Marshal Ridgeway filled you in?"

"Well, he didn't tell me what color you are, but he told me something about the situation here. He told me about Archie Young Bull and his crew. He said they set fire to the office after they beat up Dan Wingate. I can still smell charred wood and smoke."

Marshal Brown pointed to a chair opposite his desk. "The fire took pretty much everything that would burn," he said. "Hide buyer was leavin' town last week. He sold me this desk. I borrowed that chair from the Legal Tender Saloon. Have a seat."

The room still showed the fire's damage. New beams supported the roof and ceiling, and the flooring was new, as well. Both the front door and the door that led from the office to the jail cells in the rear had been replaced.

"Looks like you're back in business," I said. "Any word as to where Archie and his boys are now?"

The marshal shook his head. "Some say they went north to steal horses from the Blackfeet. Others say they're down in Wyoming, with the Shoshone. All I know is they haven't been in town since I got here."

A coffee pot simmered atop a cannon stove at the room's center, and Marshal Brown poured a cup and handed it to me. "No guarantees regardin' the quality," he said, "but it's hot, and strong. Have you had supper?"

"No," I said. "I just got in. Stayed at Fort Custer last night."

"That's a good ride. I expect you're hungry. The City Café is still open—we can talk while we eat."

"I like the way you think," I told him.

We walked together to the corner and turned left on Trail Street. Ahead, at the end of the block, the action at the Legal Tender was in full swing. Inside, the piano player thumped out melodies as before, and the babble of the patrons at the bar grew louder.

"The Rimfire cowboys are in town tonight," the marshal said. "They work for John Wesley DuFresne, one of those southern cowmen I mentioned. Not a bad bunch, but they tend to get a little wild when they're drinkin.'"

I grinned. "That describes about ninety percent of the cowpunchers I know."

The marshal slowed his pace as we reached the Legal Tender, looking in through one of the saloon's big front windows. For a moment he paused, studying the interior. Then he turned back to me. "Hardest part of the job is keepin' the peace without clampin' down too hard. Town council likes the money DuFresne and his cowhands spend in town, but it don't like things to get out of hand. We're supposed to get a city attorney some time this spring, but at present you and me are the law in Medicine Lodge.

"The Legal Tender is open from noon to two in the mornin'," he continued. "City ordinance says customers have to check their guns with the barkeep while they're inside. Whiskey and gunpowder make a bad mix."

"What about Indians?" I asked.

"It's against the law to sell whiskey to Indians. Both the government and the tribal leaders are firm on that point. Most saloon owners keep the law, out of self-interest if nothin' else. There's no profit to a man in gettin' his business shut down."

The marshal turned back for another look inside, his face serious. "But not everyone is so high-minded. Whiskey does get sold to Indians, one way or another. That's when the trouble begins."

Marshal Brown stepped off the boardwalk and into the street. He nodded toward a brightly lit building directly across from the saloon. "Yonder is the City Café," he said. "Let's surround a couple of their T-bones and get better acquainted."

"You ain't waitin' on me," I told him. "I only hope they don't run out of grub before I fill up."

Inside, the café was nearly as busy as the saloon had been, but the marshal led the way through the crowd to an empty table at the back. As we walked toward it, we neared two cowboys who sat joking and laughing over their coffee, the way men will when they're having a good time.

Suddenly, the laughter stopped when the bigger of the two looked up and saw Marshal Brown. The cowhand nudged his partner, and the men stared at us with hard eyes. They stood abruptly as we went by, and walked toward the door. I heard the big man's words, left behind him like a skunk's foul odor: "Goddam coon marshal and his nigger-lovin' deputy."

I spun on my heel, turned to go after the men. They were just going through the doorway when I felt the marshal grasp my arm like a steel trap. "Whoa, Deputy," he said, "You've only been in town an hour or so. You'll hear worse than that if you stay."

"Turn me loose!" I said. "I'm not letting them get away with that!"

"Yes, you are. Keeping the peace calls for a cool head and a steady hand. If you don't have those things, you'd best collect your horses and go on back to where you came from. I can't use you."

He spoke softly, but his hand on my arm hadn't relaxed at all. I looked into his eyes and felt my rage melt away.

"I—I'm sorry, Marshal. I brought a cool head when I came here. I just forgot where I put it for a minute there."

The marshal laughed. He let go of my arm. "Then let's have us some supper," he said. "And if you're stayin' on, maybe you'd better start callin' me Jeff. It don't make much sense, us goin' 'marshal' and 'deputy' like we been doin.'"

"Are you sure?"

He sat down at the table, tipped his hat back, and smiled his flash of a smile. "I'm sure," he said. "Long as you don't call me what those fellers did, I expect we'll get along fine."

CHAPTER 3

▼

We sat together at the table. A sad-eyed waiter took our orders and scuttled back into the kitchen. Marshal Brown—Jeff Brown—seemed unruffled by the incident with the cowhands, but I found their remark still rankled.

"How did those boys know who I am?" I asked.

"Oh, they heard it over the grapevine, I expect. Your comin' has been the talk of the town the past few days."

"Are there many people who feel the way they do?"

Jeff shrugged. "Some," he said. "That's their problem, not ours."

"I just hope it don't get to be ours. All men may be created equal, but some folks seem to figure they're a little more equal than everybody else."

Jeff nodded. "Besides which, there's some who just don't like peace officers."

The waiter came out of the kitchen with two heavy china cups and a coffee pot. He set the cups before us and filled them from the pot.

"Your steaks will be out in a jiffy," he said. His breath smelled like a well-seasoned fruitcake. He ambled back to the kitchen, but not in a jiffy.

I looked at Jeff. "All right," I said. "Where do we go from here?"

"After supper, we'll get you settled. I'm livin' in a cabin near the jail. You can bunk there, too, if you've a mind to."

"Suits me. I'll fetch my bed from the livery stable."

I sipped my coffee. The dining room was nearly full. The drone of voices and the soft scrape of eating tools on china was a constant sound in the background. I noticed Jeff had taken a chair that put his back to the wall and provided a clear view of the room. He appeared relaxed and easy, but I noticed his eyes stayed watchful.

"How did you come to be a peace officer?" I asked.

"I expect it had somethin' to do with makin' things right. I came to the gold-fields at Alder Gulch with my daddy when I was just a button. Brain fever took his life when I wasn't but ten years old. I made my way runnin' errands and doin' odd jobs around Virginia City. I was there when the vigilantes cleaned out the Plummer gang.

"When I was old enough, I joined the cavalry. Was a buffalo soldier down in Arizona. Fought Apaches till eighty-four. Came back north. Signed on as deputy marshal down in Cheyenne. Then they offered me the job here.

"It always seemed to me there was a whole lot of wrong in the world. Folks hurtin' others. Robbin.' Killin.' Like I said, I guess I just wanted to be part of makin' things right."

Right then the waiter showed up with our grub, and we fell to forking it in. We talked, and we ate, the marshal keeping a close eye on the room all the while. As I watched him, I decided I liked Jeff Brown, whatever color he was.

The next morning, Jeff took me over to the Legal Tender Saloon and introduced me to Kyle Haddon, the owner. Haddon was a stocky man of about my height, with broad shoulders and careful brown eyes. He wore a dove-gray frock coat over a fancy embroidered vest, and his graying hair and moustache were neatly trimmed. He shook my hand.

"Welcome to the Legal Tender, Deputy," he said, "Can I buy you gents a drink?"

A beer would have gone good about then. I glanced at Jeff and raised an eyebrow.

Jeff shook his head. "No thanks, Mistuh Haddon," he said, "not just now. Deputy Fanshaw and me are still on duty."

Haddon laughed. "You're mighty conscientious, Marshal Brown. Seems to me you're always pretty much on duty."

Jeff chuckled. "Yes, suh," he said, "it seems like that to me, too, sometimes."

Haddon was watching Jeff through narrowed eyes. I had the impression he was appraising Jeff, as if he still hadn't decided what manner of man the new town marshal was.

"Well," the saloonkeeper said, "You both have a rain check—any time."

It was just past eleven in the morning, and the Legal Tender was quiet at that hour. Besides us, the only other people in the room were the swamper, scattering fresh sawdust over the oiled wood of the floor, and a redheaded bartender, polishing glasses.

Jeff and Haddon talked briefly of the weather, of cattle prices, and of local folks I didn't know. Then I shook Haddon's hand, and Jeff and me went on our way.

Outside, we turned left on Trail Street and walked south toward the bank.

"The Legal Tender is the biggest saloon within two days' ride," Jeff said. "Kyle Haddon has a money-maker on his hands, and he knows it."

"That means the last thing he'd want is trouble with the law," I said. "I don't expect we'll have any problems with Kyle Haddon, or his customers."

It just goes to show you how wrong a man can be.

Jeff gave me the next day off, so I saddled Rutherford after breakfast and rode out to explore the countryside. The morning was warm and bright, with big-bellied clouds adrift on a sky of sapphire blue. Medicine Lodge Creek twisted its way through the valley, its path marked by stands of cottonwood, wild plum, and willow. White-tailed deer watched from its banks, and beaver and muskrat swam in its green waters. I resolved to bring a fishing pole on some future trip and discover what else might make its home in that crooked stream.

A narrow road stretched out along the base of low hills, parallel to the creek. I saw cabins and outbuildings among the trees and on the flat, and one farmer who had already begun his spring plowing. Farther along, I met four riders on the road, bound for town. Three of the men looked to be working cowpunchers, about my age or a little younger. The fourth was a man of about thirty, tall and dark-haired. He was dressed in black from his hat to his boots, and his silver-mounted saddle had been custom-built by a craftsman. The cowhands nodded in greeting as they passed, but the tall man looked straight ahead and rode by as if he didn't see me.

Off to the southwest rose the cool blue mass of the Bighorn range, snow still dusting its peaks. I turned Rutherford up a low hill and drew rein overlooking the valley. Wildflowers grew in reckless profusion, and rich grass rippled in the breeze. It was easy to see why the ranchers and farmers had pushed their way onto the reservation. The Crows would have their work cut out for them if they were to protect their land from settlement by outsiders. I wished them luck.

It was two in the afternoon by the time I got back to town. The Legal Tender was open for business, and already horses lined its hitch rack. Most wore the Rimfire brand—a circle with a short bar inside at the circle's edge—that Jeff said was the mark of DuFresne's spread. I tied Rutherford alongside the other horses and went inside. The three riders I'd met on the road stood at the bar, drinking beer. The tall man sat at a table, playing poker with three other gents. I walked up to the bar and set my elbows on the hardwood.

Kyle Haddon greeted me from a doorway off the big room. "Afternoon, Deputy," he said. "You off-duty this time, or on?"

I smiled. "I've just been out looking the country over," I replied. "I guess you could say I'm off-duty."

"Then I'll buy you that drink I offered last time you were in. What will you have?"

"I wouldn't say no to a beer."

Haddon laughed. Speaking to the bartender, he said, "Draw the deputy a beer, Jerry. He's collecting on a rain check."

One of the men at the bar turned toward Haddon. "How come he don't have to check his gun with the barkeep?" he asked. "What makes him so special?"

"He's the new deputy marshal in town, Curly," Haddon said. "The law doesn't have to check its irons."

There was something familiar about the man called Curly. He had been on the road with the other three, but it seemed to me I'd seen him somewhere before that. Then, suddenly, I remembered. He was the gent who'd passed the remark about Jeff and me at the café. I felt my anger rise like hot water in a kettle—my heart commenced to pound, and I turned to face the cowpuncher called Curly.

It was then I remembered Jeff's words. *Keepin' the peace calls for a cool head and a steady hand. If you don't have those things, you'd best collect your horses and go on back to where you came from. I can't use you.*

I took a deep breath. My shirt collar felt tight. I threw a checkrein on my temper, and set the brake. But as I tried to pull back from my boiling point, I went too far the other way.

"He's right," I told Haddon. "I'm not on duty. I'll check my gun like everyone else." I pulled my Colt from the leather and slid it over to the barkeep.

Now, I don't know about you, but when I make a bad decision it ofttimes seems the consequences fall upon me the very next second. Anyway, that's the way it was that day in the Legal Tender. No sooner had I shucked my shooter than I saw the tall man at the poker table kick his chair back and jump to his feet. The man who was seated across from him had been dealing, and he still held the deck in his hands.

"You're a damned cheat!" the tall man said. His hand flashed beneath his coat and came out holding a cocked revolver!

The dealer dropped the cards and tried to dodge sideways out of his chair, but the tall man fired at point-blank range. The sound of the shot was loud in the big room. The bullet caught the dealer in the shoulder and slammed him to the floor.

I stepped away from the bar. My hand flashed to my waist, but my gun, of course, was not in its place. The tall man had caught my move. He spun, pointing his pistol at me!

Something moved at the doorway. I turned my head to look, and saw Jeff Brown coming fast through the door. He held a sawed-off shotgun at the ready, and his eyes were on the man with the revolver. "Drop it!" Jeff commanded.

The tall man lowered his gun, but he didn't let it fall. "Who the hell says so?" he asked.

"Man with a shotgun says so," Jeff replied. "Town marshal says so. Drop it!"

The tall man smiled. "So you're the new John Law I've been hearin' about," he said. "Easy with that scattergun, Smoky."

Jeff strode toward the man, cocking the hammers of the shotgun as he came. "I told you twice to drop that pistol," he said. "That gun is fixin' to hit the floor, whether you're still holdin' it or not."

This time the tall man let the weapon fall. The gun was a Colt's Peacemaker, I saw, silver-mounted and fancy. Carved longhorn steer heads decorated its ivory grips. "Just so you know who you're talkin' to, boy," the man said, "my name is Buck DuFresne."

Keeping the shotgun trained on the man, Jeff bent down and picked up the revolver. Quickly, he moved to the wounded dealer and knelt beside him. The man grimaced with pain, pressing his right hand to his wound.

"How bad are you hit?" Jeff asked.

"Shoulder," the man grunted. "Sonofabitch shot me."

"Shot you because you're a goddam cheat," said the tall man. "You were reading every card you dealt with that shiner on your left hand."

Jeff took hold of the dealer's hand and forced open his clenched fingers. Sure enough, a highly polished silver ring caught sunlight.

"Looks like you made a mistake," Jeff told the dealer. "We'll find Doc Westby and get him to patch up that shoulder. Then I want you out of town on the next stage."

I had been watching the tall man. He wore handmade boots and a suit of black wool. His face was ruddy, and he looked as if he'd just come from the barbershop. He stood, his feet planted wide apart, and looked at Jeff.

"Like I told you—Marshal—I'm Buck DuFresne. J. W. DuFresne's son. Does that name ring any bells?"

Jeff put a hand on DuFresne and turned him around. Next thing I knew, the tall man's hands were cuffed behind him. "You're under arrest, Mistuh DuFresne," Jeff said. "Aggravated assault, assault with a deadly weapon, and violation of a city ordinance. Looks like you'll be spending a little time in our jail."

Rage twisted DuFresne's features. His face turned a deep red, and his eyes bulged. He glared at Jeff, contempt plain on his face. "Now hold on," he said. "No goddam nigger marshal is goin' to arrest me! I'm Buck DuFresne!"

"You already told me your name," Jeff said." Now are you going to walk over to the jail with me, or do I have to charge you with resisting arrest, too?"

"Those boys there at the bar ride for the Rimfire brand," DuFresne said. "Just one word from me and you'll have more damn trouble than you can handle."

"You don't want to say that word," Jeff said pleasantly. "So far, nobody's dead."

I have to admit I'd been enjoying the show. I admired the way Jeff had taken charge, and the way he'd stood up to the cattleman. I just leaned there against the bar with a foolish grin on my face. Then, suddenly, it was my turn.

"Well, Deputy?" Jeff said, looking at me. "Get your gun back from the bartender and take that wounded cardsharp to the doctor. Or are you still on vacation?"

I heard one of the cowhands at the bar chuckle, but I was so ashamed of myself I didn't even take offense.

I found Doc Westby in the yard behind his house, next to the dry goods store. The doc was on his knees, planting a rose bush, when I walked up with the wounded dealer. He took in the situation at a glance.

"Bullet wound, eh?" he said, getting to his feet. "Take him inside. I'll wash up, and have a look."

"How'd you know it was a bullet wound?" I asked.

The doc removed his gardening gloves and turned toward the house. "It's a quiet day," he said, "and sound carries. I heard the gunshot about ten minutes ago."

Up to that time, the dealer hadn't complained much. He had pressed his handkerchief over the wound, holding it tightly with his right hand to stanch the bleeding, and had come along quietly enough. But now that he had an audience, he commenced to moan and grimace something awful. Doc Westby never paid him much mind, but simply looked at the wound and commenced to clean and bandage it.

"Not too bad," the doc said. "Bullet went straight through, in one side and out the other. Didn't strike bone, or do any real damage." He finished the bandage, and stepped back. "You'll be fine," he told the gambler.

I took it on myself to give the man some advice. "You might consider keeping your card-playing on the level," I said. "Next time somebody shoots you, you might not be so lucky."

Once the man saw he wasn't going to get any sympathy from Doc or me, he gave up his moaning. "Free advice is worth just about what you pay for it," he said. "Where do I catch the stage?"

"Main Street," I said. "Next to the hotel." I turned to Doc Westby. "What does this feller owe you, Doc?"

"I guess five dollars will cover it."

"Suppose I don't pay?" the dealer asked.

"In that case," I said, "I'll take you over to the jail and lock you in with Buck DuFresne. I don't think he's through with you yet."

There was no further talk of not paying. The dealer produced a five-spot and handed it to Doc. "I can't wait to get shut of this town," he muttered.

"I expect the town feels pretty much the same about you," I said.

Jeff Brown met me before I got to the marshal's office. He stood on the boardwalk in front of the saddle shop, watching as I walked up. "Did you get that dealer taken care of?" he asked.

"Yes. Doc Westby patched up his shoulder, and I walked him over to the stage office."

"I never like to criticize a man," Jeff said, "but you made a few mistakes back there, Merlin."

I couldn't meet his eyes. I looked down, watching a party of ants amble across the boardwalk. "I'm sorry, Jeff. Checking my gun with the barkeep was a fool thing. I wasn't thinking."

"Your gun ain't your own anymore, Merlin," Jeff said. "It belongs to the people you're paid to protect. Belongs to the law."

I kept my eyes on the ants. Jeff's voice was quiet, measured. I believe I'd have felt better if he'd bawled me out in anger. I heard disappointment in his tone, and that was worse by far.

Jeff put his big hand on my shoulder. "Lawman can't afford to be careless, Merlin," he said. "Folks depend on him. I depend on you. Can I do that?"

I had a lump in my throat the size of a hen's egg. I looked up into Jeff Brown's honest, open face and nodded. It was a second or two before I could answer him. "You sure can, Jeff," I said. "I'm sorry as hell."

Jeff smiled. His eyes went wide. "Sorry as hell? Man—you must really be sorry! From what the preachers say, hell is a mighty sorry place." Then he laughed his big laugh and slapped me on the back.

Back at the jail, Buck DuFresne paced his narrow cell and gave vent to his anger. "You've got no call to jail me, boy," he said to Jeff. "That tinhorn was dealin' a crooked game!"

Jeff had just poured himself a cup of coffee from the pot on the stove. He took a sip and sat down on the edge of his desk. "First off," he said, "I'm no 'boy'— haven't been such for many a year now. Second, catchin' a man cheatin' at cards don't mean you have the right to put a bullet in him.

"You're goin' to be with us for a while, Mistuh DuFresne," Jeff said. "Why don't you settle down and decide what you'd like for supper?"

DuFresne gripped the bars so hard his knuckles went white. For a minute there, I thought he'd tear the jail down through sheer determination.

"It don't matter what you bring me," he said. "I won't be in your damn jail long enough to eat it!"

Jeff smiled. "You're a gamblin' man, Mistuh DuFresne," he said. "Would you like to bet twenty dollars on that?"

News of the shooting got around pretty fast. By the time I went down to the City Café to fetch supper for DuFresne, the incident was the talk of Medicine Lodge. The victim had left town on the afternoon stage, but the talk still ran high. The main topic of discussion had to do with what would happen next. Most folks seemed to think John Wesley DuFresne—Buck's daddy—would come down like an avenging angel and spring his boy from the calaboose. The DuFresne name—and bankroll—carried a good deal of weight, not only in town but throughout the reservation and the territory.

People figured Jeff Brown's days as marshal of Medicine Lodge were numbered. They felt certain the town council would send him packing. I had no idea what was going to happen, but if I had to bet one way or the other, I figured I'd put my money on Jeff.

When I got back to the jail with Buck's supper, Jeff asked me to stay and keep an eye on the prisoner while he went uptown. The town council had called a special meeting and wanted Jeff to attend. He had no doubts about why they wanted to see him.

"There's no call to worry," he said. "They can't very well fire me for doin' my job too well. Besides, they still remember how the town was before I came. They know Archie Young Bull and his boys could come back any time."

He glanced at the heavy door that set the office off from the jail cells, and shrugged. "I don't guess we can keep Mistuh Buck DuFresne much longer than overnight, anyway. That dealer he winged sure won't be preferrin' charges. Come morning, we'll fine Buck for failin' to check his gun, and turn him loose. We'll have made our point."

After Jeff left the office, I looked in on the prisoner and found that his mood hadn't improved all that much.

"You look like a man who's been around some," Buck said. "What are you doin' workin' for that spade?"

"You look like a man who got caught breakin' the law," I told him. "Law breakers are the dumbest people alive."

DuFresne was quiet for a moment. He sat on the edge of his bunk, studying me. I noticed he hadn't touched the supper I'd brought him.

"I'll give you a hundred dollars if you'll turn me loose right now." DuFresne said.

"You've got a bad habit of misjudging people," I told him. "You can't bluff Marshal Brown, and you can't bribe me." At the doorway to the office, I turned back and grinned. "Tell you what I will do, though—I'll turn you loose when the marshal says to. And it won't cost you a cent."

While I waited for Jeff to return, I took a walk around outside the jail. It occurred to me that some of DuFresne's cowboys might try to break their boss out, but I found nothing of a suspicious nature and went back inside. The evening had turned cold with the setting of the sun, and I built up the fire and made a fresh pot of coffee. I was working on my second cup when Jeff came back.

"How was the meeting?" I asked.

Jeff went over to the stove and rubbed his hands together, warming them. He grinned. "Short and to the point." he said. "The mayor wanted to make it clear that the DuFresnes are very important people to Medicine Lodge. The council expressed some concern that I might not be aware of that, me being so new on the job and all."

Jeff's grin grew wider. "'Oh,' I said. 'Does that mean you don't want me to arrest them when they break the law?'"

I chuckled. "What did they say to that?"

"'Heavens no!' they said. 'We're not saying that! We just want the DuFresnes to know we appreciate what they contribute to the town's economy.'"

"I asked if they meant I should treat the DuFresnes different than everyone else," Jeff said. "They stammered and said, 'Of course not—the law must be enforced impartially.' I thanked them for their guidance and went to supper over at the café."

I laughed aloud. "Council puts me in mind of the feller who took a big drink of hot soup," I said. "Made him mighty uncomfortable. Soup was too hot to swallow, but the feller was too polite to spit it out.

"The day we met, you summed it up. You said the council likes the money DuFresne spends here in town, but it doesn't like things to get out of hand. Enforcing the law and keeping the council happy at the same time means we're going to be under a good deal of pressure."

Jeff shrugged. "Pressure," he said, "is what turns coal into diamonds."

CHAPTER 4

▼

Next morning, Jeff did just what he said he would. He unlocked the cell door, fined Buck DuFresne ten dollars for failing to check his gun at the Legal Tender, charged him another ten for disturbing the peace, and told him he was free to go. Buck paid without protest, but it was plain to see he'd enjoyed better mornings. His straight black hair was tangled and unkempt, his eyes were red-rimmed, and his clothes looked as though he'd slept in them—which, of course, he had.

Beneath the blue-black stubble of his beard, his jaw muscles clenched and knotted like cables. It was clear to me he was a man trying, with some difficulty, to control his temper.

Jeff took his money, gave him a receipt, and returned his six-gun and cartridge belt. "Now you take care, Mistuh DuFresne," Jeff said. "I hope our next meeting will be under better circumstances."

Buck's hands trembled as he buckled on his gun. "Next time I see you, boy," he muttered, "will be too damn soon, whenever it is." He slammed the office door behind him as he stepped outside.

After Buck had gone, Jeff turned his attention to writing a report. He smoothed a sheet of paper on the desk before him and dipped a pen in the ink well. He made a face, and sighed. "Worst thing about the peace officer trade is the paperwork," he said, "but it is part of the job. I expect I'll be at this for an hour or so."

He raised his head and smiled. "Why don't you go along and get acquainted with the town some, Merlin? I expect I can find you if I need you."

"Maybe I will," I said. "I'll be back before noon."

I walked out into one of those spring mornings a man dreams about during most of the previous winter. April in Montana tends to be unsettled and fickle, sometimes changing its mood and its mind a dozen times a day. The month arrives on wobbly legs like a newborn foal, and grows more sure and steady as the days pass. An April day may hold a sudden snowstorm or a gentle rain. It can be sunny or dark, windy or still, warm or cold, or all of these in turn. And sometimes a morning in April comes in on a sunbeam, with a promise that's like music. This day I'm talking about was one of those.

I turned left on Main Street, walked past the saddle shop, and headed for the bank on the corner. One of only two brick buildings in Medicine Lodge, the Cattlemen's Bank stood two stories proud, shaded on its east side by a board awning above the first floor windows. On the veranda in front, a silver-haired man in a black frock coat watched me as I strode toward him. As I drew near, he smiled.

"Merlin Fanshaw?" he said. "I'm Junius Drysdale. I'm president of the bank, and mayor of Medicine Lodge. Welcome to our town."

He offered his hand and I took it. It was a soft hand, but its grip was firm.

"Thank you, Mayor," I said. "I'm looking forward to my stay here."

Drysdale's laugh was jovial—practiced, I thought.

"A good town, by George," he said. "Made up of good, honest people. You'll like it."

"I'm sure I will," I told him. "A peace officer mostly has to associate with bad, dishonest people."

Drysdale laughed again. He seemed to be a man who laughed easily and often, but his eyes were guarded. "I daresay," he said, glancing at my badge. "How long have you been a deputy U.S. marshal?"

"Just about a year now."

"Well, by George, it's good to have you here. Marshal Brown can certainly use your help. Any idea how long you'll be in Medicine Lodge?"

"Until Marshal Ridgeway tells me otherwise," I said.

"Well, enjoy your stay. Anything I can do for you?"

"No, thanks. I'm just out getting acquainted with the town."

"By George, I envy you, Deputy. Glorious day for a stroll."

Drysdale removed a gold watch from his vest pocket and snapped open its case. He sighed. His expression was that of a convict returning to work on the rock pile. "Must get back to my desk, I'm afraid," he said. "It was good to meet you, Deputy."

"Likewise, Mayor," I said.

Drysdale turned and walked into the bank. It occurred to me that our palaver was marked more by what wasn't said than by what was. Drysdale had made no mention of Buck DuFresne's arrest, nor had he asked the reason I'd been sent to Medicine Lodge. I figured both topics were much on his mind.

I stood for a moment where the banker had, watching the activity on Trail Street. Up beyond the City Café, Arnie Moss, the liveryman, drove a work team as the horses pulled a heavy drag to level the ruts and potholes of the street. A young Crow man in flat-brimmed hat and a farmer's overalls drove past in a rickety wagon, his wife on the seat beside him wrapped to her eyes in a red woolen blanket. Three children rode the wagon box, their black hair shining in the sunlight. Tied to the tailgate of the wagon was a pinto mare, followed by a nursing colt.

Jeff had told me the Indian agent began teaching the Crows how to farm back in 1880 in an attempt to make them self-sufficient. Jeff said some of the Crows were growing potatoes, hay, and wheat, but that farming was not popular with a people who had previously known only hunting and tribal warfare. The Crows had my sympathy. Most of the sodbusters I knew found farming to be long on labor and short on profit.

Directly across the street from the bank, on the opposite corner, stood a small, whitewashed house. This cottage—and cottage it surely was—occupied the rear of a spacious corner lot. At the front of the lot stood a frame building with a sign that read "Ed's Barbershop." A red-and-white striped pole beside the doorway further identified the enterprise.

It had been some time since my last haircut. I imagined I looked more like a sheepdog than a deputy marshal. I made a mental note to visit Ed's establishment in the near future. I crossed the street, and was about to go on to the livery stable when I noticed a woman, standing in the doorway.

She was short in stature, and slender, perhaps a few years older than me. She wore a short-sleeved blouse of white cotton with a low neckline, and a long, tight-fitting skirt. Her hair was blonde, swept up and dressed high in front, and she smiled as I neared the doorway of the shop.

"Good morning," she said, stepping out into the light. "You're the new lawman in town, aren't you?"

She had caught me by surprise, and no mistake. I snatched my hat off. "Yes, ma'am," I said. "M-Merlin Fanshaw, d-deputy U.S. m-marshal." I was astonished at myself. I had worked hard to break the habit of stammering, and until that moment believed I had succeeded.

Her smile grew wider. She held out her hand, palm down, and I took it. "Bonnie Jo Hutchins," she said. "I didn't mean to spook you, Deputy."

I laughed. "I guess my mind was somewhere else, ma'am."

"Please," she said, "call me Bonnie Jo. Everyone does."

"All right," I said. "Bonnie Jo."

She smiled at the sound of her name. She was looking up at me through a pair of big brown eyes, and for a moment there I thought I might go back to stammering again.

I said, "I guess I just never expected to see a pretty young lady like yourself in a barbershop, Bonnie Jo."

Her laughter was like music. "I spend a good deal of my time here," she said. "I am the barber."

"You are? I don't believe I ever met a lady barber before. The sign says Ed's."

Her smile faded. Bonnie Jo lowered her eyes and was silent for a moment. When she spoke, her voice was so soft I could barely hear her. "Ed was my husband. I lost him three months ago."

"I'm sorry," I said.

She smiled again, a wistful, plucky smile. "A lady has to make a living," she said, "and I really am a good barber. Maybe even better than Ed."

Bonnie Jo placed her hands on her hips and looked me over. "Speaking of barbers," she said, "you really do need a haircut and a shave. Why don't you come inside and let me prove my boast? No charge—my way of saying welcome to Medicine Lodge."

"I—I couldn't let you do that, ma'am. I'd be happy to pay—"

Bonnie Jo gave me a reproachful look, and took me by the arm. She led me inside to a hardwood barber chair with red plush upholstery. She was wearing that plucky look again.

"You should never look a gift horse in the mouth," she said, "and you should never offer to pay for a gift. Take a seat, Deputy."

Well, what could I do? I hung my hat on a peg, stepped into the chair, and put my feet up. Her smile was my reward.

I have always liked barbershops. While Bonnie Jo heated water, I took time to look Ed's shop over. There was the usual coat and hat rack, and a painted wooden bench where customers could sit and read old copies of *The Police Gazette* and *Scribner's Magazine* while they waited. There was a countertop arrayed with barber tools and bottles of hair tonic, shampoo, and bay rum, and a large, brass cash register.

A sectioned display case containing a dozen or so shaving mugs belonging to regular customers hung on the wall beside a beveled-glass mirror. Pictures of prizefighters and racehorses and a calendar from a barber supply company graced the patterned wallpaper. Above the chair, an oil lamp hung suspended from the ceiling, and coils of flypaper dangled, awaiting their prey.

I heard Bonnie Jo's footsteps behind me, and then her voice at my ear: "I'm going to lower your chair back, Merlin, so I can wash your hair." The chair back went down, and I felt Bonnie Jo's fingers touch my temples. She raised a large pitcher with her other hand. "Close your eyes," she said.

Warm water cascaded from the pitcher's spout, soaking my hair and flowing into a china bowl on a stand behind me. I felt Bonnie Jo's fingers in my hair, lathering the soap, massaging my scalp. Her touch was gentle, and I lay back, eyes closed, and gave myself to the feeling.

Afterward, she rinsed the soap away with more water from the pitcher, toweled the excess dry, and raised the chair back. Then, standing close behind me, she began to cut my hair with scissors and clippers. I could smell her perfume, hear her voice at my ear, feel the warmth of her body as she clipped and snipped away.

"You might think this shop would be a gold mine," she said, "but that isn't the case. Ed used to say barbering was a good business because hair and whiskers always grow back. That's true, of course, but not everyone can afford a barber on a regular basis. Cowboys don't have the money until they get paid off after the roundup, and most of them shave themselves. They mostly let their hair grow, or get one of the other cowhands to cut it.

"And the Indians, of course, have no need of a barbershop at all! They grow their hair long, and braid it—and they pluck what few whiskers grow with a pair of tweezers. Barbering is a living, but as I said, it's no gold mine."

When Bonnie Jo finished cutting my hair, she reclined the chair again. A moment later, she placed a steaming towel over my face, leaving only my nose exposed. As I breathed in steam and Bonnie Jo's perfume, I found I was more aware with every passing minute that Bonnie Jo Hutchins was a woman, and that I was not.

For some reason, I thought about Pandora, back home in Dry Creek, and durned if I didn't go to feeling guilty, although there was no earthly reason I should. Then Bonnie Jo took the towel away and began to lather my face with shaving soap and a brush, and the guilty feeling went away.

I felt her body press close against me, felt her fingers soft upon my face, felt the smooth glide of the razor across cheek and jaw, neck and chin. I had never cared much about money, but right then I found a reason to be rich. If I was a man of means I could go to Bonnie Jo for a shave every day, and maybe a haircut too, every month or so.

At last—all too soon—she finished the shave, and rubbed bay rum onto my face. She gave my cheeks a final pat, raised the chair to its upright position, and handed me a mirror. I hardly knew myself. The face that stared back at me was mine, all right, but it looked better than I was accustomed to seeing it. My hair was slicked back and parted on the side, my sideburns looked as if they'd been drawed on, and my clean-shaven face tingled in a mighty pleasant way. Smiling, Bonnie Jo took the cloth away, brushed the stray clippings off me, and let me get up from the chair.

"I never knew a shave and haircut could be so pleasuresome, Bonnie Jo. Are you sure I can't pay you something?"

"Next time, Merlin," she said. "Again, welcome to Medicine Lodge."

My hat was loose when I put it on. At the door, I looked back at Bonnie Jo and we exchanged smiles. Then I turned and stepped out onto the street.

No sooner had I left the barbershop than I saw Arnie Moss running toward me from the direction of the livery barn.

"Deputy!" he called. "Wait up!"

I suppose I was distracted some. I guess I was still thinking about my time with Bonnie Jo, and it took me a moment to recognize the man. Arnie Moss had not struck me as excitable, but he was stampeding my way like a locoed steer. Behind him, I saw people rushing toward the livery stable, men walking fast and talking to each other, youngsters running.

"Glad I found you," Arnie said. "Curly Bunton just brought in a dead Indian— says he caught him cutting up a DuFresne steer and shot him on the spot!"

I turned toward the livery stable. "Send someone for Marshal Brown," I said. "He's up at his office."

"Hell, I'll fetch him myself," Arnie gasped. "Soon as I catch my breath."

Inside the barn, men had formed a circle, the way men do when they're watching a fight. Squirming, ducking between the legs of the onlookers, schoolboys joined the crowd. A grizzled old-timer pulled one boy away by his collar and pushed him toward the barn's open door.

"Get out, you kids! Ain't nothin' here for you to see!"

I raised my voice, speaking above the hubbub. "Deputy marshal! Make way!"

The voices grew silent. The crowd parted. Men shuffled aside to let me through. I felt their eyes on me as I passed.

Curly Bunton stood, his thumbs hooked in his cartridge belt. His shaps and boots were bloodstained. He looked proud, a half smile on his face, like a hunter who had killed a trophy animal.

"Caught the damn redskin butcherin' a DuFresne steer," he said. "Right on the road, he was—just two miles beyond ranch headquarters. He's sure a good Injun now."

The body of a young Indian male lay on its back in the dirty straw and muck of the barn's floor. Wide and unseeing, the eyes of the corpse stared upward. The mouth was open as well, as if the dead man was trying to tell his side of the story. The body was clad in a ragged shirt and work pants, and his moccasins were thin and patched. He had been, I guessed, thirteen or fourteen years old. He would never be older.

The body bore a gaping chest wound, and had lost a great deal of blood. Kneeling down, I turned the corpse over. The chest wound was an exit wound. The boy had been shot in the back.

I looked up at Curly. "What did you shoot him with?" I asked.

"Winchester," Curly said. "He was bent over the steer he'd killed. I shot him at about seventy-five yards."

"From the back. Did he have a weapon?"

"He had a butcher knife."

"Anyone else see you shoot him?"

"Hell, no! I came on him, like I said, and I killed the thievin' bastard."

"Good riddance," a man in the crowd said.

"Man has a right to protect his property," muttered another.

I stood up. "I'll tell you how I see this," I said, looking Curly in the eye. "You killed this boy in an act of willful murder. I'm placing you under arrest."

Curly laughed. "You're what? You've got no authority to arrest me! You're a town deputy—I killed this redskin on DuFresne land!"

"You mean on Crow land, trespassed on by DuFresne. And you're wrong, Curly—happens I'm a federal deputy. Crow land is under federal jurisdiction."

Curly's face went red. He took a step back, his right hand near his holstered revolver. "You ain't takin' me in, you damn—" he started, and it was then I swung the barrel of my .44 up hard just behind his left ear. The heavy revolver struck bone with a satisfying thump. Curly's eyes rolled up and his knees buckled. He slipped sideways and fell like a toppled tree, coming to rest just a few feet from the body of the Indian boy.

Someone behind me said, "That ain't right. Curly caught that Injun butcherin' a DuFresne steer!"

"Killin' a Injun ain't murder!" someone else said.

I turned to face the crowd and showed them my .44. "Show's over, boys," I said. "You don't want to draw cards in this game."

The crowd broke then. Slowly, they moved away and out onto the street. Most of the men went quietly, but one big man stood his ground, glaring at me. Another, smaller man stood at his side. I figured they were the two that spoke earlier.

"If you arrest Curly," the smaller man said, "you may wish you'd never come to Medicine Lodge. J. W. DuFresne won't stand for it."

Suddenly, Jeff Brown was in the doorway, with Arnie Moss at his side. Jeff held the shotgun he favored, and he spoke to the two men. "Why, I expect he'll have to stand for it," he said, pleasantly. "From what I heard, there ain't no 'if' to it—seems like Deputy Fanshaw has already made his arrest."

Jeff waved the two men along with the barrel of the shotgun. "You boys just go on along now, if you please. You don't want any trouble, do you?"

The men looked as if they knew just what kind of trouble a sawed-off ten-gauge could produce. Slowly, they moved out into the sunlight and walked across the street.

Two horses, a saddled black cowpony and a starveling paint, stood loose-tied to the stable's hitch rack.

Arnie nodded his head in their direction and said, "Curly's horse, and the Indian boy's. You want me to take 'em in?"

"I'd be obliged, Arnie," Jeff said. "Any idea who the dead boy is?"

Arnie shook his head. "No. I can ask around."

"Yes. Do that."

I asked, "Does this town have an undertaker?"

Jeff shook his head. "There's a storage shed out behind the jail. We can take the body there for now."

Curly had begun to come around by that time, though he was still pretty groggy from the thump I'd given him. I handcuffed him, and we loaded both him and his victim in a buckboard from the livery stable. It was only two city blocks from the livery to the jail, but we had onlookers aplenty watching us pass. I figured we'd be the talk of the reservation by nightfall.

Back at the marshal's office, we took the cuffs off Curly and locked him in a cell. We wrapped the corpse in a canvas tarp, laid it out on a workbench in the shed, and locked the door. By the time I'd returned the buckboard and walked back to the office, a half dozen town dogs had already picked up the scent of the corpse and were sniffing around the shed.

Jeff had brewed a fresh pot of coffee while I was gone. When I got back, he poured us each a cup, and we sat down together at his desk. "How's our guest?" I asked.

"Curly? I expect he's felt better," Jeff said. "What did he tell you about the shooting?"

"Said he caught the boy cutting up one of DuFresne's steers. Curly said he shot him with a Winchester. In the back. No witnesses. I asked if the boy was armed, and Curly said he had a butcher knife. That's when I arrested him. It wasn't a popular decision with the crowd."

"It is with me," Jeff said, "but I reckon J. W. DuFresne won't like it much."

"According to Curly, the shooting happened on the road, just two miles from ranch headquarters. I think I'll ride out there tomorrow and investigate some. The steer should still be there, and whatever the boy used to bring it down. He sure didn't kill the critter with any butcher knife."

Jeff nodded. "I'll send word to the agent at Crow Agency—let him know what happened. Hard to say how the Crows will take this."

"Well," I said, "they'll take it better if we bring the killer to justice."

Jeff nodded. For the first time since I'd met him, he looked troubled. "Let's hope so," he said.

I had banked the fire in the cook stove the night before, but the coals had died anyway, and the cabin was cold as a crypt. Jeff's steady breathing from the small room next door told me he was still asleep, and I walked soft so as not to wake him. I slipped out of my blankets, got dressed, and made my way outside under a sky scattershot with stars. It was still dark, but the position of the Dipper told me it was just past four o'clock in the morning.

Over at the shed, town dogs still snuffled around the door to the shed where the body lay, whimpering and fussing. I chunked a rock, and went back inside.

By four-thirty, I had built up the fire, breakfasted on bacon and beans, and was on my way down to the livery barn. There was a chill to the air at that early hour but there was no wind, and the clear skies bespoke a pleasant day.

Arnie Moss was up and doing at the barn. He greeted me with a nod. "I figured you'd be riding out to DuFresne's this mornin'," he said. Nodding toward the back of the barn, he added, "And so did he."

Looking in the direction of Arnie's nod, I saw a short, chubby gent in a wool jacket and riding britches. Behind thick spectacles, his eyes were steady and alert. His hair was close-cropped, and a walrus moustache screened a set of strong, white teeth. He smiled when he saw me, and stepped out of the shadows.

"Deputy Fanshaw?" he said. "I'm Clifford Bidwell, editor, publisher, and janitor of *The Medicine Lodge Star*. Arnie is quite right. I thought you might be riding out to DuFresne's this morning."

He stuck his hand out, and I took it.

"Well, you thought right, Cliff," I said, "but I don't have much to say for publication."

"I'm afraid you'll think I'm a bit cheeky, but I'd like to ride along, if I may."

I was trying hard to remain aloof, but the man's smile was honest, and his eyes were bright and alert. "Why would that be, Clifford?" I asked.

"Just to observe, and to provide such help as I can," he said. "For example, I can show you the shortest way to the ranch."

"And while you're helping and observing, I suppose you might ask me a few questions?"

"I would consider it bad manners to ride all that way with you, and ask nothing," he said, smiling.

I lost the battle. I found myself liking the man. It might be good to have company on my ride, at that. If anyone could answer my questions, it would surely be the publisher, editor, and janitor of *The Medicine Lodge Star*. I gave him back his smile and shook his hand. "Well," I said, "Let's ride then. We're burning daylight."

That last remark of mine wasn't strictly true, of course. Daylight was still a half hour away, by any reckoning. Clifford nodded, and walked back to the barn's stalls to saddle a horse.

While I brushed and saddled Rutherford, I asked Arnie if he'd learned anything more about the dead boy's identity.

"No," he said, "but I passed the word. Charlie Babcock runs a trading store at the agency. He was through here last night, and I told him. By this afternoon, most of the Crows will have heard about the killing by way of the moccasin telegraph."

I led Rutherford outside, slid my rifle into its scabbard, and stepped up into the saddle. A minute later, Clifford Bidwell appeared, leading a rat-tailed bay mare. He clambered on board, and I led out on the Medicine Lodge Creek road. Behind us, above the Wolf Mountains to the east, the sky had grown lighter. Then, twenty minutes later, the sun exploded over the rim of the world and sent our shadows far out before us to lead the way.

CHAPTER 5

▼

Clifford Bidwell was not accustomed to life in the saddle, but the mare he rode was neither barn sour nor a camp staller, and we took to the road at a brisk trot. The little newspaperman seemed anxious to interview me, but the choppy gait of our horses made talk difficult. Clifford mostly just bounced along in the saddle, looking game, but unhappy. After we'd gone about three miles, I slowed my horse to a walk, and Clifford looked relieved.

"That gait is hard on the anatomy," he said, smiling. "I'd hate to travel very far that way."

"A trot is the best gait for covering distance," I told him. "Some horses can hold that pace all day."

Doubt passed over his face like a cloud, and his smile faded. I took pity on him.

"We'll mostly switch back and forth from a trot to a walk today," I said. "Ride on your feet. That will make it easier on your—disposition."

Clifford nodded. After a moment, he asked: "Why did you come to Medicine Lodge, Deputy?"

"Call me Merlin. A deputy marshal goes where he's sent. My boss sent me here."

"All right—Merlin. Can you tell me what your assignment is?"

"Enforce the law. Keep the peace. Provide assistance to town marshal Jeff Brown."

"Nothing more?"

"Keeping the peace, in this place, means standing between the settlers and the Crows. Doing whatever it takes to head off an uprising."

Clifford nodded. "And you think the shooting of this young Crow boy could lead to an uprising?"

"You tell me. How big a spark does it take to start a forest fire?"

"There have been plenty of sparks already," Clifford said, his expression grim. "Three years ago white men stole a number of horses from a Crow chief named Crazy Head. When his brother tried to talk to them, they killed him. Over the past few years hundreds of Crow horses have been stolen, or killed. Nothing has been done about it, and the problems between the Indians and the whites have grown worse.

"Indians slaughter the white man's cattle—because they're hungry, mostly. White men steal and kill Indian horses to clear the range for their cattle."

"I thought the government provided beef rations for the tribe," I said.

"Beef rations are never enough," Clifford said. "Every year, the tribal council asks for more rations, and each year the government gives them less. Two years ago, in eighty-four, each Indian received only a third of a pound of flour, three-fourths of a pound of beef, six-hundredths of a pound of bacon, and a half ration of hominy and beans—every other week!

"The government wants the Crows to support themselves by farming, but only a few Indians farm. The agent has even gone so far as to say he thought a little starving would be good for them!

"Meanwhile, ranchers and settlers continue to move onto the reservation, and the Crows' protests go unheard and unanswered."

"Well," I said, "maybe this time I can head off a protest."

"You've already taken a good first step. When I heard about the shooting of the Crow boy and your arrest of Curly Bunton, I knew I wanted to talk to you."

"Time to kick these horses into a trot again," I said. "How far is DuFresne's ranch headquarters, as the crow flies?"

"Maybe fifteen miles," Clifford said, grinning, "but most of the Crows I know don't fly."

We left the main road about two hours later and turned north onto a grass-grown wagon track that led to DuFresne's headquarters ranch. Clifford and me turned our horses uphill along a rise that wound through stands of juniper and jack pine, and then we broke out on the hill's crest and looked down on the ranch layout itself.

The buildings had been constructed of cottonwood logs, inside a curve of Medicine Lodge Creek that nearly doubled back on itself. The main house was long and low, fenced all about with a single rail to keep the horses out of the yard.

Beyond lay the cook shack, blacksmith shop, bunkhouse, barn, and corrals, all sheltered by low hills on both sides of the creek. Thick stands of trees bordered the creek and offered shelter from the wind.

Minutes later, we descended the hill. Smoke rose from the chimney at the cook shack, but there seemed to be no people about. We rode over to the shack and drew rein. There was no need to announce our presence. A pair of ranch dogs dashed out from behind the house, barking a challenge. Our horses pretty much ignored the yapping, while we tried to, with mixed success. We sat our saddles and waited for someone to come out and call off the dogs.

The door swung open, and an older man wearing a flour-sack apron stepped outside. "That'll do!" he said to the dogs, "Come here!"

Dutifully, the dogs stopped their racket. Tails wagging, they went to the man and lay down. Squinting up against the sun, the gent took our measure. He didn't ask us to get down.

"My name's Fanshaw," I told him. "Deputy U.S. marshal." I nodded toward Clifford. "That's Clifford Bidwell. He runs the newspaper in Medicine Lodge. We're looking for the boss."

The man wiped his hands on his apron. "I cook for the outfit," he said. "Nobody here but me. Boss is down at the cow camp on Willow Creek with some of the boys, brandin' strays." He shaded his eyes, studying me. "You the feller who arrested Curly Bunton?"

"I am. Curly said he shot that Indian boy two miles from here. Said the boy killed a Rimfire steer. I'd like to see that steer."

The cook didn't meet my gaze. He dropped his eyes, his boot toe scuffing the dirt before him. "Don't know nothin' about no steer."

"No? According to Curly, the boy killed it just two miles from here. What's your name, if you don't mind my asking?"

"Leo. Leo LeBreche. Like I said, I don't know nothin' about no steer."

"Well, Leo LeBreche, it strikes me as peculiar you wouldn't know about a dead steer just two miles down the road. I don't suppose you'd know the name of the dead boy, either."

LeBreche frowned. "No, sir, I wouldn't. I never seen him before."

"Before when? Before Curly killed him? So you saw the Indian boy, but not the steer."

"I—I never said that. You're tryin' to trick me—"

"Curly is in the Medicine Lodge jail on a murder charge. If I decide you're concealing information about the killing, I might just have to take you in, too."

LeBreche looked nervous. "I ain't goin' back to no prison," he muttered. "No, sir."

I waited for the rest of it.

"Maybe—" LeBreche said, "Maybe there wasn't no steer."

I dismounted. "Maybe there wasn't. You want to tell me about it?"

"Merlin," Clifford said. "Riders coming."

I looked up. The horsemen came from beyond the tree line, three men riding in at a brisk trot. As they drew nearer, I recognized Buck DuFresne and one of the cowboys I'd seen in the Legal Tender the day Buck shot the tinhorn. The third rider, tall and straight-backed, rode slightly ahead of the others. I judged him to be a man in his fifties, and his face, beneath the shadow of a high-crowned Stetson, was dark from the sun and proud as Lucifer. He could only be one man—John Wesley DuFresne himself.

The three riders reined up, their eyes hard. Buck DuFresne, as usual, was dressed in black from his boots to his hat. He gave me a curt nod. All three men wore revolvers at their waists.

"Ah'm J. W. DuFresne," the tall man said. "You looking for me?"

I felt at a disadvantage. Only LeBreche and me were not on horseback. Now it was my turn to squint up against the sun.

"Merlin Fanshaw, deputy marshal," I said. "I'm looking for evidence in a murder case."

The senior DuFresne looked down at me without expression. His snow-white hair and moustache made his skin seem even darker. "A case involving one of mah men, Ah hear. You're mistaken, Deputy—there's been no murder."

"How's that, Mr. DuFresne? Curly admitted shooting the boy."

"Every killing is not a murder, Deputy." He glanced at Clifford, nodded in recognition. "Isn't that right, Clifford?"

Clifford made no reply, and DuFresne turned his gaze back to me. "For example, suppose one of mah men caught a thief in the act of butchering a Rimfire steer," he began, "and suppose the thief opened fire on him. Now, if mah man fired back and killed the thief, that wouldn't be murder, would it, Deputy?"

"You saying it happened that way?"

"You saying it didn't?"

"Curly Bunton didn't tell it that way. No weapon." I glanced at the cook, LeBreche. "No proof a steer was killed. Can you show me the carcass?"

DuFresne shifted in the saddle. When he spoke again, there was a hard edge of anger in his voice. "Ah've lost thirty-five head to Indians since last fall," he said. "The damn government cuts back on the tribe's beef rations, and the Indians get hungry and butcher mah steers. Up to now, Ah've tolerated it, but a man has to draw the line somewhere. Ah'll put up with it no longer."

DuFresne's eyes were cold when they met mine. "And no, Ah will not show you the carcass. Get the hell off mah land."

"Your land?" I asked. "This is Crow land, under federal jurisdiction. As a deputy U.S. marshal, I have more right to be here than you have."

DuFresne looked as if I'd struck him. His eyes widened. His hand trembled. Abruptly, he turned to his son, Buck. "Ah thought you said he was deputy to that nigger marshal!" he said. "You never told me he was federal law!"

Buck wavered before his father's anger. "I—I didn't know, Pa," he said.

J. W. DuFresne turned back to me. Beneath his tan, his face was flushed, but his voice was steady. "Ah seldom repeat myself, Deputy," he said, "but Ah will this one time. Get the hell off mah place!"

Jeff would have been proud of me. I held on to my composure, and even gave the boss cowman a smile. I swung up into my saddle, touched my hat brim, and said, "I'm obliged for your hospitality, Mr. DuFresne. You boys have a good day now, you hear?"

Then Clifford and me turned our horses and rode back up through the trees, the way we had come.

On the far side of the ridge, we reined up to let the horses breathe.

Behind his spectacles, Clifford's eyes were wide with fear. "You do tend to go at things head-on, don't you?" he said. "Next time you want to put our lives in jeopardy, why don't you just snatch food out of a grizzly's mouth?"

I grinned. "I thought the investigation went pretty well," I said. "We learned the cook has served time in prison, and really doesn't want to go back. And we learned there was no butchered steer. That means Curly lied."

"You also pushed John Wesley DuFresne pretty hard," Clifford said. "People don't usually talk to him the way you did."

I shrugged. "Maybe somebody should, now and then."

Back in the cabin at Medicine Lodge, I gave Jeff an account of my trip to the ranch and my conversations with LeBreche and J.W. DuFresne. "I know Curly murdered the Indian boy," I told him. "I just don't know if we can prove it in a court of law."

Jeff looked thoughtful. "It doesn't look good. I surely will hate it if we have to turn him loose for lack of evidence."

"If that happens, the Crows will be hard to live with. I reckon they know injustice when they see it."

"They should," Jeff said. "They've had plenty of practice."

Jeff had cooked up a beef stew and had baked a batch of sourdough biscuits for our supper that evening, and the good smells from the cook stove reminded me of just how hungry I was. While Jeff put the coffee on, I walked over to the window and looked out at Main Street.

The sun had dropped behind the hills to the west, and dusk had settled over the town like a blanket. Distant trees stood sharp-edged against a brilliant sky. Darkness chased the light away, blurring and softening details of the landscape. I thought about my meeting with DuFresne earlier in the day, and about Curly, across the way in a jail cell for a cruel and senseless killing.

Jeff and I agreed that one or the other of us should spend the night at the jail to guard the prisoner while he was in our custody. I would be going over after supper, but I wasn't looking forward to it much. Curly's mood usually varied between self-pity and arrogance, and I had no wish to deal with either that evening.

I was just turning away from the window when I saw the boy. He was a young Indian, not much older than the dead youth had been. He wore a cotton work shirt, moccasins, and a breechcloth, and he sat his pinto pony in the twilight, his eyes fixed on the cabin.

For a moment, I wasn't sure I really saw him. He and his pony were completely motionless. I watched for what seemed minutes; then the pony lowered its head and began to graze.

"Jeff," I said. "What do you make of this?"

Jeff came over and stood beside me. "Young Crow," he said. "Looks like he wants to talk."

"Do you know the language?"

"Enough to get by. I savvy sign language better."

"Well," I said. "It's your cabin. Go invite him in while I heat up the coffee."

I watched from the window as Jeff left the cabin and made his way across the street. I saw the pinto raise its head, its ears erect. Motionless as a statue, the youth sat his pony, observing Jeff's approach. When Jeff was about six feet from the boy, he stopped. Jeff's hands moved swiftly, forming words and phrases in sign talk. The boy watched. Then his own hands moved, answering. Jeff pointed back toward the cabin. The boy nodded, sliding easily from his pony to the ground. Leading the animal, he walked with Jeff back to the cabin.

Jeff came though the door first. "Smile when he comes in," he told me, "and say, '*Kahé iilpáache.*'"

"What does it mean?" I whispered.

"I'll tell you later—just say it."

The boy ducked beneath the lintel and entered the cabin. He looked nervous, uncertain. He also looked hungry. I gave him my best smile, and said, "*Kahé, iilpáache.*"

The boy seemed to relax. He raised his eyes. He seemed, almost, to smile. "*Ahó,*" he replied.

Jeff rubbed his belly, put his hand to his mouth in the "to eat" sign. He offered the boy a chair at the table. Shyly, the boy sat down, his eyes on the stew that simmered atop the stove.

"All right," I said to Jeff. "What did I say?"

Jeff smiled his big smile. "You said, 'welcome, friend,' except the way you pronounced it, I'm not sure what you said. The boy thanked you, and I asked him to join us for supper."

I dished up the stew and biscuits while Jeff poured the coffee and spoke to our guest. The boy answered briefly, and then fell on the stew as if he hadn't eaten in a week. It didn't take Jeff and me long to join him, and the three of us made short work of our portions. While I cleared away the dishes Jeff leaned toward the boy and began to speak in earnest. The Crow tongue was strange to me, phrases and words that seemed to rise and quaver, with harsh sounds, as if the speaker had something caught in his throat.

At length, the conversation ended. Jeff turned to me. "The boy says his name is Gray Owl. He tells me he was a friend of the young man we've got laid out in our shed, and that his name was Goes to the Water. He also says he was with his friend—'when the white man shot him.'"

During the next several minutes, the boy told Jeff the his story of the shooting. He said he and Goes to the Water had gone hunting together that day on Willow Creek, above DuFresne's headquarters. They were leading their horses, he said, while they tracked a deer on foot through a grove of trees.

They had no gun, he said; only one bow and six arrows between them. He—Gray Owl—was carrying the bow, while Goes to the Water followed. As they stalked through the timber, they spooked a good whitetail buck from its bed. Gray Owl loosed an arrow at the deer, but missed. The buck broke out of the trees, crossed an open meadow, and re-entered the timber on the other side. Caught up in the chase, Goes to the Water led his horse past his friend and out onto the meadow, pursuing the deer.

Then, Gray Owl said, he saw a white man riding a black horse. The rider saw Goes to the Water running and reined up, pulling his saddle gun as he dismounted. When the white man raised the rifle to his shoulder, Goes to the Water turned away, and the white man shot him in the back. Fearing for his own life, Gray Owl remained hidden in the grove while the rider loaded his friend's body on his pinto and led the animal away.

"I was ashamed," he told Jeff. "I wanted to kill the white man, but I was afraid." He had waited until the rider was well away before he came out of hiding and made his way back home.

"This rider," Jeff had asked him. "What did he look like?"

"A big man," came the reply, "with curly hair."

Gray Owl lowered his eyes. He was silent for a moment. Then he said, "I remember something else. It is a thing that makes my heart bad. The white man laughed after he killed Goes to the Water."

When Jeff told me that last part, I answered him in English. "It makes my heart bad, too."

We took supper over to the jail for Curly, and Gray Owl went with us. While Jeff passed the plate and cup through the bars I held the lamp high, illuminating the cell. Gray Owl's face went hard when he saw Curly.

"Yes," he said, in the Crow tongue. "That is the man."

Afterward, we took Gray Owl out to the shed. Unwrapping the body was not a pleasant task. The stench of death was strong in the small space. Again, I held the lamp high.

Gray Owl nodded. "It is my friend, Goes to the Water," he said.

He spoke briefly with Jeff, and then swung up onto his horse and rode away into the darkness.

As we watched him go, Jeff said, "He said he'll tell the boy's parents they can come and claim the body. I believe, in at least some small way, he has come to trust us."

Jeff chuckled. "I also learned the Crows have their own names for us. They call you Law Bringer."

I grinned. "I'll settle for that. What do they call you?"

Jeff laughed his deep rumble of a laugh. "Black White Man," he said.

Over at the office, I lay awake for a long time that night. My thoughts went back to the day Ridgeway sent me to Medicine Lodge, and the reason. I was to assist Jeff Brown in his duties as town marshal, and do what I could to prevent trouble between the Indians and the whites. Now, the trouble seemed near at hand. White ranchers and settlers were trespassing on Crow land. Indians were being denied the rations the government had promised them. Worse than that, the Indian agent was using the threat of starvation to force the Crows to become farmers. Indians stole or butchered white men's cattle, and bad blood increased. An uprising had become a very real possibility.

Now one of DuFresne's riders had killed an Indian boy, casually, as a man might kill a coyote. He seemed surprised, even offended, that he had been called to account for the murder. He had lied about the circumstances of the killing, and he had even expected other white men to admire him!

The dead boy's friend—Gray Owl—had come forward to tell another story. We now had evidence that the shooting had been cold-blooded, deliberate murder. Curly's conviction would help prove to the Crows that white man's law would be enforced fairly, whether the lawbreaker was Indian or white. And yet I wondered—would he be indicted? And if he was, would a white jury convict him on the evidence of an Indian boy's testimony?

I resolved to send a full report to Ridgeway. I would lay the case before him, and trust in his decision. I was finding law enforcement to be harder than I thought it would be. I was also learning that justice is a lot easier to pursue than to catch.

Medicine Lodge Creek marked the town's southern boundary, and clearly established the town. The creek began its journey as a clear stream a child could step across, high in the Bighorn Mountains. It snaked down through the valleys and lowlands, recruiting tributaries as it ran, until at last it joined the Little Bighorn River just south of town. North of the creek was the town itself, where white merchants and boosters invested their cash and their labor to build the growing settlement.

Just across the creek, on a broad plain, was an area where many Crow families lived. Most of their dwellings were tepees, but a growing number of cabins and even a few frame houses had begun to appear. A log dance hall and meetinghouse provided a place for tribal councils and celebrations, while dancers and singers circled outdoor fires to the drummers' rhythms.

The drums and the singing could be clearly heard in Medicine Lodge. As I lay on the cot in the marshal's office that evening, I listened to the steady drumming and the high-pitched wailing of voices in mourning and knew they were for Goes to the Water.

The boy's parents came just at sunup. They drove up to the jail in a weathered wagon pulled by a team of skinny horses, and asked us for the body of their son. Jeff and me helped load the corpse into the wagon bed. Neither father nor mother showed their grief much, but the woman wore her hair loose and cut short, and her arms were bandaged where she had slashed them with a knife in her mourning. The boy's father carried himself with pride, his head high and his mouth set in a tight line. He kept looking at the jail, hot anger in his eyes. There was no doubt he knew his son's killer was just inside.

They didn't tarry. Once their boy's body was loaded, the old man clambered up into the wagon seat beside the woman. He gave us a curt nod, shook the reins, and the wagon clattered away on the road out of town. We heard later they buried their son in a shallow grave on a high bench overlooking the valley.

Jeff said that, like the other Plains tribes, the Crows used to place their dead on scaffolds or in the forks of a tree, giving the departed a head start toward the spirit world. "Didn't make sense to put their dead down in a grave," he said. "Not if you wanted to help 'em go up yonder."

Jeff looked thoughtful. "I heard a story about an early missionary to the Crows," he continued. "I don't know if it's true or not. Seems this missionary had considerable success—he converted and baptized a good many members of the tribe. But try as he might, he couldn't persuade the Indians to bury their dead in the ground. They listened politely to his arguments regarding Christian burial, and went on putting corpses on scaffolds and in trees.

"Shortly afterward, the missionary lost one of his own children to death. Deep in his grief, he invited the entire tribe to the funeral, which he and his wife conducted themselves. The Indians looked on, sharing his sorrow. At the end of the service, the missionary placed the body of his little child in a grave he'd dug himself, and committed the child's spirit to the Almighty.

"After that, the story goes, the Indians began at last to bury their dead in the earth, too. Guess they figured if it was good enough for the missionary, it was good enough for them.

"But they hedged their bets. They began to bury their dead in the ground, all right, but they usually chose ground that was as high on a ridge or hilltop as they could find!"

Jeff was silent for a while. Then he said, "That's the story, as I heard it. Like I say, I don't know whether it's true or not."

"Well," I said, "it's a good story, either way."

Early the next morning, I sat down at Jeff's desk and wrote out a letter containing a full report of the killing of Goes to the Water. Afterward, I looked over what I had written, polished up the writing some, and carried the missive down to the express office. When the stage left Medicine Lodge that afternoon, my letter went with it, bound for U.S. Marshal Chance Ridgeway in Helena.

CHAPTER 6

▼

The case against Curly Bunton began to fall apart almost immediately. Early in the week, I rode out to DuFresne's ranch to further question the outfit's cook, Leo LeBreche. LeBreche wasn't there, and neither were J. W. DuFresne or his son, Buck. Cowpunchers at the stable said they'd heard LeBreche had quit the outfit and left the reservation. Nobody seemed to know where he'd gone.

Jeff and I found Gray Owl's folks at their cabin on Good Luck Creek. The boy's father told us their son had gone away. They didn't know where he had gone—maybe hunting, they said—or when he'd be back. Jeff said it was very important that we talk with him. He asked the couple if they would please let us know when he came home. They said they would.

As we rode back to town, I asked the question that was on both our minds. "Has it struck you, too, that it's a strange coincidence our only two witnesses have disappeared?"

Jeff's expression was somber. "Most coincidences I've seen," he said, "have been manmade. I figure Gray Owl's folks sent him away to protect him from the DuFresnes, and the DuFresnes sent LeBreche away to protect Curly from the law."

"Yeah," I said, "but in both cases, we're fresh out of witnesses."

We had scarcely been back in the office an hour when Major Weede arrived. The Indian agent occupied the full rear seat of a top surrey, his great bulk clad in a rumpled suit of white linen. A wide-brimmed straw hat and a pair of smoked spectacles helped to protect his pale skin from the sun. Across from him, riding backward in the surrey, sat a thin, dark-suited man who seemed to take note of everything about him with quick, careful eyes. The same Indian policeman I'd seen during my visit to the agency occupied the front seat, and drove the team. He drew rein, and Weede and the thin man stepped down. Jeff met them at the door.

"Good mornin', Major," Jeff said. "Come in."

The agent nodded. He stepped inside, followed by the thin man.

"Good morning, Marshal," Weede said. Seeing me behind Jeff, he said, "Deputy."

"Hello, Major," I said. "What brings you to Medicine Lodge?"

"Official business," the agent said. He turned to the thin man. "This is Hartford Canfield, attorney for the DuFresne Land and Cattle Company. Hartford, this is City Marshal Jeff Brown and Deputy Marshal Merlin Fanshaw."

The lawyer nodded. "Gentlemen," he said, "I'll get right to the point. I understand you're holding an employee of DuFresne Land and Cattle, one Curly Bunton."

"That's right," I said. "He's inside."

Canfield smiled a thin smile. "I represent Mr. Bunton, Deputy. Can you tell me why he's being held?"

"Curly killed an Indian boy. He's being held on a murder charge."

The smile faded. "I see. Upon what evidence did you make that charge?"

"His own admission, and the testimony of witnesses."

"Mr. Bunton admitted to murder?"

"No—but he admitted shooting the boy. Said he caught him butchering a DuFresne steer."

"So—he was protecting his employer's property."

"Witnesses say otherwise."

"Can you produce these witnesses? Their depositions?"

"Well—no. Not at the moment."

"Did you have a court-issued warrant to arrest my client?"

"No, but—"

The lawyer removed a folded document from an inside coat pocket. "Then I'm afraid you must release Mr. Bunton forthwith. This is an order from the district judge in Miles City."

I looked at Weede. "This isn't right, Major," I said.

The agent's face showed no expression at all. "I'm afraid this is a matter of law, Deputy. You must comply."

I turned to Jeff, hoping for some kind of support. Jeff had heard Gray Owl's testimony; he had watched the grieving parents take the body of their murdered son away. Jeff's eyes were sad when they met mine. He shook his head slightly, and lowered his gaze.

I took the cell key from its peg. "All right," I said, but it wasn't all right, not at all.

If ever I needed to keep a tight rein on my temper, it was when I unlocked the cell door and let Curly Bunton out. The big man looked down his nose at me and grinned a smile that had more malice in it than humor. I gave him back his hat, gun belt, and personal effects.

"Sorry you have to leave so soon," I told him. "Maybe you can come back sometime when you can stay longer."

Curly held his grin, but there was hatred behind his eyes. "I still owe you for that pistol-whippin', Deputy," he said. "I hope to pay you back one day soon—with interest."

"Any time, back shooter," I said.

I stood outside the office door and watched the surrey drive away. Curly sat on the front seat beside the driver, looking back. He pointed a finger at me as if it was a gun, took aim, and jerked his hand sharply upward as if firing a shot. Then he turned his back, and I watched the rig move on down Main Street.

I have never been much of a drinking man. I guess I saw too much of my pa's struggle with booze for me to take to it much. But just for a moment there I thought about seeing how much whiskey I could drink and still remain conscious. Knowing Curly murdered Goes to the Water the way a man might step on a bug, and watching him ride off scot-free, left a mighty bad taste in my mouth.

I stepped back inside the office. Jeff Brown sat behind his desk, looking as glum as I felt. He didn't meet my eyes when he spoke.

"Old story, Merlin," he said. "White man kills a black man or Indian, he goes free. Lady Justice may be blind, but she don't appear to be colorblind."

He took something out of his shirt pocket and tapped it on the palm of his hand. "Bought this here mouth organ from a trooper down in New Mexico," he said. "I play it sometimes when I get the blues. She's got sixteen double holes and thirty-two super-fine reeds. This evenin,' I expect I'll need them all."

I stretched out on the cot in the office and stared at the ceiling. Eyes closed, Jeff breathed into the harmonica, his hands cupped around it the way a man might shield a match flame from the wind. A low chord trembled and grew into a wail, sad as a broken heart. Jeff took the melody from a whisper to a growl, puffing in his rhythms and harmonies, playing from his soul, and making the music cry.

I tilted my hat down over my eyes, letting the sadness and the anger in the music speak to me. It occurred to me that most people never really listen to music, and I had to admit I was one of those people. But as Jeff poured his feelings into the instrument, I marveled. I had no musical skills myself, but I like to think I recognize talent when I hear it. As I listened, Jeff gave himself to the playing with such skill I seemed to feel the sadness of the whole world.

Jeff's harmonica may only have been an object of metal and wood, with holes and reeds, but on that day it seemed like a living thing. The music sobbed and stormed; it spoke of heartbreak and hurt, of injustice and grief; and it shouted in protest even when it whispered.

At last the music slowed, faded, and died. In the shadow beneath my hat brim, my eyes were wet.

I was having a late lunch in the City Café the following Thursday afternoon when I happened to see the latest edition of the weekly *Medicine Lodge Star*. Fresh from Clifford Bidwell's flatbed press, copies of the newspapers lay in a neat stack on the counter, beside the cash register. I paid my dime, picked up a copy, and sat down to read it. The story was there, on page one. In bold, black letters, the headline proclaimed:

ACCUSED SLAYER OF CROW YOUTH FREED, COURT RULES EVIDENCE INSUFFICIENT

The U.S. District Court at Miles City today ordered the release of Alfred "Curly" Bunton, employee of the DuFresne Land and Cattle Company. Mr. Bunton was arrested earlier in the week by Deputy U.S. Marshal Merlin Fanshaw on suspicion of the willful murder of Goes to the Water, son of Old Eagle and Dog Woman of Medicine Lodge. Mr. Bunton was incarcerated in the Medicine Lodge jail.

At the time of his arrest, Mr. Bunton confessed to shooting Goes to the Water, but claimed the action was justified because he caught the youth in the act of butchering a steer belonging to the DuFresne Land and Cattle Company. Mr. Bunton also said that when he confronted Goes to the Water, the youth was armed with a rifle and threatened to use it.

"I hated to shoot the boy," Bunton said, "but it was either him or me."

There was more to the story, but I had read all I could stand. I left the café, stomped up the street, and flung the newspaper onto Clifford Bidwell's desk. "You missed your calling," I told him. "You ought to be writing dime novels!"

My outburst didn't bother Clifford. He wiped his ink-stained fingers on his apron and said, "Everything in that story is true. You did arrest Curly. The court did order him released. And he did say what I wrote he said. Those are his words, not mine, Merlin."

"But they're lies, Clifford! You were with me when we talked to DuFresne's cook—you know Curly murdered that boy!"

"Maybe. But I can't say so without proof. Arresting lawbreakers and gathering evidence is your job, not mine."

I was coming off my mad. It wasn't Clifford's fault the court had turned Curly loose. "Oh, I know that," I said. "I just wish my witnesses hadn't disappeared. I keep seeing the faces of the dead boy's folks when they came to pick up his body."

"You're up against DuFresne's money and power, Merlin. He doesn't like anything to get in his way, not even the law."

I walked to the doorway and looked out at the street. "No man is above the law," I said, "not even Mr. DuFresne. I aim to teach him that."

Clifford smiled. "If you ever do, I can promise you another front-page story."

I stepped out into the sun. "See you, Clifford," I said, "I think I'll go get myself a shave."

When I reached Ed's barbershop I found a note tacked to the door that read: "Running errands—Back in twenty minutes." I rubbed a hand over my beard stubble. I hadn't shaved that morning, or the morning before. My whiskers had passed from casual and carefree to scruffy and unsightly. It was important, I thought, that a deputy U.S. marshal look clean and well groomed.

I pondered the note, written in Bonnie Jo's tight, schoolgirl hand. Twenty minutes? When had she written the note? Five minutes ago? Ten? Had she just left, or had she been gone for a while? Well, I thought, I'd better not wait. There's no telling how long her errands might take her.

I had just turned to walk away when she spoke. Bonnie Jo had this soft, sort of breathy voice that made the hair on the back of my neck stand up.

"Hello, Merlin," she said. "Been waiting long?"

I snatched my hat off and turned to face her. She wore a form-fitting skirt of green wool and a yellow blouse with the top three buttons undone. Her eyes were deep and warm.

"Uh—no, Bonnie Jo. I—I just got here a minute ago." She was pretty as a sunrise, and her smile was inviting.

"I'm sorry," she said. "I had to step out for a bit. I'm so glad I didn't miss you."

"I c-could use a sh-shave," I said. Funny how my stammer seemed to return whenever I spoke to Bonnie Jo.

Her laugh was a demure giggle. "Well, this is a barbershop. You sure came to the right place, Deputy," she said.

I took a seat in the barber chair and put my feet up on the footrest. Bonnie Jo covered me with a cloth, raised the headrest, and tilted the chair back. "Just lie back and relax, Merlin," she said. "I'll bring you a hot towel."

I closed my eyes and lay back, but I sure didn't relax. I could hear Bonnie Jo walking about the shop; I could smell that perfume she favored. I heard her come up behind me, felt her hands cover my face with a hot, steaming towel. I lay still, enjoying the feeling. I felt my mood grow lighter. My anger at having to turn Curly loose began to fade. I heard the rhythmic clink of the shaving brush on a china mug, the slap and glide of a razor on the leather strop that hung from the chair.

Then she was beside me, taking the towel away, lathering my face with smooth strokes of the shaving brush, bending low to scrape away my beard. The touch of her fingers was as light as the landing of a butterfly. I felt her breathing close to my ear, inhaled her scent. This time she didn't speak. There was only the sound of the razor, of her breathing, of my heartbeat.

Bonnie Jo stepped back, folded the razor and placed it on the counter beside the shaving mug. As she had done the first time, her soft hands rubbed bay rum onto my face and left it glowing. She moved to the door and closed it. Then she drew the shades over the big front window. Bonnie Jo turned back to me. Again, her small hands gently brushed my face. She touched my lips, tracing my mouth with her fingertips. Her eyes were large and liquid in the dim light.

"I—I've been wondering since the day we met," she said, "how it would feel to kiss you."

I was taken aback by her boldness, but only for a moment. I felt a hot wave sweep through my belly, heard my heart pounding loud in my ears. I reached up, touching Bonnie Jo's hair, and pulled her face down to mine. There, in the half-light of Ed's Barbershop, I lost myself in the deep, hot sweetness of her kiss.

Now I believe there are some things a gentleman shouldn't talk about. I have never been inclined to tell tales out of school, nor to speak of matters that might damage a lady's reputation. So, just as Bonnie Jo did with the window shades of the shop, I'll close the curtains on what happened next.

There's one thing I can tell you, though—Ed's Barbershop stayed closed for the rest of that afternoon.

Dusk had descended by the time we finished saying our farewells. I watched Bonnie Jo trip lightly up the walkway to her house and open the screen door. For a moment she hesitated, her eyes big and dark in the twilight. Then, with a smile and a wave, she went quickly inside. Seconds after she had passed from my sight, I found myself still returning her wave.

I don't recall walking back to the marshal's office, but next thing I knew I was standing at its front door. Through the window I could see Jeff, seated behind his desk. The lamp was turned low, and the shadow of Jeff's hat brim hid his face as it had the day I met him. I put away my memories of Bonnie Jo and our afternoon together, and walked in.

"Evenin', Merlin," Jeff said. "I was just fixin' to make rounds. Thought maybe we could get us some supper down at the café afterward."

I shook my head. "I'll help you make rounds, but I believe I'll pass on supper at the café. I don't much feel like being around people tonight." Jeff looked at me, and nodded. "I understand," he said. "Our having to turn Curly loose will be the talk of the town."

Jeff took his sawed-off ten-gauge down from the gun rack and checked its loads. "I expect DuFresne and his cowboys will be feelin' their oats about now. They just might figure they've got the law on the run."

I grinned. "If they figure that, I figure they just might be wrong. What do you figure?"

Jeff closed the scattergun with a flip of his wrist. His smile was bright against the darkness of his skin. "Law don't run from lawbreakers," he said. "Lawbreakers run from the law."

Together, we stepped outside and set our faces toward Trail Street.

We walked south, checking the locks of the saddle shop and bank. The streetlight on the corner lit the intersection of Trail and Main, its yellow circle taking in the pickets of Bonnie Jo's fence. I checked the lock on the barbershop door, my memories of the afternoon heady and strong.

Across the street, Jeff had moved on to the darkened pawnshop. Next door, the hanging lamps inside Sharp's pool hall cast squares of light out onto the street. Looking in though the window, Jeff watched for a time and then he turned, waiting for me. I checked the doors of the post office and mercantile, and crossed the street.

Six horses were tied to the hitch rack in front of the Legal Tender, including a steel-gray thoroughbred wearing Buck DuFresne's silver-mounted saddle. I passed among the animals, checking their brands. "Four of these horses carry the Rimfire brand," I said. "That means four DuFresne men are inside, including Buck."

Jeff nodded. "Buck is in town 'most every night," he said. "The hired help don't get in near as often."

"What say we go in and socialize some?" I asked. "If there's to be trouble, let's have it now."

Jeff's grin told me he was ready, too. "My old mammy used to say, 'never trouble trouble till trouble troubles you,' but I've always preferred to meet it head-on."

I bowed at the waist, and waved Jeff toward the doorway with a sweep of my hat. "After you, Marshal Brown," I said.

It was a slow night at the Legal Tender. The long bar was occupied by three of DuFresne's cowboys, including Curly Bunton. Buck DuFresne sat at a table near the window, talking with Kyle Haddon. Across the room, two farmers from up Medicine Lodge Creek sat together, drinking beer. On the sober side of the bar, bartender Jerry Paddock stood, polishing glassware with a towel. He raised his eyes to the door as we came in. The DuFresne men turned their heads, watching as we approached.

Jeff was the very soul of affability. "Good evenin', gentlemen," he said. "How are you boys doin' tonight?"

At the bar, Curly Bunton turned to face us, elbows on the bar behind him. "Evenin', Marshal," he said. Nodding at me, he added, "Deputy."

Buck DuFresne stood up and turned to face us. "We're doing fine, thank you, Marshal," he said, "just having a drink or two, and enjoying good company. As you can see, we've all checked our weapons with Jerry. This town is peaceful as a church."

"Well, now," Jeff said, "I am glad to hear that, Mistuh DuFresne. There's nothin' we like better than a peaceable town. Ain't that so, Deputy?"

"That's right," I said. "And we hope it stays that way."

Buck glanced at Jeff's shotgun. "Goin' bird-huntin', Marshal?" he asked.

Jeff looked at the weapon in his hands as if he was surprised to see it. "Why, no," he said. "This here is my 'just in case' gun. I carry it just in case the peace gets disturbed."

Buck's face was expressionless. He smiled, but his eyes were hard as flint. "I don't believe you'll be needing it, Marshal," he said, "not tonight."

Buck's meaning was clear. There would be no trouble from him or his riders that evening, but he was making no promises regarding the future.

Jeff turned back toward the door. "Glad to hear that, Mistuh DuFresne, mighty glad," he said. Then, to the boys at the bar, he added, "Now you gents have yourselves a pleasant evenin', you hear?"

Out on the street, Jeff looked back at the lighted windows of the Legal Tender and frowned. "Those men ain't near as friendly as they seem," he said. "I've got a feelin' they're just bidin' their time."

I felt tense, annoyed, somehow. Jeff and me had prepared ourselves for a showdown that hadn't come. "I feel like the feller who got all dressed up and had no place to go," I said.

Jeff smiled. "I guess sometimes when a man's ready to face up to trouble, trouble ain't quite ready to face up to him."

The following week began with a change in the weather. I lay on the bunk in the marshal's office, listening to the patter of rain on the roof, and thought about Bonnie Jo. I recalled our time together in the dim half-light of the barbershop. I remembered her touch, and the urgent, breathless words she whispered in my ear. I recalled her kisses, and the way the flame we kindled turned into a wildfire. I saw her face in memory—her small, turned-up nose, her tender smile, and her big, deep eyes that held my own and would not let them go.

I have ofttimes been a mystery to myself. I have sometimes said and done things I neither planned nor expected to, and that afternoon with Bonnie Jo had been one of those times. I hardly knew the woman, and yet what happened that day had little to do with knowing. I knew Pandora, back home in Dry Creek, but she and I had never let things get so out of hand. Not only did I know Pandora, I loved her. *Well,* I told myself, *if that's so, you surely have a strange way of showing it.* I can't explain the way I felt just then except to say that Pandora was in my heart, but Bonnie Jo was in my blood.

The town stayed peaceful all through the next few weeks. DuFresne's cowboys came in at night, as usual. They drank and gambled at the Legal Tender and at the Mint, over on Front Street. They checked their guns, rode easy when they came and went, and were as law abiding as anyone could wish. Jeff and me stayed watchful, not wanting to let our guard down, and waited.

A letter came from Ridgeway, acknowledging my report. He had already heard about our having to turn Curly loose, and while he seemed to sympathize, he was nowhere near as upset as I was. He wrote that I was doing well, and that I had his full confidence. He even included a draft on the Cattlemen's Bank, covering my wages for the month of April. I was glad Ridgeway seemed to think I was doing well, but I'd have been a good deal more glad if I had thought so, too.

It will come as no surprise that I spent a good deal of my time during those weeks in the company of Bonnie Jo Hutchins. Just watching her face light up when I came around made me feel like I'd hung the moon, and the sweet hours we spent alone together made me crave her company like a drowning man craves dry.

One day I rented a rig from the livery stable and drove us out to a picnic in the nearby Wolf Mountains. We spread our blankets on the grass and dined on fried chicken, biscuits, and apple pie. Bonnie Jo read poetry to me from a book she'd brought. Later, we lay there on our backs amid the wildflowers, watching the great clouds drifting by overhead. We tried to outdo each other in telling of the shapes and forms we imagined. We drank lemonade, we laughed and talked of childish things, and she called me her sweet cavalier.

We made love by the tumbling waters of Owl Creek, and for a time I forgot all about the DuFresnes, Jeff Brown, and the troubles I believed were coming. I turned my thoughts away from the world I knew, and found a new world in the person of Bonnie Jo Hutchins.

A week later, I saddled Rutherford and the bay and took Bonnie Jo for a ride in the country around Medicine Lodge. Bonnie Jo didn't ride sidesaddle like a lady is supposed to, but rode cross-saddle like a man. I suppose such conduct would be considered pretty scandalous in some quarters, but it didn't bother me none. Bonnie Jo was a good rider, and seeing her fork the bay in her divided riding skirt just seemed natural somehow. Anyway, I never worried about it. She and I explored the creeks and the draws, rode to the tops of hills and looked down at the country below.

We watched the beaver and muskrat at play, and we surprised white tail deer along the brushy bottoms. Finally, as the sun dropped low in the sky, Bonnie Jo grew restless. She inquired about the time of day, and asked that we return to town. As far as Bonnie Jo was concerned, our outing had ended. Nothing would do but that I take her back to her house, and so, of course, I did.

As we continued to see each other, I learned it was Bonnie Jo's wish and her rule that she be back at her home alone well before sundown. I soon discovered there was no use teasing or coaxing her at such a time. I didn't understand the why of it, but I figured if that was what she wanted, the least I could do was comply with her wishes. Sometimes she put me in mind of one of those enchanted princesses in the storybooks. You know, the kind who had to be back in the castle before sundown or her coach would turn into a pumpkin and her coachmen into mice or something.

Bonnie Jo always seemed to enjoy our time together, whether we rode the country or spent a rainy afternoon inside at her house. But always, as evening drew nigh, that restlessness would come upon her and our time together would end.

When I asked to see her in the evening, she always told me no. "I just can't," she would say. "I'll see you tomorrow, my sweet cavalier." And sure enough, when we met the next day she would seem as pleased to see me as if I'd been gone for a month.

If Jeff knew about Bonnie Jo and me—and I reckon he did—he never said a word. As for me, I made it a point to make evening rounds with him, and to man the office when he needed to be away. We both still expected some move by the DuFresnes, but the days passed without incident and little by little we dropped our guard.

There was precious little to do during those weeks in April and early May. Jeff made a trip to the agency on business. I broke up a fight one afternoon between a farmer and his neighbor. Late one night we had to jail the sad-eyed waiter at the City Café for drunkenness. The Richardson boy broke a window at the dry goods store, and I had to call on his old man to make it right with the storekeeper. Such was the state of law enforcement in Medicine Lodge during that time.

And then, just when we least expected it, Archie Young Bull came back to town.

CHAPTER 7

▼

Arnie Moss brought the news. He burst into the marshal's office at ten o'clock in the morning, out of breath and out of sorts.

"I'm too damn old to be runnin' in the hot sun," he said, mopping his brow with his shirtsleeve, "but I figured you boys would want to know—I just got word Archie Young Bull and his friends are across the creek at the campground."

I had been sweeping out the office when Arnie came in, and I nearly dropped my broom.

Jeff closed the file he'd been reading, and stood up at his desk. "I don't really believe in coincidence," he said, "but I'm starting to think there may be somethin' to it. I've just been looking at Archie's file."

Arnie sat down in the chair across from Jeff. "Well, you can go look at him in person, if you hurry," he said. "Freddy Two Bears, the kid that works for me down at the livery, just saw him. Archie and the bunch he runs with are over there, throwin' arrows for sport like they don't have a care in the world."

"I expect Archie figures the heat is off, by this time," Jeff said. "Let's go welcome him home, Merlin."

I took Jeff's "just in case" gun from the rack and handed it to him, but Jeff shook his head.

"No guns, Merlin. Not this time. We'll just ride on over and introduce ourselves."

I could hardly believe my ears. "I don't mean to question your orders, Jeff, but we're talking about the boys who nearly killed Dan Wingate! I have a feeling they don't respect the law all that much."

"Maybe they will," Jeff said pleasantly, "after today."

Jeff stepped out toward the livery barn at a rapid pace. It was all I could do to keep up with him.

"All right," I said. "We'll do this your way. But if what happens is what I think is going to happen, I'm sure going to hold it against you."

Jeff chuckled. "Where's your sense of adventure, Deputy? Didn't you ever face up to bullies in the schoolyard?"

"Yes, and I got my butt kicked about eighty percent of the time. Besides, this ain't no schoolyard and Archie Young Bull ain't no schoolboy!"

Jeff laughed out loud. I was beginning to doubt his sanity. "No, he ain't," Jeff said, "but that don't mean he's too old to get an education."

We saddled our horses at the livery barn and rode out for the campground at a trot. But instead of following the road and crossing the bridge over Medicine Lodge Creek, Jeff turned his horse down into the willows and brush and drew rein at the creek bank.

"I figure they'll be watching the road," Jeff said. "We'll ford the creek and go in the back way."

Jeff kicked his horse in the flanks, and drove the animal off into the creek. I stood in the stirrups and reined Rutherford in after him. A moment later, we were across and in the brush and trees on the other side.

"According to his file," Jeff said, whispering now, "Archie Young Bull is eighteen years old, and he lives with his grandmother when he's not raisin' hell somewhere in the territory. He learned to speak English at the Crow boarding school before he broke out and went on the dodge. He's five foot eleven in his moccasins, and he's mean when he's drinkin,' which is most of the time." Jeff stepped down and tied his horse to the tree branch. "I'll walk in from here," he said. "You follow and back me up." Then he was gone.

"Arrow-throwing" is a game played by Crow boys and men. An arrow is cast and serves as a target for as many as ten players, five on each side. Whoever hits the arrow with his arrow, or comes closest to it, wins all the arrows. Sometimes, other items of value are wagered, and I'm told the competition at such times gets downright intense. Anyway, that's where we found Archie Young Bull that day. Archie, and four of his followers, were competing against five older men. Their attention was on the game, not on us.

Most of the men were naked from the waist up, clad only in breechcloths and moccasins. A handsome youth, his jet-black hair unbraided and falling well below his shoulders, took aim with his bow and fired. A roar went up from his friends as his shot struck the ground just inches from the target arrow.

Jeff stepped out of the woods and walked toward the players. I don't believe they even knew he was there until he was nearly upon them. I watched Jeff turn toward the young man who had just made the shot, and I heard him speak.

"Archie Young Bull!"

The youth spun sharply about and faced Jeff. Surprise flashed briefly across his face, but was quickly replaced by arrogance. Jeff had embarrassed the players. He had come into their midst without being detected by any of them. The young man's eyes blazed. He still held his bow, but his arrows lay in his quiver on the ground beside him. He kept glancing down at them, then back at Jeff. I felt the hair rise on the back of my neck. It was clear the young Indian was considering whether to kill Jeff outright.

In the end, curiosity got the better of his murderous instincts. He looked Jeff up and down, then looked beyond Jeff at me. Maybe, I thought, he was wondering how many more men were behind us in the brush. For just a moment his hot eyes looked directly into mine, and then he turned his attention back to Jeff.

"I am Archie Young Bull," he said. "I have heard about you, Black White Man. You are younger than old man Wingate, but you are as weak. You had the killer of Goes to the Water in your jail, and you set him free."

He looked at Jeff, waiting for his reply.

For a moment, Jeff was silent. Then he said, "I am the marshal of Medicine Lodge. My deputy, Law Bringer, works with me to protect the people of the town and capture those who do wrong. Others, not us, set the killer of Goes to the Water free."

Archie glanced again at the arrows on the ground, then back at Jeff. "If you are law men, where are your guns?"

"Marshal Wingate was an old man when you and your friends beat him and took his gun. Maybe you would like to give it back."

Archie frowned. Clearly, this marshal was a different sort than he was used to. "I think your name should be Crazy Black White Man," Archie said. "Maybe I will kill you today."

Jeff took a step closer to the young Indian. They were now no more than ten feet apart. "Maybe you will not," Jeff said. "You are a thief and a coward, and I am not a weak and feeble old man."

Archie stiffened. Suddenly, he hurled himself at Jeff, swinging his bow like a flail. Jeff feinted left, then dodged to the right, avoiding the charge. As Archie swept past, Jeff set his feet and swung his right fist sharply into the young man's temple. Stunned and confused, Archie faltered, and Jeff snatched the bow from his hand. Off balance, Archie fell to one knee, but scrambled quickly to his feet.

Jeff was waiting for him. Holding the captured bow in his left hand, he struck Archie a stinging blow across the face and neck, then clubbed him hard with his fist, dropping him face-down onto the grass.

Jeff stood over the fallen youth, Archie's bow in his hand, and turned to face the others. I held my breath. The only sound I could hear in all that broad meadow was the beating of my own heart. The other Indians were silent, unmoving. Then a young Indian, his eyes wide and his face twisted by rage, suddenly nocked an arrow to his bowstring and drew it back, aiming at Jeff.

Uh-oh, I thought, *the apple cart is about to upset.*

Behind the youth, an older man with thin gray braids spoke sharply in the Crow language. I have no idea what he said, but his words had an immediate effect. The young man released the tension on the bowstring and lowered his bow, hatred still hot in his eyes.

Jeff played to the crowd. He raised the captured bow above his head, and slowly stepped away from the unconscious youth. I watched the men behind him as he walked toward me, well aware there was little I could do if they chose to attack us.

As he reached me, he said quietly, "Just turn, and follow me. Walk slow, but proud."

My mouth was dry and the palms of my hands were wet, which is just the opposite of the way they're supposed to be.

With nerves stretched taut as fiddle strings, I did as Jeff told me, but it's hard to strut when your knees are knocking. We slowly walked into the brush and out of sight. A moment later, and we had mounted our horses, crossed the creek, and were headed back to town.

I think I mentioned that I seldom drink hard liquor. Well, on that day I was ready to make an exception to my rule. It seemed to me that attempting suicide by getting pushy with a passel of armed Indians—and surviving—just might be reason enough to fall off the wagon.

As for Jeff, I didn't know whether he was brave or just lacking imagination, and I told him so.

Jeff grinned his bright, big-toothed smile, and said, "A man can't help being scared sometimes, but he doesn't have to show it. If there's one thing Indians respect, it's courage."

"They respect crazy people, too, so I guess you qualify either way. I can't believe we got away with that! What did we accomplish, anyway? You didn't even take Archie into custody—you left him where you found him!"

"I decided to play by their rules," Jeff said. "There are four war deeds the Crows require for a man wishing to become a chief, and they all involve risking his life. First, touching or striking the first enemy to fall, whether alive or dead. Second, wrestling a weapon away from an enemy warrior. Third, commanding a war party successfully. And fourth, entering an enemy camp at night and stealing a horse. I figure I accomplished three out of four, anyway."

"No wonder they were impressed. I suppose you'll want to go back tonight for Archie's horse! Well, if you do, you're on your own."

Jeff laughed aloud. "No, suh! That would be pushin' my luck. Anyway, I already have a horse."

Some people steady their nerves with drink or soft music, but I've always found that three or four eggs, a T-bone steak, and a double handful of fried spuds will do it for me. Later that night, over supper at the City Café, I asked Jeff how he'd come to know so much about the Crow Indians.

"Truth is," he said, "I'm still learnin' about the Crows. But most of the tribes seem to have pretty much the same values. Chasin' Victorio with the Tenth down in New Mexico taught me plenty about Apaches."

"You made Archie look small," I said. "He won't forget."

"I hope not," Jeff said.

I have to admit I had my doubts about what our encounter with Archie had accomplished. Jeff had surely taken a bold step. He had met the young warrior head-on, and he had won the day. But I couldn't believe Archie would let it end there. Some day, some night, when we least expected him, I figured Archie would strike back. I kept glancing back over my shoulder, waiting for the other moccasin to drop.

Two days later, returning to the marshal's office just before sundown, I found the package. It was a small bundle, wrapped in a square of white buckskin and tied with thongs, and it had been left on the boardwalk just outside the front door. Jeff was sitting at his desk when I brought the bundle in and handed it to him.

"Looks like somebody brought us a May basket," I said.

Jeff untied the thongs and carefully unrolled the buckskin. There, in the center of the square, lay an old Starr revolver and a nickel-plated city marshal's badge!

"Don't tell me," I said. "That's the gun and badge Archie took from Dan Wingate."

Jeff nodded. "The very same," he said. "It appears Archie is a renegade, but an honorable one. There may be hope for that young man yet."

It was my custom to give Rutherford and the bay horse some riding at least once a week, and I generally spent a little time with Arnie Moss, the liveryman, on those occasions. It was Arnie, you may recall, who first told us that Archie Young Bull was back in the area. My account of our encounter with the young Indian had both edified and entertained Arnie, and he had asked me several times to repeat the story.

It was on a Monday afternoon about a week after the bundle arrived that I next visited the livery barn. The day was hot, and both the front and back barn doors stood open to let a cooling breeze blow through. Arnie came in from the corral out back, mopping his face with a bandanna. He grinned when he saw me. "Hot enough for you?" he asked.

I gave his grin back. "Just about, Arnie. How about you?"

He sat down on a hay bale and took his hat off. Wiping the inside band with his bandanna, he put the hat back on, and cleared his throat. "I've been wantin' to ask you a favor," he said. "I've seen enough men pass through here to know a bronc stomper when I see one. I'm guessing you have set a few of the wild and snuffy ones in your time."

"One or two," I admitted.

"Well, I have this little four-year-old gelding I believe would make a fine cow horse," he said, "if the right man had the time to work with him."

"Meaning me?"

"If you're interested."

I thought the idea over. Aside from making rounds with Jeff in the evening and being on call at the office when he wasn't there, I did have some time on my hands.

"I don't rough-break a horse," I said. "You'll find no bear sign or panther tracks on the horses I handle. I like to bring an animal along with patience and kindness. It takes longer, but you wind up with a more reliable mount."

"That's what I'm lookin' for," Arnie said. "When can you start?"

I looked out through the doorway. Heat waves shimmered along the sun-baked street. "First thing in the morning, while the day is cool."

"I'll see you then," Arnie said. "I'll pay ten dollars cash, or you can take ten off your livery bill."

"That's generous. Five is the going rate."

"It's the goin' rate for breakin' a horse quick, and rough," Arnie said. "I already said that ain't what I want."

I gave him a grin and my hand. "All right," I said. "You've got a deal. I'll see you in the morning."

Back out on the sun-baked street, the day seemed even hotter than before. I walked up Main and turned the corner, passing the barbershop and Bonnie Jo's house. I considered paying Bonnie Jo a visit and maybe passing a pleasant hour in her company, but then I thought better of it. As I passed the shop's open door, I saw she was shaving a customer, with two other fellers waiting their turn. Bonnie Jo looked up, smiling as she saw me. I tipped my hat, and walked on. I thought, *that woman surely has taken up a homestead in my mind—danged if I'm not half jealous of her customers.*

Behind the livery barn, and the pens and wagon yard that joined it, was a round corral designed for working broncs. It was there I found Arnie Moss the next morning, waiting for me.

"Mornin'," he said. "Come on over and meet your pupil."

Inside the corral stood a handsome gray gelding with black mane and tail, watching me warily as I approached the corral. The animal appeared to be steady and sound, with a deep chest and good legs. I could see why Arnie wanted special handling for the horse. I shook out a loop in my catch rope and opened the gate.

"Well," I said, "Let's call the class to order."

With Arnie acting as helper, I forefooted the gray and threw him. While Arnie held the gelding's head, I tied up its front feet and slipped the hackamore over its nose. At first, the little horse fought the hobbles, struggling to stand and falling in the soft dirt of the corral. When at last he stopped fighting for a moment and regained his feet, I cross-hobbled him as well, and he was ready for the saddle.

Then came a time for patience. Time after time I laid the saddle blanket upon his back, and each time the gray shied and dodged away from it. Finally, when he came to believe the blanket would do him no harm, he hesitated. I swung the saddle into place and settled it atop his withers. The gray slipped from under the rig and let it drop. I picked it up and eased it onto his back. Twice more, the little horse dodged the saddle, and twice more, I returned it to its place. As had been the case with the blanket, a time came when the little horse hesitated. Quickly, I passed the latigo through the cinch ring and snugged the saddle up tight.

The gray stood, quivering, nostrils flaring. Keeping my moves slow and deliberate, I took off the hobbles. At first, the little horse didn't realize his restraints were gone. Seizing the moment, I stepped in close. I gripped the hackamore reins and a handful of the gelding's mane in my left hand, grasped the saddle horn with my right, and swung lightly up onto his back.

For just a moment, the little horse remained motionless. Then, as I gave a tug on the reins, he took a halting step or two and discovered he was no longer hobbled. He bawled and jumped straight up, but I was ready for him. I took a deep seat and clung to the saddle like glue. Down the gray dropped with a jolt, front legs stiff, forefeet slamming into the dirt, back legs drawn up and cocked for his next jump.

Again he leapt, black mane whipping like a flag. Back he came to earth, twisting, throwing himself right and left, trying to shake me as he circled the corral. Somewhere in the tip-tilted blur of sky and earth, I heard Arnie's voice.

"Ride him, Merlin," he said. "Stay with him!"

The little horse circled the corral, leaping and warping his backbone. He twisted; he spun, growing desperate in his attempts to throw me. He bawled again, and grunted each time his hooves struck the earth. I knew what was coming next. All of the gelding's attempts to get me off his back had come to nothing, thus far. Next, he would sulk, then rear and throw himself backward. I took a short hold on the reins, loosened my feet in the stirrups, and prepared to step off if I had to.

Sure enough, the little gray suddenly stood tall, quick-stepping backward on his hind legs while I hung on with everything I had. Just when I thought I'd have to quit him, he suddenly pitched forward again. His front feet struck the earth like a hammer, and I lost my off stirrup. The gelding redoubled his efforts, bucking and bawling. I tried to find the flopping stirrup with the toe of my boot, but without success.

I held the reins with a death grip, trying to regain my balance. I was slipping, losing my seat. Suddenly, I was flying free, over the gray's head. The corral post rushed to meet me. I twisted, throwing my hands out. The shock of the impact was blinding. Pain exploded behind my eyes, and took my breath away. Then darkness fell like a curtain, and with it, a kind of peace.

CHAPTER 8

▼

When next I came to myself I found, somewhat to my surprise, that I was still alive. I knew I was because of the pain that throbbed behind my eyes and the queasiness that troubled my paunch. My head pounded like a drumbeat at a war dance. I figured if a person still felt such a grievous hurt after he had gave up the ghost there wasn't much point to dying in the first place.

I lay still, barely breathing. Like some great cat, the pain prowled, watching me. I tried my best not to provoke it. I believed if I dared to move or open my eyes, the pain would pounce upon and maul me. I waited, and little by little my tribulation grew less. I came to believe I just might be able to stand the hurt after all.

Where was I? I lay on my back in a bed someplace. My mouth was dry as cotton. I could hear the pulsing of my heart, loud in my ears. The odor of alcohol, and of ether, came wafting to my nostrils. There were sounds—the clink of glass, the slow shuffle of feet. Someone was moving quietly nearby. I opened one eye a crack, and light stabbed in.

"Easy, son," said a calm voice. "Just lie easy. You've taken a hard hit to the head, but you'll be all right."

I tried to speak, but I couldn't make the words come out the way I wanted them to. Finally, I put three of them together. It was a start, anyway. "Who—are you?" I asked.

"Doc Westby," the voice said. "You've had yourself a horse wreck, son. Tried to take out a corral post with your head. Bad idea."

I felt a glass at my lips, felt water moisten my dry mouth. "The good news," said the voice, "is you don't have a skull fracture. The bad news is you've lost some blood, and you may have a concussion. Judging by the old scars, it appears you've had head injuries before."

The water helped. I managed to get out two more words. "A few," I croaked.

"Arnie Moss and Freddy Two Bears, the boy who works for him, brought you in an hour ago. Arnie thought you were dead."

"I'm not," I said. "Am I?"

Doc Westby chuckled. "No, son, not just yet. You're in a room here in my house, just off the parlor. I've sewed up your scalp and applied a cold compress to the wound. You need to keep your head low and try not to move."

A glass was at my lips again. "This is a little something for the pain, and to help you sleep," Doc Westby said. "Now you rest easy. I'll come back to check on you directly." I heard the curtain that served as room divider slide open, and I listened to Doc's quiet tread going away. I quit fighting, laid back, and let the pain have its way with me.

The sick room was dark and quiet, and already I felt sleep tugging at the edges of my consciousness. Just as I was about to slip off into slumber, I heard the brisk ring of Doc's doorbell. Then I heard him walk across the parlor and open the door.

"Howdy, Fletch," said the voice.

The voice belonged to an older man. It sounded strained, maybe a little nervous.

"J. W.," Doc Westby said. "Long time. Come in."

Footfall. The door closed. I heard the soft chime of spurs. Then I heard Doc's voice again. "Sit down, J. W. What can I do for you?"

"Ah need to talk, Fletch. About mah boy. About Buck."

I knew that voice. Where had I heard it? Doc had called his visitor J. W.—John Wesley! John Wesley DuFresne!

"What about Buck?" Doc asked. "Is he in trouble?"

John Wesley's voice was touched by bitterness. "Most of the time, Ah fear. Ah'm worried about him."

"A father worries," Doc said. "How can I help?"

J. W. didn't answer right away. After a moment, he cleared his throat, and said, "It's his drinking, Fletch. It's getting worse. Seems like Ah'm spending half my time bailing him out of one scrape or another. Whiskey seems to bring out the meanness in that boy."

There was another pause. Then J. W. said, "He tore up a hotel room in Billings last week. Got throwed in jail there for beating up a woman. For beating up a woman, Fletch."

"I'm sorry for your trouble," Doc said. "But I don't know what—"

"You're a doctor. Ah thought maybe some medicine, some treatment—"

"For alcoholism? Oh, there are pills, nostrums, and such. Snake-oil peddlers promise a cure. I've even read—and I quote—'some cases have been helped by the application of electricity along the spine.' In my opinion, such remedies are worthless."

"You don't give a man much hope, do you?"

"There's always hope, J. W. I've known people who quit."

"But not many?"

"No. Not many."

There was another long pause. Then I heard the creak of springs as J. W. stood up from the chair. Again, I heard the soft chime of his spurs. J. W. seemed to be pacing the parlor. Then the pacing stopped.

"Buck is mah only boy," J. W. said. "Ah don't want to lose him."

"If memory serves," Doc said, "Buck turned thirty-one this spring. He's not a boy any longer. You can't keep standing between him and the consequences of his actions."

"Meaning Ah should abandon mah son?"

"No. I mean if you want him to be a man, you should treat him like one."

"Do you have a son, Fletch?"

"You know I don't. I lost my boy at Gettysburg."

"Yes, Ah know. Ah guess Ah'm suggesting that if our situations were reversed, you might not see things that much different than Ah do."

"Well," Doc said, "I guess we'll never know, will we?"

When J. W. replied, his voice held a kind of weary resignation. "No," he said, "Ah guess not."

I heard the door open. "Ah'm obliged for your time," J. W. said. "There ain't many people Ah can talk to thisaway."

"I wish I could be of more help," Doc said. "Luck to you—and to Buck."

Then the door closed, and the house was silent again. I knew I had overheard a conversation I wasn't meant to hear, but I didn't know what to do about it. If I should apologize for listening, or even admit I'd heard, I would only make matters worse. After thinking on it some, I decided my best course of action would be to pretend I was asleep.

As it turned out, I didn't have to pretend. By the time Doc returned to the sick room, I had fallen asleep for real.

How long I slept I cannot say. I seem to recall being awakened more than once over the next several hours by Doc Westby so he could give me something to make me sleep, which doesn't make a whole lot of sense if you think about it. Whatever it was he gave me tasted horrible, which I took as good news. Everybody knows the worse the medicine tastes, the better it is for a person.

Sometimes it was dark when I woke up, and sometimes light. The last time I came to, the sun was shining in through the window and the birds were singing outside. Best of all, the pain in my head had gone from unbearable to not too bad, and I woke up hungry as a February bear. Doc Westby took that last as a good sign.

"I'll cook you up some side pork and scramble a few eggs, Deputy," he said. "As to your medical condition, it is my considered opinion that you will not have learned anything from this experience. You'll be back trying to break that fool horse first thing tomorrow morning."

He gave me an owlish look over the tops of his spectacles and smiled. "You'll be good as new in a day or so, and you may even look halfway decent in a week or so."

"Some bedside manner," I said. "You cheer a man up with one hand, and scare him to death with the other. What's wrong with my looks?"

"See for yourself," he said, handing me a mirror.

The apparition that met my gaze resembled me, I suppose, but just barely. Both eyes were purplish-black and narrowed to slits. A big white bandage covered most of my head, making me look like pictures of a Hindu I'd seen once. A red and yellow streak spread down my right cheek. Over all, my face looked puffy, lopsided, and peculiar. I could have robbed the Cattlemen's Bank without a mask, and nobody in town would have recognized me, except Doc, maybe.

When I spoke, the words came out the side of my mouth. "Well, I'm sure not coming here for my beauty treatments anymore," I said. "Bring on them eggs and that side pork."

Doc Westby was as good as his word. He fed me a breakfast that was as tasty as it was filling. By the time I finished, I felt almost like my old self. Doc took the dishes away, and by the time he returned I had got out of bed and dressed myself. I felt a little woozy when I bent over to pull my boots on, but except for that I figured I was ready to take up living again.

"I don't suppose it would do any good to tell you to stay in that bed another day, would it?" Doc said.

I grinned. "No, I don't suppose it would."

"Well, then. Give me five dollars and get out of here so I can go back to taking care of sick people. If you don't have the five, you can owe me."

I took a five-dollar bill from my pocket and gave it to him. "It's better if I pay you now," I said. "If you let me leave here owing you, you might never see your money." I offered my hand, and he took it. "Much obliged, Doc," I said.

He smiled. "Get the hell out of here," he said.

Jeff was waiting for me when I stepped out into the sunlight. He leaned against the apple tree in Doc Westby's front yard, and his smile was bright as the sunlight.

"You're taking on my color, Deputy," he said. "Your eyes have already turned black."

"Hello, Jeff," I said. "I had me a little mishap with a gray gelding."

"So I understand. I came by when I first heard, but Doc figured you needed your rest. How you doing, Merlin?"

"A little shaky, but I'm on the mend. Anything new in town?"

Jeff opened Doc's front gate for me and stepped aside. "There was one incident of note," he said. "Archie Young Bull came by the office last night, full of whiskey and injured pride. Said he had no wish to break the white man's law. Said whiskey made him crazy, but he didn't know how to leave it alone. I figure that's about as close to an apology as we'll ever get."

"Is that all he wanted—to apologize?"

"He said he was drunk and a little crazy already. Asked me to lock him up so he wouldn't get in trouble."

"Seems like Archie figures the law should protect the citizen—even from himself."

"I wish more lawbreakers thought that way. Anyway, Archie Young Bull spent the night sleeping it off. I expect he's sick, sober, and sorry about now."

Thinking of my recent horse encounter, I said, "Remorse comes easy. All a man has to do is hurt himself bad enough."

Back at the jail, Jeff unlocked the cell door and told Archie he was free to go. The young Indian was still handsome as a hawk, but his eyes were red and his long hair was unkempt and matted. He got shakily to his feet and felt his way to the open door. As he stepped through, he saw me standing behind Jeff. Archie took a long look at my face, and then turned to Jeff. "I didn't do *that*," he said.

By Monday morning of the following week, I had lost considerable of my battered look and had returned to the breaking of Arnie Moss's gelding. Because the little horse had got away with throwing himself backward—and throwing me in the process—I figured he would try it again. If he succeeded a second time, he would most likely be on his way to becoming a bona fide outlaw. I knew the remedy, but I hated to use it.

Hanging from a nail in the tack room at the livery stable was a braided rawhide quirt. When next I stepped up into the saddle, the quirt was in my hand and ready for use. As before, the gray fell to bucking and pitching and I stayed with the animal at every jump.

Then came the moment I had expected. The gray fell into a sulk, backed up a step or two, and reared high. But this time, before he could throw himself over backward, I brought the rawhide into action. I swung the quirt forward and backward, stinging the horse about the ears and whipping back across his flanks. Startled, and distracted from his rearing and backing, the gray resumed his sulk. Ears laid back and feet spread wide, the little horse refused to answer to word, rein, or quirt.

It was then I touched the gelding with my spurs. He broke out of his balk, circling the corral until he was blowing hard and dripping sweat. For a time, I kept him working and moving, convincing him he had begun a test of wills he could not win. At last, I drew rein and stepped down, then remounted and dismounted quickly several times. Finally, I stripped the hackamore and saddle off and turned him out into the big corral. The little gelding's first day of school was over.

The next day was chiefly a repeat of the first, except that the gelding no longer tried throwing himself backward. I was pleased; the little horse was intelligent and a quick learner. His bucking had lessened, and he had begun to respond to the rein and knee pressure without need of the harsh remedies of quirt and spur. As before, I ended the day by mounting and dismounting several times before unsaddling and turning the animal out.

On the third day, I had Arnie throw open the gates and I rode the gray away into the countryside. Finding himself free of the corral, the little horse again tried some running and bucking. When he was unable to shake me and I reminded him that I still wore spurs, he seemed to remember his earlier lessons and fell to behaving himself.

By the time I rode him back to the livery barn later that morning, the breaking of Arnie's gray gelding was complete. Arnie would need to ride the animal daily for a time to reinforce the lessons, but the only thing needed to complete the gray's education would be a series of wet saddle blankets.

Over the next few days I tended to my own horses and helped Jeff man the marshal's office. Archie Young Bull and his war party seemed to have turned plum peaceful, and Archie even stopped by now and then just to talk with Jeff. From time to time, when the drink was upon him, Archie would decide an ounce of precaution was worth a pound of whatever and would check into our jail until he sobered up. It was an unusual practice for a wild Indian, but it seemed to work for Archie.

I stopped by Bonnie Jo's house a couple of times, but on each occasion the barbershop was closed and her house was locked up and dark. Clifford Bidwell, down at the newspaper office, said he thought she'd left town for a few days. Nobody seemed to know where she'd gone. I played a few games of pool with Clifford and teased him some about being the editor-publisher of *The Medicine Lodge Star*.

"The trouble with running a small town newspaper," I told him, "is that everybody knows all the news before you can get it in print."

"That may be true," Clifford said, "but they still have to buy the *Star* to find out what they ought to *think* about the news."

I said the real reason folks bought his paper was so they could have something to wrap their garbage in, and to have a week's worth of paper for their outhouses. Clifford let on that my remarks didn't bother him none, but he scratched on an easy shot right after that, and that allowed me to run the table and win the game. Clifford is a better pool player than I am, but I figure if you're short on skill you can at least rattle your opponent.

I gave some thought to the conversation I'd overheard between Doc Westby and J. W. DuFresne. I sure hadn't meant to eavesdrop, but that hadn't kept it from happening. The trouble was, I couldn't very well unhear what I'd heard. All I could do was try not to think about it, but that didn't work the way I hoped it would. It was like when someone tells you not to think of a purple elephant— from that moment on, all you can think of is a durned purple elephant.

The trouble came, sudden and unexpected, as trouble often does. The worst of storms begin with a breeze and a raindrop, a prairie fire with the smallest of sparks. This time, a spark lit a fuse that led to a major clash of men and wills, and to a chain of events that few could have foreseen.

Late on a Friday night in May, Jeff and me were once again making our rounds. As usual, Jeff carried his sawed-off "just in case" gun. It had become our habit to take opposite sides of a street, keeping each other in sight, in order to speed the task and avoid duplicating our efforts. We were doing so that night.

Across Trail Street, Jeff had checked the doors of the Cattlemen's Bank and the pawnshop, and had once again stopped to survey the activity inside Sharp's pool hall through its big front windows. Just beyond, horses lined the hitch rack at the Legal Tender, and rough laughter and piano music—if you could call it music—drifted out through the open door. The piano player's name was Paul, but I had taken to calling him "Thumbs" for reasons that would be apparent if ever you heard him play. To be charitable, I can only say he made up in raw determination what he lacked in musical ability.

On my side of Trail Street, I could see a light in the window at Bonnie Jo's house, although the hour was well past midnight. I was glad she had returned from wherever her travels had taken her, but I remember being concerned that she might be ill. As a rule, Jeff and me made our rounds earlier in the evening, so I didn't know if being up so late was Bonnie Jo's usual habit or not. For a moment I considered knocking at her door to inquire, but thought better of the impulse and moved on up the street.

I checked the locks at the post office and the mercantile, and was about to move on when I heard a clatter in the alley nearby. I pulled my gun and stepped into the shadows. Keeping close to the wall, I held my breath, listening. Then, suddenly, Doc Westby's tomcat exploded out of a trash barrel, screeched a yowl that could have raised goose bumps on a dead man, and streaked away into the night!

I had to laugh at myself. My heart was pounding like a trip-hammer, and I had very nearly touched off a shot from my .44. That would sure have brought Jeff running, I thought.

Just as I stepped out of the alley, a tall man crossed the street in front of me, headed for the Legal Tender. I could see he had already taken on enough booze to interfere with his walking. His gait was unsteady, and his course was far from direct. As he stepped up onto the boardwalk and into the light from the saloon windows, I suddenly recognized him—Buck DuFresne!

The cattleman's hat was pushed back, his black hair was mussed, and his shirt was open halfway down its front. Buck swayed, surveying the room over the tops of the batwing doors. He pushed them open and stumbled inside. Back on the street, I saw Jeff approaching the saloon. He looked my way and stopped, waiting for me to join him. In a moment, I had crossed over.

"Was that who I think it was?" I asked.

Jeff nodded. "Yep. Buck DuFresne, big as life and twice as natural," he said. "Strikes me as curious, the way he came walking up that way. His horse is already tied there at the hitch rack."

I looked. Sure enough, the steel-gray thoroughbred stood hitched with the others.

"I wonder where he was coming from," Jeff said.

We might have speculated further, but all at once we were interrupted by sounds from inside—a scuffle, angry words, breaking glass, voices raised in surprise. I have said that Jeff Brown was a stocky man, big-shouldered and solid. He was all of that, but he was far from slow. Before I could react, Jeff had swept through the doors and was headed straight for a group of men at the bar.

Buck stood, his back to us, at the center of the long bar. On each side, men leaned back, surprise on their faces, frozen in various attitudes like actors in a stage play. Across from Buck, bartender Jerry Paddock fell back against the bottles and glasses, his right hand extended in defense and his left covering his face. Bright blood flowed from beneath his hand, staining his shirt and spattering his vest. Buck raised his arm, and I saw the broken bottle he held in his hand.

All this I took in at a glance, moving toward the bar, but Jeff was already there. Wild-eyed, Buck turned, swinging the broken bottle up by its neck to meet Jeff's advance. He was too late. Jeff set his feet and swung the butt of the ten-gauge up sharply beneath the cattleman's jaw. The impact sounded like an axe striking a chopping block. Buck's eyes glazed, his knees buckled. Then he folded, loose-limbed, and collapsed in a heap among the booted feet at the rail.

"What happened here?" Jeff demanded. For a moment, no one spoke. The Rimfire cowboys stared silently at Jeff, their eyes hard, their jaws set. Curly Bunton was not among them.

A familiar figure—Arnie Moss, from the livery table—stepped away from the bar. "Buck was in here earlier," he said. "Checked his gun, drank some, and left. When he came back, he was mean drunk. He told Jerry he wanted a quart of his best whiskey. Jerry set a bottle out, but told Buck he'd maybe had enough already. Buck went crazy then. Yelled at Jerry. Broke the bottle on the bar, and caught Jerry full in the face with the broken top. Buck can be a sonofabitch when he's drunk."

Behind the bar, Jerry held a bar towel to his face. The towel was already soaked with blood. "God damn him," the barman said, "He cut me bad. I can't see."

I ducked under the pass-through and went to Jerry. "It's me, Jerry—Merlin Fanshaw. Let's have a look."

Carefully, I took the towel away. Jerry's eyes were tightly closed, the left side of his face slashed by the broken glass, and bleeding. I grabbed a couple of fresh towels from behind the bar and put them in Jerry's hands. "It's not so bad," I lied. "Let's get you over to Doc's."

Kyle Haddon burst out of his office and rushed toward the bar. He took in the scene at a glance—his bartender in my care, stunned and bloody, Buck DuFresne unconscious on the floor, Jeff bending over, handcuffing him. "What the hell?" Haddon said.

"Your barkeep told Buck DuFresne he'd had enough to drink, and Buck took offense," I said. "Buck cut up Jerry's face with a broken bottle. When Marshal Brown tried to stop him, Buck turned on him, too, and the marshal put him down."

"Damn!" Haddon said. "How bad is Jerry hurt?"

"Bad enough, boss," Jerry muttered. "I'm bleedin' like a stuck pig, and I can't see. Face feels like it's on fire."

Kyle Haddon seemed frustrated. He stood, poised for action, but found nothing to do. I could almost read his thoughts. The DuFresnes and their cowboys were the Legal Tender's best customers. They provided the bulk of Haddon's income through the money the Rimfire riders spent on whiskey and beer and lost at the gambling tables. Hot-tempered Buck DuFresne had caused trouble before, but this time he had attacked Haddon's principal bartender. Worst of all, the law—Jeff and me—had been on the scene when the attack happened. There was no way to protect Buck, no way to gloss over the incident.

As usual, Haddon was immaculate in white shirt, dove gray frock coat, and fancy vest. To his credit, he gave his clothing no thought, but put his arm around Jerry's bloody shoulders and pulled him close. "I'll take him over to Doc Westby," he said. "Jerry's my bartender, and my friend."

"That's good, Mistuh Haddon," Jeff said. "Merlin and me will be takin' Buck on down to the jail now."

Together, Jeff and me got the cattleman on his feet and leaned him against the bar. Still groggy from the booze he'd consumed—and the butt stroke from Jeff's scattergun—Buck struggled to regain his senses. I picked his hat up from the saloon floor and put it on his head.

"What are you gonna do with him?" one of the cowboys asked.

"Lock him up until the circuit judge gets here," Jeff said. "Mistuh Buck DuF-resne is under arrest for assault, battery, and mayhem, for openers."

The cowboy frowned. "The old man—J. W.—ain't gonna like that."

"I expect not," Jeff said pleasantly. "I don't like it much myself. But his son cut up Jerry with a broken whiskey bottle, and he'll have to answer for it."

"You're a hard man, Marshal," said the cowboy.

"Yes, I am," said Jeff.

CHAPTER 9

By the time we got Buck to the office and took the handcuffs off, he had sobered up some. Jeff took his belt from him and asked him to turn his pockets out. After I lit the lamp, we took him back to a cell and locked him in. He seemed confused.

"What the hell is this?" he grumbled. "What are you arrestin' me for this time?"

"You don't know?"

"Hell, no! I had me a few drinks earlier this evenin' and then—"

"And then you left the Legal Tender, and walked somewhere. You came back a little after midnight. You told Jerry, the barkeep, you wanted whiskey. Jerry set out a bottle, but said he thought you'd had enough already.

"That's when your famous temper showed itself. You yelled at Jerry some, and then you broke the bottle and slashed his face."

Buck looked shocked. "Slashed Jerry! I wouldn't do that—I like Jerry!"

"If you like him any better he's liable to be dead," Jeff said dryly. "This is the second time in a month I've had to run you in. This time you're going to trial."

Buck scowled. He ran his fingers through his hair. "Now wait a minute," he said. "I raised a little hell, I guess, and I'm sorry about Jerry. I'll make it right with him. But you'd best remember who I am, nigger—there's no way you're keepin' me locked up, and no goddamn way I'm goin' to trial."

Jeff ignored Buck's insult and his bluster. He turned and opened the door to the office. When I took the lamp inside, Buck's cell went dark as a mineshaft.

"Get some sleep," Jeff said, and closed the door behind him.

Back in the office, Jeff hung the cell key on its peg and sat down at his desk.

I opened the front door and looked out into the night. "If it's all right with you," I said, "I believe I'll go down to Doc Westby's and see how Jerry is doing. I might get his statement, if he's up to it."

Jeff had already begun to write his report. "Go ahead," he said. "Maybe you could stop by the Legal Tender and pick up Buck's gun on your way back."

"I'll do that. It's a good thing he wasn't packin' it tonight. He'd likely be looking at a murder charge about now."

"Good thing for Jerry, too," Jeff observed.

It was nearly one-thirty when I turned the corner at the bank and headed north toward Doc Westby's place. Across the street, Bonnie Jo's house was dark and silent, and I assumed she had finally gone to bed.

The Legal Tender was still open—it would be until two—but the cowboys had called it a night, and their horses were gone from the hitch rack. Looking in the window, I saw that only Kyle Haddon and Arnie Moss remained in the saloon. Haddon sat, drinking with Arnie at a small table near the front. He had loosened his collar, and he looked bone-tired. His usually immaculate frock coat was stained with Jerry Paddock's blood.

The front door was locked, but I knocked until Haddon got up and let me in. "I was just having a nightcap with Arnie," he said. "Will you join us?"

"No, thanks," I said. "I just wanted to check on Jerry. How is he?"

"Doc says he'll be all right. No damage to his eyes, but he'll have some ugly scars. The cuts from that damned bottle run deep."

"I expect he's hurting pretty bad."

"He was. Doc gave him some laudanum and sewed him up. He was asleep when I left just now."

"I'll stop by in the morning and see him," I said. "I'll need to get his statement."

"Yeah," Haddon said. "Jerry's got his Irish up. Talking about preferring charges. Says he plans to get a lawyer and bring a damage suit against Buck."

"I'd say he's got a case," I said. "Do you still have Buck's gun?"

"Yes," Haddon said, walking toward the bar. "The Rimfire cowboys took his horse over to the livery. Asked me for his gun, too, but I figured the marshal would want it."

Haddon brought the holstered gun and cartridge belt out from beneath the bar and handed them to me. The fancy ivory grips with the carved longhorn heads almost seemed to glow in the lamplight.

"Much obliged," I said. "We'll lock these up with the rest of his effects."

Arnie still sat at the table.

I nodded at him, and at Kyle Haddon. "See you gents tomorrow," I said, and walked outside.

Medicine Lodge was silent at that hour of the morning. Overhead, stars beyond counting flickered and winked in the blackness. Except for the streetlights and the dull glow of a hanging lamp inside the Legal Tender, the town was peaceful and dark. After the bustle of the day and the early-morning havoc at the Legal Tender, quiet covered Medicine Lodge like a blanket.

I wrapped the gunbelt around Buck's holstered revolver and made my way back toward the marshal's office. There were questions I wanted answers to, and troubles I knew would come, but there would be time later to deal with them. Sufficient unto the day is the evil thereof, says the Good Book. My questions could wait.

I woke up in my bunk at the office a half hour before dawn the next morning. The fire in the stove had long since gone to ashes, and the office was cold as charity. I tried to go back to sleep, but my mind got to working and next thing I knew the rest of me was awake, too. I put my hat on and sat up at the edge of the bunk. Piece by piece, the events of early morning returned to memory, like ducks alighting on a pond. I recalled Buck's attack on Jerry and Jeff's arrest of the cattleman, and I shook my head at the folly and waste of it all.

I fed the stove some kindling and lit a fire to take the chill off. There was still a cup or two of coffee left from the day before, so I set the pot on while I pulled on my britches and boots. Minutes later, the sun topped out above the mountains east of town, and the stove was commencing to ping. I took the coffee off and was just pouring myself a cup when I heard Jeff's boots clump across the boardwalk outside.

"Good morning,'" he said, stepping inside. "How is our prisoner doin'?"

"Sleepin' like a baby, last time I checked," I said. "A big, mean baby."

Jeff frowned. "He's liable to be even meaner when he wakes up," he said. "I cooked up some bacon and beans over at the cabin. Why don't you go have yourself some breakfast and bring a plate back for Buck? I'll take over here."

"I'll do that," I said, "but if Buck comes off his drunk like my pa used to, he won't be much interested in breakin' the fast."

Jeff shrugged. "Eat or not, his choice—but he'll get no hair of the dog at this hotel."

Doc Westby was rumpled, and grumpy as a wet owl when he opened his door. He peered at me through bloodshot eyes and said, "It's damned early for a visit, Deputy—some of us haven't been to bed yet."

"Sorry, Doc," I said.

"You're sorry, but you still want to see my patient. Is that about it?"

I lowered my eyes. "Yes, sir. If he's up to it, I surely do."

Doc eased the door open a little wider. "He's awake, and full of laudanum. I've been most of the morning sewing him up. All right—go on back, but keep it short."

I found Jerry Paddock in the small room off Doc's parlor, propped up in the bed I had so recently occupied myself. The little barkeep's face was swathed in bandages, and his mood was feisty.

"Top o' the morning, Deputy," he said. "So you've come to see the incredible patchwork man, have you?"

There was a chair beside the bed. I smiled and sat down.

"How you doin,' Jerry?"

"I don't suppose I'll know that until these bandages come off. Doc Westby put on quite a quilting bee this morning. I can only hope he didn't sew my ear back where my nose used to be."

"For what it's worth, Buck DuFresne is sorry he cut you up."

"He'll be a hell of a lot sorrier when I take him to court. My lawyer is part bull terrier, and mercy does not abide in him."

"Do you plan to prefer criminal charges?"

"Damn straight I do. And sue his ass, too."

I stood up. "Doc told me to keep my visit short. Is there anything I can do for you?"

"One thing," Jerry said. "Keep that crazy bastard in jail until he's ninety."

Leaving Doc's house, I found Clifford Bidwell waiting for me. "How is Jerry?" he asked.

"How do you think? His face has been cut up like a jigsaw puzzle, and it's mostly covered by bandages. Hell, I'm not even sure that is Jerry in there."

"You think he'd talk to me?"

"You mean for the newspaper? Yeah, he probably would—but Doc is liable to run you off with a shotgun. He spent most of the morning putting Jerry back together. He hasn't been to bed all night, and he's cranky as a constipated bear."

Clifford struck a heroic pose. "Nevertheless," he said, "I must try. Gathering news for the multitudes is not for the faint-hearted."

I grinned. "Don't say I didn't warn you. Maybe I should wait around in case I have to arrest Doc for assault, too."

"Not necessary, Deputy. I'll come by later and lodge a complaint if I'm attacked or murdered."

"Luck to you, Clifford," I said, and walked on up the street.

It was the following day when I thought about visiting Bonnie Jo. I'd not seen her since she came back from her trip, but I'd heard she was in town. I had seen a light on at her house the night before when we arrested Buck. I had meant to check on her then, but had not. Because of our agreement, I guess I had grown accustomed to seeing her only during the daytime. It had not occurred to me to call on her so late. I found that I missed her. I longed to be with her again.

It was nearly ten o'clock in the morning when I walked down to Bonnie Jo's, but I noticed the barbershop was still closed. I opened the gate beside the shop and made my way up the walk to her house. Reaching her front door, I found it ajar, but I knocked anyway.

"Bonnie Jo?" I called out. "It's me, Merlin. Are you all right?"

Her voice was hesitant when she answered. She sounded shy, almost timid. "Merlin? I—I'm in the parlor. Come in."

The drapes had been drawn in Bonnie Jo's parlor, and the room was deep-shadowed and dim. Coming in out of the bright sunlight as I had, I found it hard to make out detail. Hat in hand, I stopped at the entrance to the room, waiting for my eyes to adjust.

"Bonnie Jo?" I said. "Where are you, darlin'? Why is the room so dark?"

I heard movement, saw a slender figure rise in the gloom from a chair and cross to the window. Then the draperies were opened, and sunlight flooded the room. Bonnie Jo stood at the window, silhouetted by the light. She wore her hair down about her shoulders that morning, and her slender figure was clad in a floor-length dressing gown. She turned to face me, and I gasped at what I saw.

An ugly bruise, purple as a plum, marked the left side of her face. Her left eye was black, and swollen nearly closed. Bonnie Jo smiled when she saw me, but winced and turned quickly away. Before she did, though, I saw that her lip was also swollen, and split.

When she spoke, her voice was soft, and wistful. "I have made a better appearance," she said.

I dropped my hat and reached for her. Holding her at arm's length, I tried to look at her more closely, but she turned away and covered her face.

"I didn't want you to see me like this," she said.

I took her into my arms and held her. "Bonnie Jo!" I said. "What—how did this happen?"

For a long moment, Bonnie Jo said nothing. I felt her body stiffen within my embrace, and then relax. "It—it was Buck," she said, "Buck DuFresne."

I stepped back a pace. "Buck?" I asked. "What about Buck?"

Bonnie Jo bowed her head. "He came here night before last," she said. "He was drunk, and he—he forced himself on me."

She buried her face in her hands then, and began to weep. "When I resisted his advances, he—he—"

"Lordamighty! He hit you? Buck DuFresne took advantage of you?"

Bonnie Jo was crying in earnest at that point. She said nothing, but nodded her head vigorously.

"Damn him!" I said. "Why, he must have been coming from your house when Jeff and me saw him! Just after he left you, he walked over to the Legal Tender and cut up Jerry Paddock's face with a broken bottle! We've got him locked up right now, over at the jail!"

I picked my hat up off Bonnie Jo's oriental rug and put it on. "Don't you worry," I told her. "Buck DuFresne won't be bothering you again! I'm fixin' to break his durn neck!"

I don't remember leaving Bonnie Jo's house, but I must have. The next thing I recall, I was going past the bank like a runaway locomotive, heading for the marshal's office. Looking back on it now, I reckon I had a loco motive myself—I intended to take Buck out of his jail cell and beat him to within an inch of his miserable life. When I thought about him forcing himself on Bonnie Jo—beating and ravishing the poor little thing—it was more than I could bear. I plum forgot I was an officer of the law; all I could think of was making Buck DuFresne pay for what he'd done.

Jeff was at his desk when I burst through the door. I must have appeared plenty war-like as I came in, because Jeff took one look at my face and moved to head off my stampede. I snatched the cell key off its peg and was almost to the door that led to the jail cells when Jeff blocked my path.

"Whoa, Deputy," he said. "Slow down, Merlin—talk to me some."

"Get out of my way, Jeff," I said. "I'm gonna beat the meanness out of Buck DuFresne."

Solid as an oak tree, Jeff took a wide stance before the doorway. "I'm not sayin' that ain't a worthy goal," he said, "but you know I can't let you do it."

"I said, get out of my way, Jeff." My voice didn't sound like my own.

"Now you ain't aimin' to fight me, are you, Merlin?" Jeff drawled. He had placed himself between me and the doorway, and he showed no sign of moving. "I'm just an old country marshal, tryin' to do my job."

I don't know. Maybe it was Jeff's smile that broke the spell. Or maybe it was the way he stood, calm but ready to stop me if he had to. Whatever the cause, I came to myself again and didn't try to push my mad any further.

"Sorry, Jeff," I said. "I just learned Buck beat and raped Bonnie Jo Hutchins. Happened the other night, just before we arrested Buck for slashing Jerry."

Jeff's eyebrows lifted. "You say rape, Merlin?"

I nodded. "According to Bonnie Jo. Said Buck was drunk, and forced himself on her."

"Uh-huh. Bonnie Jo willing to prefer charges, is she?"

"Well, of course she is! I mean—she didn't say so, but anybody would!"

Jeff took the cell key from my hand and opened the door. "All right," he said. "Let's go ask Buck about it. But there'll be no more talk of beating the man up. He's our prisoner, and he's under our protection. We can't very well jail a man for assault, and then threaten to commit the crime ourselves."

"No," I said, feeling sheepish. "I know that. I'm sorry, Jeff—I don't know what came over me."

Buck had been lying on his bunk inside his cell when we came in. As we approached, he swung his legs over and got to his feet. "Well, if it ain't Black Sambo and his white nigger deputy," he said. "To what do I owe the honor of this visit?"

"Just wanted to let you know there's another charge against you," I said. "Bonnie Jo Hutchins says you raped her night before last."

Buck didn't exactly take the news the way I expected him to. He threw his head back and laughed. "That's not exactly how it was, Deputy. I don't know what the law says about rape, but I would suppose the victim has to say no or resist, or somethin.' I don't believe Bonnie Jo has ever told a man no."

"Are you calling her a liar?" I could feel my anger rising again.

"I am if she says I raped her. I've been ticklin' Bonnie Jo's fancy, if you take my meaning, two or three evenings a week for better than a year now, and she never called it rape before. Sometimes I get a little rough, but that's the way she likes it."

"Watch your damned mouth!" I said. "You're talking about a lady!"

"No, I'm talking about Bonnie Jo. And I'm not telling you anything the whole town doesn't know. Bonnie Jo and me have been keeping company evenings since her husband went away. She likes men, and men like her. That's the truth, and I don't give a damn whether you believe me or not."

I made a grab for Buck through the bars, but he saw it coming and eased back just out of reach. Suddenly, he looked at me with a new awareness. "Wait a minute!" he said. "You really didn't know about her and me! You've been doin' her, too! Well, I'll be damned—that Bonnie Jo is a caution!"

Buck fell back onto his bunk, roaring with laughter. Rage warred with doubt in my mind. I didn't know whether to pull my gun and shoot him or hang my head in shame. Could there be truth in what he said? I looked at Jeff and saw that he was watching me. His face held no expression I could put a name to, only the calm, careful look he seemed to wear as a matter of custom. I felt his big hand grip my shoulder.

"Let's go back into the office, Merlin," he said. "We can set and talk a bit, if you've a mind to."

I nodded, and let Jeff lead me. Even after we had shut the door behind us, I could still hear Buck's laughter.

Back in the office, Jeff sat me down in a chair at his desk. My heart was pounding as if I'd run a mile, and my breathing was fast and shallow. Buck's words had stirred up my anger, but they had also hurt and confused me. He had lied about keeping company with Bonnie Jo—hadn't he?

Jeff poured a cup of coffee and handed it to me. When I reached to take it from him, my hand shook so bad I spilled maybe a quarter of it. My rage had begun to ebb, but it left a hollow, sick feeling in its place.

Across the desk from me, Jeff sat down in his swivel chair and took a pint whiskey bottle from a desk drawer. He pulled the cork and added a generous slug of the bottle's contents to my coffee. "I always keep a little of this white mule on hand, in case of copperheads, vipers, and such," he said. "Looks to me like you've been snake-bit for sure."

I took a sip. The whiskey was strong, but it didn't help all that much. "Was Buck telling the truth?" I asked. "Is it true what he said about Bonnie Jo?"

"Pretty much," Jeff said. "Bonnie Jo Hutchins is a pretty lady, and she does seem to enjoy the company of men."

"About Buck and her—do you think—?"

"I don't know for sure, but yes, I believe it is true."

I remembered those times I had asked Bonnie Jo if we could be together evenings, and her telling me no. She would see me at other times, but she insisted on being home alone after sundown. Now I knew why.

I took another sip of Jeff's fortified coffee. "I thought she was a widow," I said. "She told me she lost her husband. I guess that was a lie, too."

"Oh, no," Jeff said. "She lost him, all right, for a while, anyway. Story is, Bonnie Jo took up with a travelin' man while her husband, Ed, was at work. They say Ed came home early one afternoon and caught them together. Shot the salesman, and the circuit judge sent Ed to the territorial prison at Deer Lodge. Folks who know Ed say he's a mighty jealous man."

"Looks like he had reason to be. I feel like a durn fool, Jeff."

Jeff's chuckle was warm and knowing. "You're not the first man to be misled by his feelings for a woman. You may not believe this, but it has even happened to me, once or twice."

"Once or twice?"

He laughed aloud. "More like eight or ten times. And I don't expect I'm immune to it yet."

Jeff pushed back his chair and got to his feet. "I think I'll mosey on down to Doc's and talk to Jerry. Then I may ask Bonnie Jo if she wants to prefer charges against Buck. You reckon Buck will be safe if I leave him in your care?"

I finished the contents of my coffee cup and stood up. "He'll be safe," I said. "I'm more mad at myself than I am at him."

When Jeff had gone, I slumped into a chair and studied the toes of my boots. They were nearly as scuffed as my pride.

CHAPTER 10

▼

Pride goeth before destruction, says the Good Book, and a haughty spirit before a fall. Well, if I had been haughty, I sure wasn't anymore. The way things were going, it didn't appear I was going to have much chance to become overly proud, either. It seemed like every time I began to think I was finally gaining a little wisdom I'd say or do something so durn dumb I'd want to go far away from people and cover up my head.

I could forgive myself for taking up with Bonnie Jo Hutchins—the woman had some mighty fetching ways—but I had built her up in my mind as something she wasn't and never could be. For a while there, I had even entertained the thought that I had fallen in love with her. Now it seemed I had merely fallen in lust.

Back when I was a shirttail kid, growing up on the home place with my pa, it seemed like I was forever pulling off one bonehead stunt or another. I recall one summer Pa and me gathered twenty head of mustangs up in the Brimstone Mountains and pushed them down to a horse corral above our place. Pa put me in charge of the gate, and I rode on ahead and hunkered down out of sight to wait.

Directly, he came riding, pushing those *mesteños* ahead of him, and ran all twenty into the corral. Once they were inside, I jumped up and closed the gate behind them, just as I was supposed to. Pa was pleased. He patted me on the back and told me I'd done a good job. Then we rolled out our beds and settled in for a good night's sleep.

Come morning, we went back to the corral—and found it empty! Had someone come in the night and turned our horses loose? Had those ponies grown wings? No. Puffed up and flummoxed by Pa's praise, I had neglected to latch the gate!

I can't tell you how bad I felt. It seemed to me I was dumb as a post and worthless as a road apple. It had taken us two weeks of hard riding and sweat to gather those mustangs. Thanks to me, it had all been for nothing. I figured Pa would blow up like a charge of dynamite. I expected him to bawl me out, or maybe even take a stick to me. Whatever he decided to do, I figured I deserved it.

But Pa never said a word. He didn't have to. The expression on his face said it all. I would never forget the look of puzzlement he wore, or the disappointment in his eyes. He looked at me like I was some strange, alien critter he had never seen before. He just sighed, shook his head, got on his horse, and we began the gather all over again.

Pa had died a few years later, the year I turned eighteen. I had made a few new tracks since then, mostly plain and straight. I had grown some, and I had done my share of learning. But as I recalled my recent adventures with Bonnie Jo, it seemed to me I hadn't made much progress after all. There, in the marshal's office at Medicine Lodge, I looked into the mirror above the washstand and saw Pa's face looking back.

I'm not sure what it was that made me realize I wasn't alone. I stood in the open doorway of the office, looking out at the quiet street, still lost in my thoughts. I don't recall hearing any particular sound or seeing any unusual movement, but a feeling commenced to grow on me that something—or someone— was nearby. I took a half step back inside the door and held my breath. Slowly and silently, in the shadows beneath the low brush west of the office, the form of a young Indian took shape, as if by magic—Archie Young Bull!

Archie was bare of chest, a necklace of bear claws strung about his neck, and his long hair shone blue-black in the sunlight. He wore fringed buckskin leggings and moccasins, and his expression was both proud and serious. He raised his right hand, palm outward, and spoke.

"Law Bringer," he said. "It is me, Archie Young Bull."

He had startled me, and no mistake. I hoped he hadn't noticed my surprise. I raised my hand, returning his greeting.

"*Kahé,*" I said. "Welcome. It is good to see you, Archie."

He narrowed his eyes, looking past me toward the interior of the office. "I come to see Black White Man," he said.

"He is not here," I said. "He went downtown, but he'll be back."

"*Shóotaleen?*" he asked. "When?"

"*Saskáate,*" I said. "Soon."

I smiled and offered him my hand. "Come inside and wait with me," I said. "We will drink *bilishpite*—coffee—and talk."

Archie thought my offer over. Then he nodded and shook my hand. "*Itche,*" he said. "Good."

There was enough coffee left in the pot for two cups. I poured a cup for Archie and refilled my own. I had learned Indians tended to like plenty of sweetening in their coffee, so I went around to the cabin and brought back the sugar bowl. Archie stirred in three big spoonfuls, and carefully placed the spoon on the desk. I offered him the extra chair and sat down on the edge of the bunk. Archie ignored the chair. Holding his coffee in both hands, he seated himself cross-legged across from me on the floor.

For what seemed a long time, Archie said nothing. He glanced about the office, sipped his coffee, and waited. I was learning the way of the Crows. I took a sip from my own cup and waited, too.

In the silence, I could hear the steady ticking of the wall clock. At the window, a housefly buzzed and battered against the pane, trying to escape the office. Three feet away, the open doorway offered an easier way.

Archie nodded toward the fly, a slight smile on his lips. "Even the flies don't want to stay in your damn jail," he said.

Just then, as if on cue, I heard the rattle of Buck DuFresne's tin cup on the bars of his cell.

"Marshal Jeff Brown, you damn coon!" he shouted. "You better let me out of here, by god!"

I got to my feet and walked to the door that separated the office from the jail cells. "Be quiet, DuFresne!" I said. "You're not going anywhere!"

Buck chuckled. "So it's you, is it, Deputy?" he said. "Better turn me loose, Fanshaw. You should know by now that locking me up is a waste of time. Besides, I need to be out of here by evening—sweet Bonnie Jo will be waiting for me, I expect."

"Only thing waiting for you is the circuit judge," I said. "Now shut up and behave yourself, before I cool you off with a bucket of water."

I closed the door that led to the cells and turned back to Archie. "Don't pay him any mind," I said. "He's only trying to get my goat. You know, *illíichee*—quarrel—with me."

Archie looked thoughtful. "This man—Buck DuFresne—he has many cattle—plenty money. His father has many men, many guns. These DuFresnes steal Crow land, kill our horses, sometimes even our people. The white man's law does nothing. Agent Weede does nothing. The Fort Custer soldiers do nothing. Now Buck DuFresne cuts up a white man, and you—Law Bringer and Black White Man—do something. You put him in your jail."

Archie drank the last of his coffee. Carefully, he handed me the empty cup. When I met his gaze, his eyes were intense. "Will your law bring justice this time?" he asked.

My first instinct was to say that it would. Justice was long overdue in the case of the DuFresnes. Both Jeff and me were eager to see Buck brought to trial at last. However, I hadn't just fell off the pumpkin wagon. I was well aware that simply because a thing should happen didn't mean it would. Money and political connections ofttimes trumped even the most airtight case, and there was no sure thing when it came to the law.

Still, I didn't want to tell Archie that. He had come to trust Jeff and me. He wanted to believe justice could, and would, be done. So did I, but I couldn't guarantee it. White men had lied to Indians from the beginning. They had made promises they hadn't kept. They had signed treaties, and broken them almost before the ink had dried. I looked into Archie Young Bull's earnest eyes, and I knew what I had to do. I would tell him the truth, as I knew it, and let the chips fall where they may.

"I don't know if the law will bring justice this time," I said, "but I know Black White Man and me will do all we can to see that it happens."

My answer sounded lame, even to me.

Archie's expression didn't change. He just looked at me for a long moment with that intense gaze of his. Then a slight smile flashed across his face and was gone. "Your words are good," he said. "If you had spoken other words, I would have known you lied."

By the time Jeff got back, Archie and me were well into our second pot of coffee. I had refilled the sugar bowl and had brought over some cold biscuits and leftover venison roast from the cabin. Archie had kept his dignity when I asked him if he wanted to eat. He had shrugged, as if food didn't matter to him all that much, but his eyes gave him away. I could see he was hungry. I figured he hadn't eaten that day, and maybe even the day before, because he sure made short work of both the biscuits and the venison.

I heard Jeff's boots cross the veranda and stop at the doorway.

"Well, well," he said. "Looks like I missed the feast. *Kahé*, Archie. Welcome."

Archie stood. "I came to see you," he told Jeff. "You were not here." He looked at me, then turned back to Jeff. "Law Bringer gave me coffee and meat."

"That is good," Jeff said. "You are always welcome at the law's house."

Archie nodded toward the door that led to the cells. He smiled. "Yes," he said, "but now you have given my room to another."

He shook hands with us both, said *"Ahó,"* and was gone.

Jeff watched the young Crow walk out into the sunlight, and then turned back to me. "What did Archie want?" he asked.

"He said he'd come to see you. He was hungry, so I fed him. We talked about law and order, and about justice."

Jeff nodded. "Interesting, how he's turned from being an outlaw to a law—and-order man."

"Maybe he's always been both," I said. "Could be Archie became an outlaw because he saw too little justice in his world."

"Could be," Jeff said. "Justice can be hard to find sometimes." He walked to the front window and looked out. He seemed troubled. "I saw Jerry, over at Doc's," he said. "He's no longer talking about suing the DuFresnes. And when I asked him about preferring criminal charges, he said he was tired. Said we could talk about that later."

"Later? When I talked to him, he couldn't wait to bring charges! He was talk-ing big about a civil suit, too!"

Jeff turned back from the window and sat down at his desk. "It appears he's had a change of heart."

"Well, now," I said. "How do you suppose *that* came about?"

"I saw Arnie Moss on my way back. He said J. W. DuFresne was in town, with his lawyer, Hartford Canfield. Quite a coincidence."

"We'd better bar the door. Last time those two hit town together, they stopped by for a visit and drove off with our prisoner."

Jeff looked weary. "Yes. Rich men have their own version of the Golden Rule. Them that have the gold—make the rules."

I turned away, looking out the window. "And—Bonnie Jo? Did you talk to her?"

"I did," Jeff said. "She doesn't wish to prefer charges, either."

Outside, the light had turned golden. Shadows stretched long as the sun began its descent toward the edge of the world. The approach of evening seemed to bring a kind of heaviness to my spirit. It seemed like the walls of the marshal's office were closing in around me. I felt trapped, the way those wild horses Pa and me had caught must have. Buck DuFresne was locked in a jail cell, and here I was the one who felt like a prisoner. I had to get out—away from the office for a while—to get myself centered again, and settled in my mind.

"I think I'll take myself a little *pasear* around town," I told Jeff, "maybe go check on my horses. I'll be back directly."

Jeff raised his head and smiled. He seemed to know just what I was feeling. "Yes, Merlin," he said. "You do that. I'll see you when I see you."

I had told Jeff I might look in on my horses, and I did mean to do so. Ever since I was just a kid, it had been my habit to talk to horses. Whoever said "there's something about the outside of a horse that's good for the inside of a man" was right on the money, as far as I was concerned. Some fellers tell their troubles to bartenders, and I suppose they get some relief from it, but I was a horse-talking man. I never failed to feel better after one of those one-sided equine conversations, and I didn't wake up the next morning with a hangover, either.

By the time I reached the livery barn the sun had already set. Arnie Moss sat in a chair near the open door, repairing harness with a wood-handled awl and steel needles.

"Evenin', Merlin," he said. "What can I do for you?"

"Evenin', Arnie," I said. "I thought I might look in on my ponies a minute, is all."

Arnie put the harness down and got to his feet. "I'm sorry, Merlin," he said. "I took your horses over to my pasture on Owl Creek this morning. Figured they could use some green grass. I didn't know you'd be needin' them."

"I don't, really. I'm not goin' anywhere."

"Are you sure? I'd be happy to fetch them in for you."

"I know you would, but no. I'm glad you put them on grass."

Arnie picked up the harness again. "Well, if you're sure—"

"I am. You have a good evening now."

"You, too, Merlin."

A cool breeze followed the sunset, sighing up from the creek. I crossed Main Street, made my way past the mercantile and the drug store, and so came to Bonnie Jo's house. For a time I just stood there in the twilight outside the white picket fence. I looked across the lawn at the house itself. In memory, I saw the rooms inside as I remembered them. I made pictures in my mind of Bonnie Jo and our times together.

Other pictures came. I saw Bonnie Jo and Buck DuFresne, together in her parlor, together in her bedroom. Laughing. Loving. Sharing a glass of wine, a late supper, together. In my mind's eye, I saw them locked in their passion, Bonnie

Jo's eyes changing to that deeper color that came when her desire was upon her. Tortured by fancy, I imagined their touching and their closeness.

My throat grew tight. There was an empty, hollow feeling in my belly, and an aching in my bones. I looked again at the little house, saw the lamplight in the window, and realized I had meant to go there all along. I opened the gate, made my way up the walkway to Bonnie Jo's front door, lifted my hand, and knocked. Then I stopped breathing, and waited.

It seemed a long time before I heard footsteps coming to the door. There was a moment's fumbling with the lock and the latch, and then the door opened. Bonnie Jo stood, looking at me. She wore the same short-sleeved blouse and form-fitting skirt she wore the day I met her. Her blond hair was swept up and dressed high in front, as usual. As I looked at her face, I could see she had tried to hide the bruises with makeup. She had mostly succeeded, but the swelling remained.

She held her head high, her hand still on the door. Her split lip trembled as she spoke. "Hello, Merlin," she said. "I didn't expect to see you here. Is this an official call?"

"No. May I come in?"

She stepped back, opening the door wider. "Please," she said.

Bonnie Jo led me into her small parlor. Dusk had fallen, and the room was obscured by shadows. Striking a match, she lit the lamp that stood next to the settee and sat down. Her smile was wistful as she patted the space beside her with her hand. "Sit by me?" she asked.

I ignored her invitation and took the easy chair facing her. "No," I said. "It's evening, and your rules say I can't be with you then. Of course, that policy may have changed some, now that the reason for the rules is locked up in a jail cell."

Her smile froze, then faded. Bonnie Jo lowered her eyes, and said nothing. Then she looked at me. "Why are you so angry?" she asked.

"Well," I said, "It does seem to me you have a hard time telling the truth. You told me you were a widow. You didn't tell me you were seeing Buck DuFresne at the same time you were seeing me. You told me Buck raped you. You said you cared for me. How about those items, for openers?"

Bonnie Jo seemed to grow smaller where she sat. "I must have hurt you terribly for you to be so cruel," she said. "Am I allowed to answer your charges?"

"Sure, darlin'," I said, "but I hope you'll understand if I don't believe you."

"First," she said, "I never said I was a widow, although I wish I was. I told you I lost my husband, and so I did. Ed is in the Territorial Prison for killing a salesman whose only crime was showing me kindness.

"I didn't tell you about Buck because I was ashamed. I told you he forced himself on me, and he did. The first time was just after Ed went away. Then Buck began to come here two or three evenings a week. Sometimes he was charming, and sometimes he was brutal, but he claimed me as his own. He helped pay my bills, and I let him. What was I to do? I was a woman alone—I owed money on this house and on the shop. Without Buck's help, I would have lost them both. So—I continued to see him.

"I came to dread his visits. Especially when he'd been drinking, he was spiteful and mean. He acted as if I was his property, like his dog or his horse. He beat me sometimes, and yes, sometimes he raped me. Taking me by force seemed to excite him.

"I felt trapped. I longed to be free, but Buck said I belonged to him, for as long as he wanted me. What could I have done? Run away? Buck would have come after me and brought me back. Hire a lawyer? Where could I find a lawyer who would stand up to the DuFresnes?

"So—I did what I had to do. I worked at the shop. I tried to keep my spirits up. I told myself my life would change, that I would be free some day. I waited—"

Bonnie Jo's voice broke in midsentence. She sat, her arms crossed before her as if she was trying to hold herself together. For a moment, she was silent. Then she raised her eyes and I saw tears glisten in the lamplight. "And then you came along," she said. "You were handsome, and bashful, and kind. You stammered when you met me, and you said I was pretty. I don't know—there was something about you. Just meeting you gave me hope."

Suddenly, Bonnie Jo left the settee. In two quick paces, she crossed the space that lay between us and knelt before me on the Oriental rug. She took my hands in hers, looking up at me. "When I kissed you that day in the barbershop, I dared to believe my life could be better. Believe what you will, but what I feel for you is honest and true. My heart is yours, my sweet cavalier."

What can I say? I suppose in the end I believed her because I wanted to. I looked into Bonnie Jo's warm, brown eyes. My fingertips wiped her tears away. Then I stood, raising her with me. I looked at her bruised face and her split lip, and I held her close. I was gentle when I kissed her.

CHAPTER 11

▼

It had become my habit to meet the stagecoach when it arrived at Medicine Lodge. I figured it was a deputy's job to be on the lookout for trouble, and to recognize it when it came. Sometimes, I thought, trouble comes by stagecoach.

And so, true to form, I was standing out in front of the hotel on a hot afternoon in late June when the mud wagon from Custer's Crossing pulled in. Milt Blessing was whip that day, and he sat straight and steady atop the box as he swung his four-horse team in off the main road. We'd had a little rain that morning, and I remember the way the coach slued through a muddy patch on Front Street and slithered to a stop at the Express Office.

It was Milt's nature to take life serious. I suppose that's why I liked to tease him some—just to bring a little fun into his life.

"Mornin', Milt," I said, "I swear, if I had that poker face of yours I'd do nothing but gamble. You look sober as a judge this morning."

Behind him, a short, older man in a linen duster and bowler hat stepped out of the coach and fixed me with a cold gaze. "I very much dislike that expression," he said. "I've been a judge for nearly twenty years, and I've only been sober twice in all that time."

I must have showed my confusion.

"I'm only joking," the man said. "Actually, I have been known to drink water on occasion." He smiled and offered his hand. "You'd be Merlin Fanshaw, deputy U.S. marshal and deputy to City Marshal Jefferson Brown. Chance Ridgeway described you well. I'm Benjamin Blackwood, district judge out of Miles City."

I took his hand. "You'd be the judge we've been waiting for. Welcome to Medicine Lodge, sir."

Behind the judge, a second passenger stepped down from the mud wagon. A young man in a rumpled suit smoothed his thinning hair with his hand and approached us.

The judge turned. "And this callow youth is Thomas Burke, Esquire. Mr. Burke is here to establish his legal practice and to serve as city attorney. Tom, meet Merlin Fanshaw."

I shook hands with the young man. He was about my age, lean and gangling as a stork. Behind a pair of gold-rimmed spectacles, his clear blue eyes looked into my own.

"Judge Blackwood is joking about judicial sobriety, Deputy," he said. "He is a teetotaler, an advocate of total abstinence from alcoholic drink. His honor really is 'sober as a judge.'"

"It's good to meet you both," I said. "We've been expecting you for a while now."

I turned toward the front door of the hotel. "I expect you'll be stopping at the hotel while you're in town. I'll give you a hand with your bags."

"That won't be necessary on my account, Deputy," the judge said. "I only have one traveling bag."

"I have a bit more than that," Burke said. "I have a Gladstone, two large bags, and a trunk full of law books. I'll be looking for a boarding house first thing tomorrow. For now, I'll leave everything except the Gladstone here at the express office."

"All right," I said. "I'll let you gents check in and get settled while I tell Marshal Brown you're here. Maybe we can take supper together later."

"That would be splendid," the judge said. "Give us an hour."

We met in the lobby of the hotel just before sundown—Jeff Brown, Tom Burke, Judge Blackwood, and me. The day had been a scorcher, and Bob Devlin, the hotel's day manager, had propped open both the front and back doors in the hope of catching a cooling breeze.

"The City Café has a good kitchen," I said, "but it's inclined to be a mite crowded on a Friday night. Jeff and me figured the dining room here at the hotel might suit us better."

"As you say," Judge Blackwood said. "We bow to your local knowledge."

Together, we walked past the front desk to the dining room at the rear of the building and stepped inside. The room was spacious and well kept, with brass hanging lamps, potted palms, and tables covered with white damask cloths. The waiter showed us to a table in the corner and handed us each a printed bill of fare.

"We have two specials this evening," he said, "pork chops with hominy and green beans, and fried chicken with new potatoes and pan gravy. Can I bring you something to drink while you're deciding?"

Judge Blackwood fanned himself with the bill of fare. "Something cold, for me. Do you have lemonade, by any chance?'

"We sure do," said the waiter, "made fresh this afternoon and cooled with ice from our own icehouse. How about you other gents? We've got cold beer, and wine, too."

Knowing the judge's feelings about alcohol, I hesitated. "Go ahead," he said. "Just because I don't indulge in spirits myself doesn't mean I don't understand their appeal. A cold beer on a warm evening might be just the thing."

I decided then and there that I liked Judge Blackwood. Jeff, Tom, and me all ordered a beer, and we spent a little time getting acquainted.

When the meal had been served, the judge got down to business. "I can only stay here for a few days," he said. "Tell me what you can about the case against Buck DuFresne."

Jeff wiped his mouth with his napkin and gathered his thoughts. "DuFresne is in jail on charges of assault and battery, disorderly conduct, and mayhem. He cut up a bartender's face with a broken bottle."

"Witnesses?"

"A room full, including Deputy Fanshaw and me."

The judge sipped his lemonade. "And the victim—is he preferring charges?"

Jeff frowned. "Well—he was, at first. He even talked of filing a civil suit. But lately, he seems to have cooled some on the matter."

"I see. Is the accused represented by an attorney?"

"Yes, suh," Jeff said. "At least I expect so. Hartford Canfield handles all the DuFresne family's legal affairs."

Judge Blackwood nodded. "Yes. I am acquainted with DuFresne Land and Cattle Company. Canfield has argued other cases on their behalf."

"There is something else," I said. "Bonnie Jo—Mrs. Hutchins—the woman who manages the barbershop here—says Buck DuFresne raped and beat her the same night he cut up the bartender."

"Sounds like DuFresne had himself quite an evening. Is the woman preferring charges?"

I couldn't meet his gaze. "Uh—no. I reckon not."

"Then there is no case. Let's get back to the bartender." The judge turned to Tom. "You'll be prosecuting," he said. "You'll need to talk with the victim, and witnesses to the crime, as soon as possible."

Tom nodded. "Yes, Judge. First thing tomorrow."

"All right," the judge said. "Now, about a place to hold the trial. Is there a community center—perhaps a dance hall—in Medicine Lodge?"

"No, suh," Jeff said. "Only place that might do is the scene of the crime. The Legal Tender Saloon."

Judge Blackwood smiled. "A teetotal judge trying a case in a hall dedicated to the sale of whiskey and beer. The judge's bench is behind the bar. Life is full of irony."

His fingertips drummed a rhythm on the tablecloth. "Would the saloon's owner allow us to use the place?

"Kyle Haddon. We can ask him," I said. "I believe he would."

"Very well," said the judge. "Tom will prepare his case, with your help. You and the marshal will inquire of Mr. Haddon regarding use of his saloon. Let's shoot for this coming Wednesday as a trial date. You're all going to be very busy over the next several days."

Judge Blackwood slid his chair back and got to his feet. "As for me," he said, "I just may do a little fishing."

The judge had said we'd be busy, and we were. J. W. DuFresne rode in with a dozen cowhands from the ranch and spent some time visiting his son at the jail. The cowhands took up residence at the Legal Tender, checked their guns, and spent their days playing cards and drinking beer. They all seemed to be on their best behavior. I figured they were in town to show support for Buck.

Hartford Canfield, the DuFresne's lawyer, took a room at the hotel and also spent time at the jail talking to Buck. I asked him one evening why he didn't try to get Buck out on bail. He said there was no need; Buck would soon be out free and clear anyway.

Mayor Drysdale and the town council confirmed Tom Burke's appointment as city attorney, and Tom kept himself busy talking to witnesses and taking depositions. He spoke at length with Jerry Paddock, who was back on his feet and out of Doc's sickbed, although his face was still swathed in bandages. Jerry was strangely subdued, in contrast to his earlier, feisty attitude. That fact worried me some. I think it worried Tom Burke, too.

Clifford Bidwell, editor and publisher of *The Medicine Lodge Star,* was everywhere, interviewing anyone and everyone who would hold still for it. The trial of Buck DuFresne was the biggest thing to happen around Medicine Lodge in a long while, and Clifford had no intention of letting his opportunities pass him by. He even interviewed me.

Kyle Haddon agreed to make the Legal Tender available as a courtroom on Wednesday. He would close the saloon for the duration of the trial. Judge Blackwood would install himself behind the bar, where the victim, barkeep Jerry Paddock, once held sway. The judge was right—life is full of irony.

There would not be a jury trial. Judge Blackwood announced that he would preside over the trial and decide its outcome. I expected Canfield to offer at least a token argument regarding that decision, but he didn't. He seemed unconcerned, and confident of the trial's outcome. That worried me, too. Canfield seemed cheerful as a gambler with a marked deck, and I couldn't help but wonder why.

Life went on as usual in Medicine Lodge. Indians sat in the shade, impassive and patient. Nesters bought supplies on tick at the mercantile and gossiped about the coming trial. Bonnie Jo's barbershop did a land office business from early morning to evening, with clients lined up inside and outside the door.

Drums throbbed in the night from over at the campground. Indian families came to visit and to dance. I saw Archie Young Bull one night, watching the jail from across the street in the twilight. Justice was on his mind, I knew. It was on mine, too.

I recalled the killing of Goes to the Water the month before, and his parents coming to claim their son's body. I remembered their grief and their pride. I had sensed their anger. Curly Bunton had murdered Goes to the Water in cold blood. The law—white man's law, the Indians would have said—had allowed the killer to go free. I looked at Archie that night and remembered the day we ate together at the marshal's office. I recalled his question, *Will your law bring justice this time?* Buck DuFresne would soon be on trial. In the eyes of the Indians especially, so would the law itself.

I had my horses brought in to the livery barn. I cleaned my guns. I marked each day off on the calendar as it passed. I hoped, and I prayed, that I would soon be able to tell Archie, "Yes. The law brought justice this time."

When Jeff and me brought Buck down for his trial on Wednesday morning, the streets were already crowded. Wagons and buckboards were parked along Trail Street. Saddle horses lined the hitch racks in front of Sharp's pool hall and the Legal Tender. Inside the saloon, spectators sat on chairs arranged to face the long bar. Blue smoke drifted in layers below the tin ceiling, and I noticed that the gents who favored chewing tobacco had appropriated the saloon's stock of brass spittoons.

The trial, Medicine Lodge's first, was a novelty for the town, and the room was abuzz with conversation. Some of the cowboys in the crowd called out to Buck when we brought him in. "Keep your chin up, Buck!" said one. "Give 'em hell, Buck!" yelled another. Some of the spectators had already had a drink or two.

Maybe the Legal Tender isn't selling whiskey today, I thought, *but somebody sure as hell is.*

Two poker tables, one for the defense and one for the prosecution, faced the bar. Hartford Canfield sat at the defense table. He looked confident, and even more smug than usual. We led Buck over to the table. We removed his handcuffs. Buck's friends among the onlookers applauded and whistled as Buck grinned and waved back.

Jerry Paddock sat in the front row. He slumped in his chair, his head bowed. Kyle Haddon sat beside him on his left. Doc Westby occupied the chair on his right.

Tom Burke, Medicine Lodge's brand-new city attorney, sat at the prosecution's table, papers and briefcase before him on the table top. Clifford Bidwell sat in the front row of spectators, his notebook open before him as he prepared to record the day's events for the *Star*. He greeted me with a nod, and then looked back at his notes. An upholstered armchair stood with its back to the bar, placed there to serve as a witness chair. There was as yet no sign of Judge Blackwood.

I looked the crowd over. There were only a handful of women among the watchers, mostly nesters' wives and a few I took to be sporting women. Bonnie Jo Hutchins was not in attendance, nor did I expect that she would be. There were no Indians at all.

I glanced over at the entrance to Kyle Haddon's private office and saw that the door was slightly ajar. Judge Blackwood stood in the opening, wearing his judicial robes. He caught my eye, and nodded. I walked to the bar, turned, and faced the crowd. The judge had given me the job of opening the trial, and I had memorized the words, sort of.

"Hear ye! Hear ye!!" I cried. "The district court for the Territory of Montana is now in session, the Honorable Benjamin Blackwood presiding! Please rise!"

Mostly, everybody did.

Judge Blackwood came out of Haddon's office, walking proud and stately as a drum major. When he drew near, I lifted the pass-through for him, and the judge stepped behind the bar and walked along the duckboards. At the center of the bar, Kyle Haddon had placed a chair somewhat taller than the others, one usually used by lookouts to keep an eye on the roulette and faro games. I thought it made a dandy judge's chair.

Judge Blackwood cleared his throat. "Thank you," he said. "You may be seated."

There was a general scuffling of feet and scraping of chair legs as the spectators took their seats.

The judge waited until the room was quiet again and said, "I know that many of you have patronized this establishment as the Legal Tender Saloon. Today, however, this place is a court of law. Instead of dispensing beer and alcoholic spirits, we are here to dispense justice.

"To that end, certain rules will apply. First, there will be no tobacco in my court. If you gents feel compelled to roll yourself a smoke, light your pipe, or fire up a stogie, you'll have to take it outside. Same for you boys who chew tobacco or dip snuff.

"Second, there will be no drinking of intoxicating liquor, whether homemade or store-bought, until court adjourns. Drunkenness, interruptions, and demonstrations of any kind—cheers, catcalls, profanity, or what you mistakenly think are witty remarks—will get you ejected from this trial, and from this building. In addition, you may be subject to a fine or jail time.

"Now, I'm sure none of you boys would sit down to a stud game in a strange town without knowing the house rules. Well, these are my house rules. Break them at your peril.

"That being said, I have asked Deputy Fanshaw to serve as bailiff for this hearing. He will administer the oath to witnesses, fetch and carry, and serve as my general factotum. Together with City Marshal Brown, the deputy will also enforce the court's decrees and keep order during these proceedings. Deputy Fanshaw and Marshal Brown are therefore officers of this court, and any interference with them in the performance of their duties will lead to serious consequences. Now—I call on City Attorney Burke to present the case for the prosecution."

Tom Burke looked again at the papers before him, and got to his feet. Buck DuFresne slouched in his chair at the defense table, and for a long moment Tom just looked at him in silence. Then he stretched out his arm, pointing to Buck, and addressed the bench.

"Your Honor, the defendant, Buck DuFresne, is charged with assault and battery, disturbing the peace, and mayhem.

"We will prove that on the night of Friday, May twenty-first, Buck DuFresne did savagely and without provocation attack Jerry Paddock with a broken whiskey bottle in this very room. We will establish that he slashed Mr. Paddock's face, causing severe lacerations and disfigurement. We will present the facts and the testimony of witnesses, and we will prove beyond the shadow of a doubt the guilt of the said defendant, Buck DuFresne."

Over the next nearly three hours, Burke did just what he said he'd do. He called witnesses to the stand who had been in the Legal Tender on the night of May 21, and asked them to recall what they had seen. He called Arnie Moss. He called Kyle Haddon. He called two of the Rimfire cowboys. He called Jeff, and he called me.

"And what did you see, Marshal Brown?" Burke asked Jeff.

"I saw the defendant, Buck DuFresne, enter the saloon," Jeff said. "A minute later, I heard a commotion from inside—breaking glass, men's voices. Sounded like trouble."

"What did you do then, Marshal?"

"I went inside."

"What, if anything, did you observe?"

"Jerry—Mistuh Paddock—was behind the bar. He had his left hand up, covering his face. Right hand held out, like he was tryin' to defend himself. There was blood on his shirt, blood flowing between his fingers."

"Were there other men nearby?"

"Yes, suh. Riders from the DuFresne ranch. Arnie Moss. Buck DuFresne—the defendant—was across the bar from Jerry. His back was to me when I came in."

"What happened then?"

"He turned around when he heard me. I saw he had a broken bottle in his hand. He raised it toward me, and I had to put him down."

"Put him down, you say. You mean you were forced to subdue him?"

"Yes, suh. I subdued him with the butt of my shotgun."

"Thank you, Marshal. Your witness, Counselor."

Hartford Canfield, Buck's lawyer, questioned nearly every witness who testified, but the facts were clear. Buck DuFresne had deliberately attacked Jerry Paddock out of pure meanness, and had hurt him bad.

Canfield spent a little extra time in cross-examining Jeff and me. He made it clear that we hadn't actually seen the attack, that we had arrived after Jerry had been cut up. Canfield was calm and businesslike in his questioning. He offered few objections to the testimony given against Buck, and was at all times polite and pleasant. I began to think Buck's conviction was pretty much a sure thing. Still, there was something about Canfield that bothered me. He seemed almost too calm, too confident. I wondered what the man had up his sleeve.

Tom Burke had just completed his questioning of Kyle Haddon. He was looking through his papers, and I thought he was preparing to call another witness.

Judge Blackwood looked up. "Are you nearly finished calling witnesses, Counselor?" he asked.

"Just about, Your Honor. I still plan to call Doctor Westby, and Mr. Paddock."

Judge Blackwood reached beneath his robes and took out a pocket watch. He snapped open the cap and looked at its face. "It is now eleven forty-five. I'm going to declare a recess until one o'clock this afternoon. Folks can get themselves a bite to eat and attend to such other physical needs as may be required." He smiled. "I'm sure some of you gents are dying for a smoke by now." He raised his gavel and brought it sharply down on the bar top. "Until one o'clock, then—this court is adjourned."

The sound of chairs sliding, the shuffle of feet, and a general murmur broke the silence. Men and women stood, stretched, and headed for the door. Jeff had returned to the front of the room and had put the manacles back on Buck DuFresne. Buck looked sullen, restless.

"I'll stay here with Buck," Jeff said. "Why don't you go to the cabin and bring back a lunch for the three of us? The eatin' places in this town are apt to be crowded today."

"I'll do that," I said. "There's some of that beef we had for supper left. I'll make us some sandwiches."

"I'm not eatin' any more of your damn jailhouse food," Buck said. "I'll be dining on oysters and sparklin' wine this evening."

"A man can dream," Jeff sighed. "Guess we'll only need lunch for two, Merlin."

I made my way through the crowd in front of the Legal Tender and started up the boardwalk toward the bank. I was about to turn the corner and go on to the cabin when I saw Bonnie Jo come out of the barbershop.

"Oh, Merlin," she called. "Can we talk a minute?"

I walked across the street. She was wearing the green woolen skirt and the yellow blouse I admired. She seemed nervous.

"Sure thing," I said. "What is it, Bonnie Jo?"

"I—I just wanted to tell you I'll be leaving town for a while. I don't want to be here if Buck gets turned loose."

"I won't let him hurt you again," I said.

"I need to get away, Merlin. So much has happened—"

"Where will you go?"

"I have a relative near Butte City. I'm taking the stage this afternoon."

"I'll miss you," I said. "Don't worry about Buck. Whether he's convicted or not, I won't let him hurt you."

She touched my arm. Her smile was wistful. "I know, my sweet cavalier. But I really do need to get away."

Some of the crowd at the Legal Tender had gone across the street to the City Café. Others were now walking down the boardwalk toward us.

"Take care, Bonnie Jo," I said. "Come back soon." Then I crossed the street again and walked to the cabin.

When the trial resumed, Tom Burke called Jerry to the stand. The little barkeep took the oath, then sat down stiffly in the witness chair.

Smiling, Tom approached the chair. "Please state your full name," he said.

"Jerome McIlhenny Paddock."

"And what is your occupation?"

"Mixologist. Bartender for Mr. Haddon, here at the Legal Tender."

"In your own words, please tell the court what occurred here on the evening of May twenty-first."

Jerry cleared his throat. "Well—I was standin' behind the bar, about where the judge is sittin' now. There were maybe half a dozen DuFresne cowboys in the place. Arnie Moss was here. Mister Haddon was in his office."

"What about Buck DuFresne? Was he here?"

"He was earlier. He came in with the cowboys, then left for a while."

"Was there a time that evening when Buck DuFresne came back?"

"Yes, sir, there was. He came in again about ten-thirty."

"How did he seem to you, Mr. Paddock?"

"Well, he was pretty drunk, sir."

Canfield was on his feet. "Objection, Your Honor," he said. "Calls for a conclusion on the part of the witness."

Tom Burke turned to the judge. "The man's a bartender, Your Honor. If a bartender can't tell when a man is drunk, who can?"

"Overruled," Judge Blackwood said. "The witness says DuFresne was drunk, and I believe him."

The judge leaned back in his chair, his eyes on Canfield. "May I remind you, Counselor—I am deciding this case, not a jury. Therefore, there should be little need for objections. Let's get on with it."

"Thank you, Your Honor," Burke said. Turning again to Jerry, he resumed his questioning. "Now you say Buck was drunk that night. How drunk? Was he staggering? Unable to speak clearly? In short, how did he manifest his condition?"

"Well, he came bustin' through the swing doors, and came straight for the bar," Jerry said. "He wanted whiskey, but it seemed to me he'd had enough. I told him so."

Burke had brought the testimony to a key point. I knew what his next question would be. He seemed to sense that victory was at hand. "Then," Burke said, "what happened?"

Jerry was silent for a moment. He looked away from the lawyer to the crowd, and to me. His eyes met mine, then looked away. "There was a bottle on the bar," he said. "Buck took hold of it. He smashed it against the bar—right there, just beyond where the judge is sitting."

"He broke the bottle—to use as a weapon?"

"No," Jerry said. "I think he just broke it because he was mad. He held it in his right hand, out in front of him."

Burke frowned. "Yes," he said. "To use as a weapon! Is that correct?"

"No, sir. I ain't sure he even knew he had it in his hand. He looked like he was going to pass out."

"But you told me earlier—"

"This is how it was, Mr. Burke. Buck looked woozy—he started to fall. I reached across the bar to catch him, and ran into the broken bottle with my face."

Burke looked desperate. "Yes, he attacked you—"

"It was a plain accident," Jerry said. "My fault. Buck didn't mean to hurt nobody."

And there it was. I heard Jeff suck in his breath, saw him stare at Jerry in disbelief. Burke asked a few more questions, but Jerry didn't budge. His face had been slashed by accident, he said. It was nobody's fault. That was all there was to it. Burke didn't call Doc Westby. He didn't call any more witnesses. He looked stunned.

"No further questions," he said. "The prosecution rests."

That pretty well ended the trial. Canfield called Buck to the stand. Buck said he couldn't remember what had happened, but that he liked Jerry and would never have hurt him intentionally. Canfield called the cowboys who had been there that night. To a man, they backed up Jerry's story. They said the slashing had been an accident, nothing more.

Burke had been sandbagged, pure and simple. Jerry had told him one story before the trial, and then changed his account on the witness stand. Jeff knew the truth. So did I. I think even Judge Blackwood did, but there was nothing he could do. The charges against Buck DuFresne were dismissed. He was declared not guilty on all counts.

CHAPTER 12

▼

I heard shouts and laughter from the cowboys, and gasps of disbelief from Jeff Brown and Tom Burke. J. W. DuFresne nodded his approval, his cold, blue eyes ablaze with a fierce light. Buck DuFresne smiled his reckless smile and gave Jeff and me a go-to-hell look. Hartford Canfield allowed himself a smirk of triumph before assuming his customary aspect of cool disdain.

Jerry Paddock, his eyes downcast, walked slowly to the Legal Tender's back door and quietly left the building. Judge Blackwood removed his robes, gathered up his books and papers, and set out for the hotel. Kyle Haddon reopened the bar, and Thumbs Carlyle took to abusing the piano again, pounding out a syncopated rhythm that was only occasionally in tune.

Jeff stood apart from the crowd, near the front door. He watched Buck and the cowboys belly up to the bar. His expression was calm, even pleasant. But Jeff was my partner, and I had come to know his moods. I saw the anger that lay just below the surface. For the third time in two months, the DuFresnes had cheated justice, and it was a hard truth for Jeff and me to live with.

At the bar, Buck was making up for lost time. He tossed back the whiskey in his glass, and poured himself another drink. He saw Jeff watching him from across the room.

"Hey, boy!" he shouted, "What the hell are you lookin' at?"

Jeff shifted his weight and walked over to where Buck stood. "You talkin' to me, Mistuh DuFresne?"

"Yeah," Buck said. "I don't like you starin' at me while I'm drinkin' with my friends."

Jeff chuckled. "Why, these boys ain't your friends," he said. "They're your hired hands. I don't expect a man like you *has* many friends."

"Sticks in your craw, don't it?" Buck said. "The court found me innocent, in spite of you. I'm a free man, and there's not a damn thing you can do about it."

Jeff smiled. "There'll be another time. I can wait."

"Go wait someplace else," Buck said, "I'm tired of bein' eyeballed by a buck nigger with a badge."

Jeff glanced down at the marshal's star, pinned to his vest. Then he raised his eyes again to Buck. "Funny thing about this badge," he said, "It even protects men like you. Drop by the office later, if you ain't too drunk. Pick up your personal effects."

I caught up with Jeff at the door. "How about an early supper, over at the café?" I asked. "I'm buyin'."

Jeff smiled, but there was sadness in his eyes. "Not tonight, Merlin," he said. "I think I'll just go on back to the cabin. I need to be alone for a little while."

I nodded. "Play a tune on that mouth organ for me, too," I said. "I'll see you later this evening."

The day that began on such a high note now seemed flat as stale beer. Like a stone cast into a pond, the trial had made its splash. Ripples had widened, washing against the shoreline. Now the day, like the pond, was still again. The crowd from the trial had mostly gone its way. A few people stood talking in groups of two or three. Some had crossed the street to the City Café.

Homesteaders had turned their wagons out on the road, headed home to their farms. Most of the buggies and buckboards had moved off as well, and the saddle horses that had lined the hitch racks were down to five in front of the Legal Tender. Buck's steel-gray thoroughbred was among them. Somebody must have been pretty sure of how the trial would turn out, I thought. If the verdict had been other than not guilty, Buck would still be behind bars.

I looked for people I knew, but everyone seemed to have gone. Clifford Bidwell had taken his notes back to the Star, no doubt to write up the story for the next edition. Arnie Moss had returned to the livery stable and the care and feeding of other people's horses. Doc Westby had gone home to his practice, and his roses. J. W. DuFresne and Hartford Canfield had turned their horses back on the road to the home ranch. I looked for Tom Burke, thinking he might want some company, but I didn't see him. Probably, I thought, he's found lodging at a boarding house and has gone there to put the trial behind him and prepare for a new day.

And where had Jerry Paddock gone? I thought I knew. If my guess was right, Jerry had taken his scarred face to another town and another bar. There was no doubt in my mind that he had been paid, and paid well, to change his testimony. If so, I hoped for his sake that he would use his windfall to become owner of his next saloon.

I would have paid a call on Bonnie Jo, but the stage had already gone. All I knew was that she was on her way to visit her relative near Butte City, and I didn't know when she'd be back. Was it true, as she feared, that Buck DuFresne would try to move back into her life? And if he did, could I stop him? Bonnie Jo seemed to be saying she would be mine if I could keep her. Did I really want to? I had more questions, by far, than answers. I turned, thinking I'd take a stroll around town before heading back to the office.

It was then I saw Archie Young Bull. He sat a handsome paint horse in the alley behind the pool hall, and he was staring directly at me. In the late-afternoon light, his eyes glittered like obsidian, and they seemed to glow with an inner fire. I raised my hand and smiled, stepping off the boardwalk and walking toward him. He straightened, his body erect and proud, and I saw that the old, defiant Archie had returned. Scorn twisted his features as he pointed his finger at me.

"White man's law is weak," he said. "You are a fool to believe in it."

Slowly, he raised his right fist to his forehead, and then brought his hand forward in a twisting motion. It was the sign for "anger." Abruptly, he turned the horse away. He dug his heels sharply into the animal's side, and in a moment was gone.

I didn't return to the office until nearly seven that evening. I walked the eight city blocks that made up downtown Medicine Lodge, looked in on my horses at the livery, and stopped for supper at the hash house on Front Street. When I passed the Legal Tender, all five horses were still tied out front. Looking inside the saloon, I saw no sign of Buck or the Rimfire cowboys. I figured they were likely at the café across the street. I skirted the west side of the pool hall and took a shortcut back to the office.

Jeff was at his desk when I walked in. He looked up and smiled. "How's everything downtown?" he asked.

"Quiet. Hard to believe it's the same place, after all the bustle this morning."

Jeff opened his desk drawer and took out Buck's holstered revolver and a large manila envelope. "Yes. I expect Buck will be coming by directly for his property. Did you see him?"

"His gray and four other Rimfire horses were still tied in front of the Legal Tender. I didn't see Buck or the cowboys. Figure they're havin' supper."

Buck stood, and walked to the window. "Speak of the devil," he said. "Here he comes on horseback, with four of his demons."

I stepped to the window and looked out. Buck and his companions from the Legal Tender were riding up to the office. Even at a distance, I could see they'd taken on enough brave-maker to make them reckless. I was too far away to smell the whiskey, but I could smell trouble just fine.

"Hey!" Buck yelled. "You in there, you black bastard? I've come for my goddam gun!"

Jeff stood in the open doorway. "Come on in and get it," he said. "I'll need you to sign for your personal effects."

"Ain't signin' nothin'!" Buck said. "Bring my property out to me, boy!"

Jeff stepped back inside. He picked up the holstered revolver and the envelope. "No point in arguin' with a drunk," he said. "Keep an eye on those other four—I'll take his things out to him."

I took a Winchester carbine down from the gun rack. "Watch yourself," I warned. "Buck's just drunk enough to be dangerous. At least, take the bullets out of his gun before you give it back to him."

Jeff shrugged. "Already did. I wouldn't give any drunk a loaded gun. Buck's just runnin' his mouth to impress his cowpunchers."

Jeff stepped out onto the raised walk in front of the office. I followed, making sure Buck's companions got a good look at the carbine.

Beyond the boardwalk, Buck DuFresne slouched in his saddle. His hat was pulled down close above his eyes, and his face was flushed. A stiff-handled quirt of Mexican design was looped over his right wrist. Silver-mounted spurs adorned his boot heels, jingle-bobs chiming faintly as the gray thoroughbred danced nervously in the street. Jeff crossed the boardwalk and stepped down into the dust.

"About time, by God," Buck muttered. "Where's your damn shotgun?"

"Didn't think I'd need it," Jeff said, passing the revolver and envelope up to Buck. "You ain't cutting up a bartender this time."

Buck looped the gun belt over his saddle horn. He stuffed the envelope in his saddlebag. "God damn you," he said. "Judge said cutting Jerry was an accident. Remember?"

Jeff didn't yield an inch. "Judge said no such thing. After your daddy and your slick lawyer bought Jerry off, there just wasn't enough evidence to prove what we both know happened."

Buck's eyes were wild. "I've got a score to settle with you, Sambo," he said. "You clubbed me with your damn scattergun. You put your black hands on a DuFresne. You may wear a badge, but you're still nothin' but a coon-ass nigger!"

Jeff sighed, as if someone had finally talked him into an unpleasant but necessary task. "All right," he said. "Step down from that horse, and I'll take my badge off."

Buck shortened his hold on the reins. The gray rolled its eyes and continued its nervous shuffle.

"Go to hell!" Buck said, slashing hard at Jeff with the quirt. The cowhide tails of the whip sliced across Jeff's face and knocked his hat off.

Jeff covered his face with his left arm, reaching out with his right hand as Buck struck again. Then Jeff's big hand closed around the quirt. He leaned back, pulling hard. The thong that bound the quirt to Buck's wrist jerked the cattleman out of the saddle, and he fell hard onto the dusty street.

Jeff took a step back, planting his feet wide. He removed his badge and put it in his vest pocket. Buck scrambled to his feet, teeth bared in a grimace of hate. He slashed savagely at Jeff again with the quirt, but Jeff stepped inside the flailing arm and struck the cowman solidly just below the right cheekbone. Shaken, Buck rushed the marshal, swinging wildly, forcing him to give way.

Jeff fell back before Buck's onrush, blocking the blows with his arms. As the two men reached the walkway, the marshal stepped to one side and hit Buck full in the face with a stinging left, followed by a hard right. When the cattleman raised his hands to protect his face, Jeff caught him with a short left just beneath his rib cage and straightened him with an uppercut.

Dazed, Buck dropped to one knee, but quickly rose. Head down, eyes closed, he rushed his attacker again, taking punishment but forcing the marshal back. Jeff stumbled at the boardwalk's edge and sprawled headlong. Immediately, Buck lashed out, kicking Jeff hard in the ribs. He aimed a second kick at the marshal, missed, but hooked him in the thigh with his spur.

Jeff rolled onto his back, caught Buck's foot in both hands, and twisted, throwing him to the ground. Buck tried to rise, but Jeff was already on his feet. He grasped Buck's hair in his left fist and clubbed him hard with his right. He struck him again, then once more, and let him fall into the dust.

One of the riders, a young cowboy with red hair, reined his horse around and drew his six-gun. "That's enough, goddammit!" he said.

I fired a quick shot with the carbine, the slug plowing up a geyser of dirt just in front of his horse's hooves. The animal reared, nearly unseating its rider, and stood quivering in the street.

"Next man who pulls a gun is a dead man!" I said.

Jeff had picked up his hat. He put it on. Taking his badge from his vest pocket, he pinned it back in place. Buck lay facedown in the dirt, struggling to raise himself. Blood dripped from his nose and mouth.

Jeff turned to the cowboys. "Load your boss and take him home. I've had a belly full of his swagger and strut. When he comes to, tell him he's posted—I don't want to see him in Medicine Lodge again."

Hardy Randall, one of the older cowhands, stepped down. "Oh, I reckon he'll come in all right," he said.

Jeff's face was hard. "Tell him to come shootin' if he does," he said.

Over the next few weeks, the weather turned hot and muggy. Medicine Lodge drowsed under the summer sun, and time seemed to slow down from a fast lope to an easy walk. Jeff and me stayed watchful, but Buck DuFresne didn't come into town, nor did his daddy. Word was, they'd gone south somewhere to buy cattle. Some of the Rimfire cowboys still rode in from time to time, but they seemed to be on their best behavior, and we had no trouble with them.

City Attorney Tom Burke moved into Hannah Redfield's boarding house and opened a law office on the second floor of the Cattlemen's Bank. Folks around Medicine Lodge seemed to have little need for legal services that summer, but Burke was optimistic.

I was still getting paid regular—which is more than I can say for Tom—so I played the big spender and bought him a beer every now and then. The way my life had run up till that time I figured it could do no harm to have a lawyer for a friend.

We were having a cold one at the Legal Tender one afternoon, and Tom said, "My fortunes will improve. I rely on human nature, Merlin. Mankind being what it is, there will always be a need for lawyers."

I nodded. "And peace officers, too," I said.

June passed into July, and Bonnie Jo still hadn't come back from her trip. The barbershop remained closed, and my hair grew longer and covered my ears. I went back to shaving myself, but somehow it just wasn't the same. There is some difference between the amateur and the professional, I find.

I thought about Bonnie Jo often in the evenings just before dropping off to sleep. I remembered our time together, and the loving, of course, but I recalled other things as well. Bonnie Jo hadn't lied to me exactly, as far as I knew, but she did tend to be sort of careless with the truth.

Now, I wasn't all that experienced with women; I thought maybe that's how they all were. But then I'd remember Pandora, back in Dry Creek, and the way she had always been honest and direct with me. I would fall to missing her, and that guilty feeling would come upon me again.

It was the strangest thing. I felt like I had lost something valuable. For all my high-minded talk about truth, I knew I could no longer be completely truthful with Pandora. Bonnie Jo had come between us, not because of how I felt about her—I didn't really know how I felt about her—but because of what we had done together.

Independence Day came and went. July continued hot, and Medicine Lodge sweltered by day under the summer sun, cooling only by degrees with the coming of night. Jeff and me took to sitting out under the stars after we finished our rounds, taking in the coolness and the quiet. Sometimes, great cloudbanks gathered in the night sky, blotting out the stars. Distant lightning stitched the horizon and dazzled the eye, and thunder rolled with a sound like watermelons spilling onto a cobbled street. At other times, heat lightning flickered among the clouds and brightened the night with spectacle.

Jeff had said little about the trial, or the fight that had followed it, but I knew those events were still much on his mind. One evening, as we sat out in front of the office, Jeff broke the silence.

"Justice is a grand idea," he said, "but it's mighty hard to come by in this world."

"Yes," I said. "Men keep making laws they hope will bring it to pass, but law and justice are sisters, not twins."

"Preacher man I met one time said man's pursuit of justice was one proof that God exists. Said all people everywhere are born believing life should be fair. But why do they think so? They sure don't get the idea from the way things are in this world."

"No," I agreed. "They sure don't."

"You asked me once how I came to be a peace officer, and I told you it had to do with makin' things right," Jeff said. "Well, it don't seem like we're makin' many things right lately."

"It's not for lack of trying, Jeff," I said. "We're peace officers, not judges nor juries. It's our job to bring in the lawbreakers, not convict and sentence them."

"I know," Jeff said. "Still, it's hard to watch the guilty go free."

He shifted in his chair. "I was thinking back to the killing of Goes to the Water two months ago," he said. "Curly Bunton shot that boy in the back, like a man might shoot a prairie dog—for sport. Cold-blooded, willful murder, and he got away with it."

"We did our part," I said. "We arrested Curly. It was DuFresne's money and power that got him off."

"I keep seeing the faces of Old Eagle and Dog Woman, the dead boy's folks. I remember how they came to us at sunup to take their son's body home. The old man, proud and straight as a lodgepole, holding his grief and his anger in check. The boy's mother, her hair hacked short and her arms slashed in mourning. They didn't get the justice they deserved."

"Nobody does," I said. "Some of us wouldn't like it if we did. You pretty well summed it up earlier—justice is a grand idea, but it's hard to come by."

Jeff was silent for a long time. Then he said, "Yeah. I guess all we can do is keep trying."

In the half-light, Jeff looked tired, and older than his years. "But sometimes," he said, "a man gets tired of trying."

You know how sometimes you'll be with a person, and out of the blue they'll say the very thing you've been thinking? Or how you and your friend will be talking, and you'll both say the same words at exactly the same time? Or maybe you'll think of a man you haven't seen or thought of in years, and the very next day you'll run into him on the street.

Well, that's sort of what happened the day after Jeff brought up the subject of Curly Bunton and the killing of Goes to the Water. Next morning, I was out sweeping off the boardwalk in front of the office and here came Dobie Jackson, one of the Rimfire cowhands. He was riding up Main Street leading a saddle horse with a dead man face-down across the saddle.

"Mornin,' Dobie," I said. "Who's that you're riding with?"

Dobie drew rein and glanced back at the corpse. "Used to be Curly Bunton," he said. "I guess it still is."

I waited for the rest of it.

"Curly was ridin' line for the outfit on upper Willow Creek," Dobie said. "Cattle up there were scattered from hell to breakfast, so J. W. had me ride up and check on Curly. I found him dead maybe fifty yards below the trail."

I stepped off the boardwalk and approached the body. I lifted the dead man's head. It was Curly, all right. Behind me, Jeff came to the door of the office and stood there watching.

"What happened?" I asked.

Dobie twisted in the saddle and looked back at the led horse and its mortal burden. "He'd been workin' that bronc he's on," he said. "Snaky, man-hatin' som'bitch. Appears Curly bucked off and hit a boulder with his head. Killed him deader than hell."

"When do you figure it happened?"

Dobie shrugged. "Day before yesterday, maybe the day before that."

Jeff came out to the edge of the walk. "Take him over to Doc Westby's," Jeff said. "Doc will have to examine the body—make out a death certificate."

Dobie nodded, turning his horse away. "Thanks for bringing him in," I said. "We'll meet you over at Doc's."

Jeff looked at me. "Ain't that somethin'," he said. "Just last night I was fussin' about Curly and justice. Now, it appears he's had some."

Doc Westby signed a certificate that confirmed the obvious—Curly Bunton was dead, all right, done in by an injury to the head apparently caused by a horse wreck. Case closed. Two days later, J. W. DuFresne and a dozen cowboys held a graveside service up at the cemetery, stopped for a drink or three at the Legal Tender, and rode back to the ranch. That should have been all there was to the story, but when fate is the dealer the cards don't always fall the way a man expects.

Just at dawn the next day, visitors arrived at the jail. They came slowly down Main Street in a battered farm wagon drawn by a thin, spiritless team. It was a team and wagon we'd seen before. At the reins was Gray Owl, friend and companion of Goes to the Water, the young Indian murdered by Curly Bunton two months before.

Beside him on the spring seat, straight-backed and proud, sat Old Eagle, father of Goes to the Water. And behind him, seated in the wagon box, was Dog Woman, the dead boy's mother. Gray Owl stopped the wagon in front of the office, stepped down, and helped the old man descend to the street. Dog Woman made no move to follow, but remained in the wagon.

Jeff met them at the door. "*Kahé*, Old Eagle," he said. "Welcome, Gray Owl. What brings you to the lodge of the law?"

"Old Eagle asked me to bring him here," Gray Owl said. "I am to tell you his words in the white man's tongue."

"It is good," Jeff said. "Come inside. Sit. We will drink coffee. We will hear your words."

As Archie Young Bull had done, Old Eagle ignored the chairs and took a seat on the office floor. Gray Owl sat cross-legged beside him. Jeff built a fire in the potbellied stove and set the coffee on to heat. I went around to the cabin to get the sugar bowl, hurrying back so as not to miss anything Old Eagle might say.

I needn't have worried. We sat in silence until the coffee had boiled and while the old man drank his first cup. Then we sat in silence awhile longer. I could hear the clock ticking. Across town, a rooster crowed, greeting the day. Somewhere in the distance, a dog barked. And still we waited.

Finally, Old Eagle finished his second cup of coffee and carefully put the cup on the floor before him. He raised his eyes, looking first at me and then at Jeff. His voice was high-pitched and reedy when he spoke. His words were in the Crow tongue, and he spoke at length. Then he was silent. He sat, his face lifted to the light. Gray Owl looked at Jeff and me, and began his translation.

"Old Eagle says he is a man of honor," the young man said. "He has broken the white man's law and has come to turn himself in. He is ready to be locked away, he says. He is even ready to die."

"What has the old one done that would call for such punishment?" Jeff asked.

"He says he has killed a white man," said Gray Owl. "He has killed Curly Bunton."

CHAPTER 13

▼

Old Eagle was silent. He looked at Jeff with neither fear nor challenge. He seemed to be saying, "I have said what I have said. I have killed the murderer of my son." Having made his statement, he waited for Jeff's verdict.

"Old Eagle's words can't be true," Jeff said carefully. "Curly Bunton died from a fall. His death was an accident."

Quickly, Gray Owl translated Jeff's words. Old Eagle stiffened. He shook his head. Then, forcefully and with great conviction, he spoke again.

"Old Eagle says he speaks the truth," Gray Owl reported. "Curly Bunton murdered Old Eagle's son, Goes to the Water, but the white man's law set him free. So he—Old Eagle—killed Curly Bunton."

"How did he kill him?" Jeff asked.

In the Crow tongue, Gray Owl asked the question. Again, Old Eagle answered, his voice high and quavering, and again, the young man translated his words to English.

"He prayed to his sacred helpers for power," Gray Owl said. "The spirits led him to the evil one. Old Eagle was riding down from the mountain. He met Curly Bunton, who was also riding a horse. Old Eagle rode straight up to him. Curly smiled as Old Eagle came near, but the evil one did not know him. Then Old Eagle struck him in the head with his war club. Curly Bunton fell from his horse and died. Now his spirit must wander the earth as a ghost."

Jeff glanced at me. His eyes said, "I don't want to hear this," and I nodded. I felt the same.

Turning back to the old man, Jeff said, "Why does Old Eagle come to us?"

Gray Owl asked the question, and again received the answer in the Crow tongue. "Old Eagle says he broke the white man's law, and now he must tell the truth and be punished."

Jeff was silent for a time. He sat on the floor across from the old Indian, looking down at his hands. He looked up. "Can Old Eagle prove his words?"

The answer came swiftly. "I have told you."

Jeff made his decision. "And we hear you," he said, looking at me, "but white man's law asks for other proof. White man's law asks for witnesses—others who saw the killing." Again, Jeff looked intently at me.

I wholeheartedly joined the conspiracy. I nodded.

Turning back to Old Eagle, Jeff rendered his verdict. His decision would probably not be legal in any court in the land, but in my opinion it was altogether righteous, and just.

"We cannot accept your words," Jeff said. "You have no witnesses. You cannot prove what you say. We cannot punish you. You must go now."

Slowly, Old Eagle got to his feet. We stood up, too. Jeff smiled, raising his right hand to shoulder level and extending his index and middle finger upward in the sign for "friend." Old Eagle responded in kind. Helped by young Gray Owl, he made his way outside and down to the wagon.

We watched from the doorway until the wagon drove up the street and disappeared from sight.

"I don't know about you, Merlin," Jeff said, "but I believe this is the best day I've had since I took this job."

The dog days of summer settled in at Medicine Lodge, and the world seemed to hunker down like a turtle on a rock. The town's dirt streets baked under a pitiless sun. Dust rose in clouds with the passage of horses and wagons. The town dads hired Arnie Moss to drive the water wagon and sprinkle the streets. Arnie did so faithfully each morning, but by noon the dirt had already dried and returned to dust.

Folks moved slower. They stayed inside during the heat of the day. Merchants and saloonkeepers opened their doors and windows, hoping for a cross-breeze. Stray dogs lay in patches of shade, panting, as they waited for sundown and cooler hunting.

Most afternoons, thunderclouds teased, promising rain but failing to deliver. The heavens grumbled and growled. Lightning stabbed. Then, at length, the clouds passed. The sun dropped behind the hills and left the sky ablaze with color. Evening came on with a sigh, and another day passed.

Jeff and me made our rounds later, in the cool of evening. We generally ate supper at the cabin, but sometimes at the City Café, and spent our evenings catching up on paperwork and talking. I wrote Pandora a five-page letter, telling her about the trial of Buck DuFresne and of the people I'd met in Medicine Lodge. I didn't mention Bonnie Jo, of course. I didn't want Pandora to get the wrong idea—or the right one, either.

The fact is, I didn't know what to say. Bonnie Jo still hadn't returned from her visit, and I hadn't heard from her since she'd gone. Sometimes I wondered if she planned to come back at all. As things turned out, it wouldn't have mattered if I had known what to say. Somehow, I never got around to finishing the letter to Pandora, and I never did mail it.

Archie Young Bull began to come around the office again. I hadn't seen him since that day after the trial, but he had apparently got over his mad, at least partly. On the one hand, he was still in a huff about Buck DuFresne getting off scot-free in the matter of the attack on the bartender. As an Indian, Archie still had his doubts about the white man's law, and I sure couldn't blame him for that.

On the other hand, he seemed to respect Jeff and me. He had heard about the fight between Jeff and Buck, and of Jeff's banishing the cowman from Medicine Lodge. He also knew of Curly Bunton's death, and of Old Eagle's visit to the marshal's office. He knew we had refused to accept the old man's confession, and that we had declined to lock him up or charge him with murder. Archie may not have had much faith in our law, but he knew justice when he saw it.

He took to hanging around the office, and Jeff said Archie even showed an interest in maybe becoming a peace officer himself. I said that would be like Jesse James showing an interest in maybe becoming a bank teller. We both laughed, but I could tell Jeff was really hoping such a thing might happen. To tell the truth, I was, too.

I had come to admire the Crow people. Getting to know Old Eagle and Archie had helped me to understand the Indians' strong sense of justice. The more I learned of the tribe's history, and especially of their dealings with whites, the more I sympathized with their plight.

In a fairly short time, the Crows had gone from buffalo to bib overalls as the Indian Department tried to turn them into farmers. They were prisoners on their reservation, unable to leave or visit other parts of the territory without a pass from the Indian agent. The only Indians who were granted passes were those who did a little work on the side for the agent. When they were allowed off the reservation they could only go in small groups, and their visits were only for brief periods. To make sure the Indians didn't cause trouble while away, the agent sometimes sent Indian police along with them.

It was against the rules for the Crows to take part in dances of any kind—the sun dance, the war dance, the scalp dance, even social dances. I had noticed that in actual practice the Crows defied that rule, but they took a risk in doing so. Indians found guilty of the crime of dancing could even be sent to prison. It was also an "Indian offense" to be a medicine man, to have more than one wife, to give presents to other Indians, or to borrow or share things under the old tribal customs. And when whiskey traders got the Indians drunk on snakehead whiskey, it was the Indians who were punished, not the bootleggers.

More and more white settlers were squatting on the reservation. Big ranchers like DuFresne continued to trespass on Crow grazing land, sometimes with a little under-the-table money going into the Indian agent's pocket. All the rules governing Indian behavior came under the jurisdiction of the Court of Indian Offenses, of which the agent was arresting officer, judge, and jury all rolled into one.

The court handled all small problems among Indians, but it did not deal with major crimes or problems between whites and Indians. The tribal council spoke on behalf of the tribe with regard to treaties and such. Jeff Brown, as marshal of Medicine Lodge, dealt only with crimes and misdemeanors committed in town. His jurisdiction ended at the city limits.

Anyway, that's a rough idea as to how the law enforcement agencies were supposed to function in Crow country. The boundaries between lawmen and their different bailiwicks were many, and ofttimes overlapped. Between the tribal council, the Territorial Code, the Court of Indian Offenses, the Custer County sheriff's office, and the U.S. marshal's office, there was more law on the reservation than a man could keep up with. As it happened, I heard from two of those outfits regarding a legal matter on the very same day. Both agreed it was my job to handle. It sure is nice to be popular.

I was playing billiards with Clifford Bidwell at Sharp's pool hall when Ivan Friendly came in. Ivan managed the express office in Medicine Lodge, and he was the town's only telegraph operator.

"Telegram for you from Helena, Merlin," he said. "Looks like you might actually have to do a little work for a change."

I took the telegram from Ivan and tried my best to look put-upon. "There's no rest for us civil servants," I sighed. "Serving the taxpayer is a full-time job and a heavy burden."

Ivan smiled. "Horse shit," he said.

I opened the telegram. "Merlin," it read. "Two accused rustlers arrested July 12 by Indian police and held at Crow Agency. Contact Major Weede and take suspects into custody. Deliver to Custer County sheriff, Miles City. Will meet you there. Please advise departure date. Signed: Chance Ridgeway, U.S. Marshal."

I put up my pool cue and told Clifford the game was his by default. "Telegram's from my boss," I said. "I have to answer this, and get ready to ride."

"I appreciate your letting me win," Clifford said, his voice dripping sarcasm, "but in all modesty I feel I should remind you that you haven't won a game from me yet."

"Well," I said, "this could have been the first time."

Clifford laughed. "That's what I like about you, Merlin," he said. "You never allow reality to interfere with your fantasies."

At the express office, I wrote out an answer to Ridgeway, telling him I'd collect the prisoners and meet him at Miles City. Then I stopped at the livery barn and asked Arnie Moss to get my horses in and ready for the trail. I found Jeff at the marshal's office, talking to an Indian policeman named Bullfrog.

"You're just in time," Jeff said. "Officer Bullfrog is here to see you."

I sized the policeman up. He was a big, sleepy-looking Indian, big of shoulder and haunch, and his skin was the color of a tobacco plug. He wore a belted Colt revolver below a paunch that told me he hadn't missed many meals lately, and a nickel-plated badge pinned to his shirtfront winked in the sunlight.

"Agent Weede say you come to agency," he said. "I take you there."

I squinted up at Bullfrog's face. His features looked as it they'd been chiseled out of granite.

"That's mighty neighborly of you, Officer," I said, "but I believe I can find the agency all right by myself."

"I take you there," he said again. It was a statement, not a question.

I showed Jeff the telegram from Ridgeway, and told him I didn't know how long I'd be gone.

"Don't worry about it," he said. "The town's peaceful as a prayer meeting these days." Then he grinned and said, "Besides, if I run into something I can't handle, I can always deputize Archie and his boys."

I returned his grin. "If you run into something you can't handle, it will probably *be* Archie and his boys."

It took but a moment to round up my gatherings and pack my war bag. Bull-frog helped me cinch my bedroll on the bay horse while Arnie Moss saddled Rutherford for me. I took hold of the bay's lead-rope, stepped up into the saddle and told Arnie goodbye.

"Much obliged, Arnie. Be seeing you."

"Watch your back trail," Arnie said.

With Bullfrog riding at my side, I put Medicine Lodge behind me and set out on the road to the Crow Agency.

The hot spell continued, with no relief in sight. Heat waves shimmered on the roadway, and the cottonwood trees along the Little Bighorn stood silent and still, their leaves motionless as leaves in a painting. Before we had gone two miles, the horses were lathered. Sweat crawled from beneath my hat brim, stinging my eyes and tasting salty on my lips. Bullfrog rode beside me, silent as a statue. I tried once or twice to talk to him about the rustlers I was to pick up, but he gave no sign he even heard me. We rode in silence the twenty-odd miles and turned our horses down the wide, dusty streets of the agency.

We found the major at his residence, seated outside on its broad veranda. He was dressed as he had been when I saw him last, in a straw hat, smoked glasses, and a rumpled linen suit. Papers and ledgers were spread before him on a writing desk, and a barefoot Indian girl stood beside his chair, shielding him from the sun with a large umbrella. He smiled as Bullfrog and me rode up, and raised a languid hand in greeting.

"Ah, Fanshaw," he said. "I see my man Bullfrog found you."

I stepped down off Rutherford and loose-tied the animal to a hitching post.

"Yes, he did," I said, "but the truth is, I had already heard from Marshal Ridgeway."

"Indeed," the major said. "The thieves were driving thirty head of good Crow ponies when the Indian police caught them. They tried to make a run for it, but the horses they were herding were considerably better than the horses they rode."

Major Weede looked at me over the tops of his eyeglasses. "You look rather done in," he said. "May I offer you some refreshment? A cold drink?"

"If it wouldn't put you out none," I said. "It is a mite warm today."

An Indian woman I took to be some kind of housekeeper stood at the screen door to the house. Catching her eye, the major made the sign for "drink."

"*Bilichilía*," he said, "cold water."

The woman nodded, and went inside the house. When she returned, she carried a large metal pitcher of water and a cup. I took a chair across from the major.

The woman set the water and cup down on a table beside me. I filled the cup and drank it at a draft.

"Much obliged," I said. "If I drink that entire pitcher it will just about replace what I lost on my way here."

Major Weede smiled tolerantly. "The prisoners are ready to go when you are," he said. "They have confessed to stealing the horses, and understand they will have to stand trial at Miles City."

I filled my cup again and drank. Weede picked up a sheaf of papers from the pile on his desk and handed them to me.

"They call themselves Jack Reed and Dooley Wymore. These are their confessions, signed and witnessed," he said. "Depositions from the Indian police who made the arrest, and my own report, are also included."

I took the papers and looked through them. "Appears you've thought of everything," I said. "Do you have their horses?"

"And their saddles and weapons. Their animals are in rather poor condition, but they've had rest, and grain."

Weede looked thoughtful. "You're welcome to stay the night. Make an early start in the morning, when it's cooler."

"Appreciate the offer," I said, "but I'd like to get those boys to Junction before dark. Catch the train to Miles City in the morning."

"Your diligence speaks well of you, Deputy," the major said. "The sooner those thieves are brought to justice, the better. I'd like to see an example made of them."

Remembering the major's intervention in the Curly Bunton case, I thought, *Your concern for law and order seems to depend on who the lawbreaker is,* but I said nothing. Considering all the times speaking my mind had got me in trouble, I was proud of myself. *Maybe,* I thought, *I'm gaining a little wisdom at last.*

I found the two prisoners in a low cabin that served as the agency jail. They were handcuffed and shackled by their ankles to a bull ring in the middle of the cabin's plank floor. They didn't seem happy.

"Howdy, boys," I said. "I'm here to take you to Miles City for a visit with the judge."

One of the two, a dark-skinned gent of about thirty, sported bad teeth and an enormous black moustache. He squinted his eyes at me and scowled. "You ain't Indian police," he said. "Who the hell are you?"

"Merlin Fanshaw, deputy U.S. marshal," I said. "Which one are you?"

"I'm Jack Reed," the man wheezed. "The smart one." His breath was so bad it stung my eyes.

"If you were smart," I observed, "you wouldn't have been caught stealing Crow horses."

I turned to the other man. He was maybe five years younger than his companion. He wore his sandy hair long, and his lower lip stuck out in a perpetual pout.

"That would make you Dooley Wymore," I said. "Let's take a little ride."

Behind me, in the doorway, Bullfrog searched through a key ring for the ones that would unlock the cuffs and leg irons.

Blinking against the brightness, the prisoners stepped out into the sunlight. Their horses, scrawny and listless, stood saddled at the hitching post.

"I hate to criticize," I said, "but when you two get out of the pokey you might try feedin' your horses once in a while. Makes them work better."

With Bullfrog watching, I got both men mounted and locked their right wrists to their saddle horns. Taking hold of the gray's lead rope, I swung up onto Rutherford and turned him toward the road. "You boys ride ahead of me. When we get to where we're going, I'll let you know."

Under a sun of brass, our procession headed north to the Yellowstone.

CHAPTER 14

▼

Miles City got its start as Milestown in the fall of 1876 when Colonel Nelson Miles grew tired of all the drifters, bums, and loafers hanging around the new army post on the Yellowstone. He ordered them to move back across the Tongue River, two miles away from the post. By sundown, the civilians had thrown up a tent or two in their new location and had two saloons and a gambling hall open for business. They named the settlement Milestown, for the man who had evicted them.

Over the next few years Milestown grew into a rip-roaring community that catered to buffalo hunters, bullwhackers, river men, troopers from the fort, and fortune seekers of every stripe. When the region turned to raising cattle and sheep in the 1880s, Milestown became Miles City. It was the trade center for the entire eastern part of the territory and the county seat of Custer County, which included the Crow Reservation.

With the horse-thieves in custody, I had taken the ferry across the Bighorn and had reached Junction City after dark. When the Northern Pacific rolled in the next morning, I loaded our horses on a stock car, installed my prisoners in a day coach, and set out for Miles.

It was just past noon when the train's whistle let us know we were nearing town. Looking out the window, I saw rolling prairie, broken hills and buttes, and a grove of big cottonwood trees along the river. We passed Fort Keogh and swept on, crossing the bridge over the Tongue, and came chuffing to a stop at the depot.

When I stepped down from the coach with my prisoners, the street that ran parallel to the tracks was busy as a beehive. Top buggies, buckboards, and hacks from the hotels jostled for position along the avenue, and men and women on foot made their way through the bustle as they walked to and from the depot. I scanned the crowd, looking for a familiar face, but saw none. The horse-thieves in my custody were growing restless, looking to me for direction, but I was as uncertain as they were about my next step. I had asked Major Weede to telegraph Marshal Ridgeway and tell him I was coming, but I had no idea whether he had done so.

And then I saw him. Lanky and lean as a heron, the marshal stood beside an army ambulance drawn by a pair of brown mules. A youth in a battered black hat sat in the driver's seat, and a stocky, barrel-chested gent with a badge stood beside the marshal. All three were watching the crowd around the train. I took off my hat and waved it back and forth a time or two, and Ridgeway caught my signal. He took the arm of the man at his side and pointed at me. Leaving the boy to mind the wagon, they made their way through the crowd to where I stood.

"Well, Deputy," said Ridgeway, "You made good time."

"Yes, sir," I said. "I set out the day your telegram came."

Ridgeway turned to the man beside him. "This is Bodie Winters, deputy sheriff of Custer County. Bodie, meet Merlin Fanshaw, my able deputy."

Winters smiled a thin half smile and looked me over, to my mind just a few seconds too long. Then he stuck out his hand and said, "Howdy."

I'm not certain, but I believe his grip could have crushed a billiard ball.

Ridgeway was sizing up the prisoners. He turned to the deputy. "Take these famous horse rustlers back to the courthouse and lock them up, if you please," he said, "and send the boy over. Deputy marshal Fanshaw and I will be along directly."

Winters nodded, and then turned to Reed and Wymore. "You heard the marshal," he said. "Get up in that ambulance over yonder."

I handed the deputy the keys to the prisoners' handcuffs. "Here," I said. "You'll be needing these."

Again, the deputy sheriff gave me that long look and the little half smile. Then he took the keys and turned away with the prisoners. I decided liking Bodie Winters was going to require some work.

I watched as Winters loaded the horse-thieves into the ambulance. I saw him speak to the boy in the black hat, and watched as the boy made his way to where Ridgeway and I stood.

"Yes, sir, Marshal?" the boy said.

Ridgeway handed the boy a silver dollar. "The railroad will be unloading deputy Fanshaw's horses down at the corral in a few minutes. I'd like you to take them down to Ringer and Johnson's Livery for me. Tell them I said to put the animals up and give them some grain. Will you do that for me, Elroy?"

The boy looked at Ridgeway like a village priest looks at a bishop. "Yes, sir!" said Elroy, and turned straightaway to attend to his mission.

I was glad to see the marshal. I smiled. "You still have persuading ways," I said.

Ridgeway didn't return my smile, but I caught a twinkle in his faded blue eyes. "A valuable talent for a leader of men," he said. "Come, let us find a restaurant. As I recall, breaking bread is one of your favorite pursuits." He paused, looking at me with his old one-eyed squint. "That hasn't changed, has it?"

"No, sir," I said. "That hasn't changed."

Over a prime dinner of antelope stew at a Main Street café, I told Ridgeway pretty much everything that had occurred in Medicine Lodge since he sent me down there. I told him about Jeff Brown and the taming of Archie Young Bull. I told him of the killing of Goes to the Water, and of how the DuFresnes used their money and influence to get Curly Bunton off. I recounted the recent news of Curly's death, but said nothing about Old Eagle and his confession.

I trusted Ridgeway, but I knew he tended to be pretty much a letter-of-the-law man. I had no wish to cause Old Eagle any more grief than he'd already known. Whether Curly Bunton cashed in his chips as the result of a horse wreck or because Old Eagle brained him with a war club, I figured justice had been done and it was best not to wake up any sleeping dogs.

I told Ridgeway how Buck cut up Jerry Paddock the bartender, and of Buck's subsequent trial and its outcome. I told him of Jeff's fight with Buck after the trial, and of Jeff's posting the cowman from Medicine Lodge. I even told him about Buck and Bonnie Jo Hutchins, and of how she had accused him of raping her the night he attacked Jerry. I didn't tell him about Bonnie Jo and me, of course. In the first place, I wasn't sure myself how I felt about that part of my life. In the second place, I didn't figure it was any of Ridgeway's business.

In short, I gave Ridgeway a thorough report of what had occurred that summer in Medicine Lodge. I described the situation there as I saw it, but I didn't tell the marshal everything. I should have known better.

The waiter came around with the coffee pot and refilled our cups. Ridgeway fished out his old briar, primed and loaded it, and lit up. Once he had the pipe going well, he studied me for a time in silence. I drank my coffee and waited. I tried to meet his gaze, but I found myself growing more restless with every passing second.

"Meaning no offense, Marshal," I said, "but sometimes you have a way of making a man feel like a bug under a microscope."

Ridgeway dropped his eyes. Beneath his silver-white moustache a faint smile played at the corners of his mouth. "Sorry, son," he said. "It's a habit I picked up from questioning evil-doers. You'd be surprised how many confessions I get just by looking men in the eye."

No, I wouldn't, I thought.

"It does seem to me," Ridgeway said, "that you're being less than candid about your association with Mrs. Hutchins. I don't pay all that much attention to gossip, you understand, but there sometimes is truth to it. Your friendship with the woman is none of my concern, unless it threatens to compromise the cause of justice. I rely on you to make certain that doesn't happen."

I felt my throat go tight. "I don't know what your spies have told you," I said, "but—" The marshal smiled. "Why, bless you, son! I don't have spies. I have sources! They provide me with information, and a lawman can't have too much information.

"Just to show you what I mean, I'll provide *you* with some information," he continued. "Mrs. Hutchins—Bonnie Jo—is not exactly a stranger to criminal investigation. She was a 'bloke buzzer' in Chicago a few years back—a 'bloke buzzer' being a pickpocket who specializes in robbing men.

"Mrs. Hutchins served a twelve-month sentence there before coming west with her husband, Ed. They operated a barbershop in Denver for a year or two, but Ed had a run-in with a customer over the man's attentions to his wife, and they left in a hurry. They moved to Medicine Lodge shortly after the town began, and opened their shop there.

"Less than a year later, Ed caught Bonnie Jo in the arms of a whiskey drummer. Ed shot the booze peddler and drew himself a ten-year stretch in prison. One month after he went away, Mrs. Hutchins—Bonnie Jo—took up with Buck DuFresne.

"Now you tell me she's away, visiting a relative near Butte City. That is a fact. She's been visiting her husband, Ed, over at the territorial pen at Deer Lodge—which, as she correctly told you, is near Butte City."

"All right," I said, "you surely have kept an eye on Bonnie Jo. I don't suppose you do that with every small time criminal in the territory, so it must have something to do with me, and my keeping company with her.

"I don't know who your sources in Medicine Lodge are, but it don't seem like you have much confidence in me. Sounds like you've pretty much felt the need to check on everything I've done."

Ridgeway's pipe had gone cold. He laid it carefully in his saucer, and looked me in the eye. "That ain't so, son. You have the potential to become the best deputy I ever had, and you have my full confidence. As to my sources, they ain't anyone you know, and they're not from Medicine Lodge. One of my other deputies has been working down Wyoming way, and I had him stop off at Medicine Lodge on his way back north. Kyle Haddon, owner of the Legal Tender, told him you were keeping company with Mrs. Hutchins. It was then I looked into her background. Like I said, a lawman can't have too much information.

"When an officer is on a man's trail, he needs to know whether that man is left-or right-handed. Is the man armed? Does he carry a belly gun? Who are his friends? Are they likely to help him? When the man enters a building, the officer needs to know whether that building has a back door. How are the rooms laid out? Are there weapons inside?"

Ridgeway closed his eyes, remembering. "I've lost six deputies since I've worn this badge," he said. "One turned his back on a killer. One trusted a whore, and got gut-shot for his trouble. Two were ambushed. One took pity on a prisoner and took the handcuffs off so the man could get himself a drink. Prisoner attacked him and killed him with his own gun.

"One failed to search a prisoner properly. Prisoner cut the officer's throat with a straight razor. I lost all six because they either lacked information or failed to exercise proper caution. I don't aim to lose a seventh, if I can help it."

I have to say that Ridgeway's words went a long way toward smoothing my ruffled feathers. The man could aggravate me like no one else. At the same time, there was no one whose good opinion I valued more. He could talk all he wanted about the value of information, but we both knew he had, on occasion, withheld information from me. He had been warm and open, and he had been cool and distant. He had at times left me totally alone; he had been a fussy mother hen at others. Chance Ridgeway was a walking contradiction, but the law was his passion, and he cared for his deputies. I liked him.

I grinned. "Well," I said, "I sure don't aim to be the seventh. Where do we go from here?"

"I got you a room over at the Macqueen House," Ridgeway said. "Best accommodations in town. Each room has its own stove, but the only bath is in the hotel barbershop. Walls are thin as paper; a man can hear a mouse fart two rooms away. Still, the service is first-rate. Take a few days and look the town over. See the sights. Try the local restaurants. Rest up some."

"And then?"

"I thought you might want to go back to Dry Creek. I see no need for you to return to Medicine Lodge unless you want to for personal reasons. That's up to you. There seems to be no imminent danger of an uprising by the Crows, and from what you say, Marshal Brown has the city marshal's office well in hand. Archie Young Bull has gone from being a renegade and a problem to being a friend of the law." Ridgeway's smile was sly. "Of course, you would have to find another barber—"

I met his smile with my own. "Well, I'm too durn young to grow a beard. I guess I'll just have to go back to shaving myself."

Ridgeway paid the bill, and we set out for the Macqueen House. The town was bustling, with bull teams and jerk-line outfits raising dust as they moved along the wide streets. A beer wagon rumbled by pulled by a sloe-black work team. Top buggies and surreys passed each other. Two men loaded a keg of nails onto a wagon in front of the hardware store. Cowboys rode by at a careless trot.

I heard the ring of a blacksmith's hammer on an anvil, caught the smell of fresh bread as we passed a bakery. A young townsman in dress shirt, sleeve garters, and straw hat came out of a café with a laughing girl on his arm. They stepped off the boardwalk ahead of us, aware of nothing but each other. I thought of Pandora, back in Dry Creek, and found myself missing her. Maybe Ridgeway was right; maybe it was time to put Medicine Lodge behind me. And yet if that was so, why did I have such a powerful feeling there was something I had left undone?

Over the next two days, I spent some time getting acquainted with Miles City. I treated myself to a shave and a haircut at a barbershop by a gent who billed himself as a "capillary manipulator, boss barber, and hairdresser." He lowered my ears, dusted me with talcum, and left me smooth-faced and smelling of bay rum. I figure that when I left his shop, dogs three blocks away picked up my scent.

I bought a new shirt and sleeve garters, but drew the line at the straw hat. Instead, I dusted off my old *sombrero* and called it good.

I struck up a conversation with townsfolk wherever I went. I met a young man my age at a billiard parlor and we played billiards until I'd lost six dollars and fifty cents, whereupon I took mercy on my opponent and ended the play.

I took to having a beer or two each forenoon at Coleman's Cottage Saloon. I have to admit I did so partly because of the free lunch. The saloon was a good deal fancier than the Oasis back in Dry Creek—it had little bowls of water on the bar for a man to use in washing his hands, and clean white towels hanging at intervals along the bar with which to dry them. The barkeep was friendly and a great source of information on everything around the area. The man was a fine bartender—he had opinions even on matters he knew nothing about.

I visited a local saddle shop and talked with the saddle-maker while he worked. The shop smelled of old wood and new leather, and the proprietor kept the coffee pot on all day. I soon learned that he not only made good saddles, he had likely worn out a few. He told me he had come up the trail with a cattle drive and was homesick for Texas. When I asked him why he didn't go on back, he said he was only homesick in the wintertime. By the time he decided to pack up and leave, it was summer again. He liked Montana just fine in the summer, he said.

I bought a copy of *The Adventures of Tom Sawyer*, by Mark Twain, and spent my evenings at the hotel reading by lamplight. It was the first I had read of Mr. Twain's writing, and I laughed out loud so often I was afraid people staying next door to my room would complain.

By the morning of my third day in Miles City, I had about decided to go on back to Dry Creek. I came down the stairway to the lobby of the Macqueen House and was leaving my key at the front desk when I saw Ridgeway sitting near the front windows. He stood up when he saw me, and waved me over.

"Mornin', Marshal," I said. "You're up early."

Ridgeway smiled. "The early marshal catches the evil-doer," he said. His expression turned serious. "The kid from the telegraph office woke me at six this morning with a message. Seems there's been a breakout at the territorial prison. Three men went over the wall night before last."

I shrugged. "Jail breaks happen now and again," I said. "What makes this one so special?"

Ridgeway took a folded paper from his coat pocket. "I know something about the men who broke out. I know two of 'em by name. I know the third man personally. So do you, Merlin."

"I do? Who—"

"The two I know by name? Abner Rale and Ed Hutchins. The one we both know—Original George Starkweather."

Early morning never has been my best time of day. I wasn't sure I'd heard Ridgeway right. "I haven't had my coffee yet, Marshal. Did you say Ed Hutchins—and George Starkweather?"

"I did. Abner Rale is a small-time safecracker, serving a ten-year stretch for grand theft. Ed Hutchins is the very gent we were talking about the other day—proprietor of Ed's Barbershop in Medicine Lodge, and Bonnie Jo's husband. And Original George, well, he—"

"—was doing life without parole for everything from robbery to murder," I said slowly. "He told me when they sentenced him that he didn't know how long he'd be staying at the prison—like it was some kind of health resort he could check out of any time."

Ridgeway looked rueful. "Yes. Well, he has, apparently."

I was having trouble getting my mind around Ridgeway's news. I had met George Starkweather back in eighty-two, the same year I met Ridgeway. I had just turned eighteen, and for a while that year I'd even ridden with Starkweather and his gang. I had helped Ridgeway capture the old wolf. And now George had escaped prison and was at large somewhere in the territory.

"George Starkweather being free in the world is bad news for law and order," I said.

Ridgeway frowned, remembering. "Yes. And for public safety, peace, and decency. Maybe they'll catch those boys soon and put them back in their cages."

"Maybe. I wonder about Ed Hutchins. You reckon he'll go back to Medicine Lodge?"

"I doubt it. He's bound to know that's the first place the law would look for him."

I gazed out the lobby window, beyond the street, beyond the line of trees along the river, staring into the distance as if I could see all the way to Medicine Lodge. "I don't know, Chance," I said. "I had about decided to go back to Dry Creek, but now—"

"There's no need to change your plans," Ridgeway said. "Let's wait and see if they catch those boys. Actually, I have a job for you for the next several days—maybe a week."

I waited for the rest of it. "Earl Biggers makes his living as shotgun messenger for the stage line," the marshal continued, "but he has lately come down with inflammation of the parotid gland—or, in laymen's terms, the mumps. The local sawbones says Earl will be good as new, if the swelling don't go to his gonads. Meanwhile, the coach to Deadwood needs a shotgun guard. I thought you might like to fill in for old Earl."

"Thought so, did you?"

"As soon as I heard the news, I said to myself, 'I'll bet Merlin would just love to set atop a swayin' Concord coach for a trip or two, seein' new country and livin' a prime, healthy life in the great out-of-doors.'"

I smiled. "Uh-huh. If it's such a healthy life, how come old Earl has come down with the mumps?"

Ridgeway's eyes twinkled. He assumed a baffled look. "That's a medical mystery, son."

"You forgot to mention the good company I'll be keeping. Who's the whip on this pleasure excursion? If he's like most I've seen, he'll be a cantankerous old coot, vain as a peacock, a chewer of tobacco, and a spitter against the wind."

"That's the very man!" Ridgeway said, his eyes wide. "You reckon you could ride guard with such a gent?"

"I expect I could," I said, laughing. "My boss seems to think I can do anything."

All right, I was wrong. When I showed up at the express office the next day, I found the driver to be a pleasant young man of about thirty. So much for "cantankerous old coot." He also didn't seem especially vain, and he turned out to be a devout Mormon who would sooner kiss a boar hog than use tobacco in any form. He handed me a sawed-off ten-gauge Greener, stepped up into the box, and took the reins. I checked the shotgun's loads, climbed up beside him, and the stage to Deadwood took to the road.

As we rounded the corner where the Macqueen House stood, I saw Ridgeway standing on the hotel's wide veranda, watching us. He raised his hand, in greeting and farewell, and we swept out of Miles City on our way south to the Black Hills.

CHAPTER 15

▼

The road to Deadwood stretched south across rolling plains and low hills, under a sky of brilliant blue. The driver sat straight-backed on the box, talking to the four-horse team through the lines he held between his fingers. I sat beside him, the sawed-off Greener in my hands and my feet braced.

The coach seemed to sail over the ground, dropping into hollows where coulees crossed the road, and then swaying on its thoroughbraces as it dipped and climbed uphill again. My mother had named me Merlin after the small prairie falcon of that name. As I swooped along, seated high behind the horses, I pretended I was the bird and thought about how fine it would be to fly.

I had never served as shotgun messenger before, and for the first several miles I fancied I saw road agents and stage robbers behind every bush. By the time we crossed Pumpkin Creek I noticed the driver watching me out of the corner of his eye, a slight smile on his lips, and I relaxed some. After that, the imaginary badmen and renegade Indians seemed to grow considerably fewer.

I still didn't know the driver's name, but I admired his skill. Steady and calm, he sat atop that swaying box and drove the team with a sure hand. He seldom touched a horse with the whip, nor did he shout and swear. The horses were not excited and nervous because their driver was not.

We changed horses and greased the axles at the Pumpkin Creek station, then rolled on across Mizpah Creek to Powderville, on the Powder River. I had long heard the old saw about the Powder, that it was "a mile wide and an inch deep, too thin to plow and too thick to drink," and as we crossed it late that afternoon

I had to agree the description fit. The Powder was indeed a broad, slow-moving stream, shallow and silt-filled.

The sun was low in the sky by that time. Beneath its high banks the river lay in shadow, sunlight just touching the tops of the cottonwoods and willows on its near side. The coach crossed, and rolled up out of the water into the badlands above. Twenty miles farther down the road, daylight gone and darkness coming on, we pulled in to the Box Elder Creek stage station.

The station consisted of a rude barn, pole corrals, and a small log building that housed the station keeper and his wife. The hostler came out to meet us as we pulled in. He unhitched the tired horses and led them away. Our passengers stepped out of the coach, stretching their legs, and I had my first good look at them. Two were mining men, returning to their holdings. The other two were an older man and his wife, intent on visiting family members at Deadwood.

We all ate supper together in the main room of the building, after which the passengers bedded down in sleeping rooms. The driver and me rolled out our blankets over at the barn.

Come morning, the station keeper's wife fed us breakfast while the hostler hitched a fresh team to the coach. The driver was the first to finish his meal. He stood up, took his plate and eating tools to the dishpan by the stove, and said quietly, "We're burnin' daylight."

We picked up the mail, got our passengers loaded, and were on the road again as the sun's first rays lit the hilltops.

The day turned out to be my day for learning names. The driver had so far said scarcely a dozen words, and I had become reconciled the trip would be a quiet one. But two miles down the road that second day he turned to me and said with a smile, "Jackson. Silent Sam Jackson. That's my name."

I was so startled I almost fell off the coach. "Uh—Merlin," I said. "I'm Merlin Fanshaw." The driver nodded, and turned his attention back to his driving. He said nothing for the rest of the morning. I supposed all that chatter had played him out.

We changed horses at Alzada, just north of the Wyoming line. While there, I learned the town had once been called Stoneville, but had changed its name three years earlier because Stoneville was sometimes confused with another town with a similar name. The settlement had been renamed Alzada, in honor of Mrs. Alzada Sheldon, wife of a local rancher. Like I said, it was my day for learning names.

At a station this side of Belle Fourche, Dakota Territory, we changed to fresh horses and doped the axles again. We made a brief stop in the town, and then drove on to a station on the Fort Meade road where we spent our second night.

As before, Jackson had us on the road at daybreak, and we rolled into Deadwood at nine o'clock in the morning.

The town had only one main street, and room for only one. Born with the gold rush of 1875, Deadwood was a mining town that had already begun to lose its luster. Like many another boomtown, placer mining had come and gone quickly. Prospectors had moved on to other camps, and the hard-rock boys had moved in with machinery and men to continue the work. There were still people aplenty in town, moving on foot and by horseback along the crooked, narrow streets. Business buildings packed the bottom of Deadwood and Whitehorn gulches, while higher up the steep hillsides settlers' dwellings clung to the slopes like magpie nests.

The folks who had built the town hadn't lost their sense of humor, at least. A stretch of false-fronted buildings, boardwalks, and signs along a muddy, crooked track bore a proud name: Wall Street.

Our passengers claimed their baggage, and Silent Sam and me carried the strongbox, mail, and freight into the express office. Hostlers unhitched the team and prepared the coach for its return trip.

I told Sam I had never been in Deadwood before. He said to go ahead and look the town over and meet him back at the office at noon. I thanked him, and set out to see the sights.

I bought myself a beer at the Number Ten Saloon, where Wild Bill Hickok got himself killed by Jack McCall ten years before. The bartender showed me the chair he said Hickok sat in when McCall shot him from behind, and he showed me the poker hand—two pairs, aces and eights—that Hickok had held. The bar-keep had the cards framed and displayed on the saloon's wall, and he claimed they were the very cards the famous gunman held at the time. Well, maybe they were, and maybe they weren't. All I knew for sure was that they hadn't done Hickok much good.

I looked into some of the stores and shops, and bought myself an early lunch across the street. At five minutes to twelve I was back at the express office. The team was harnessed and hitched, three passengers were boarded, and by half past twelve the coach was loaded and ready for the trip back to Miles City.

Silent Sam wasn't driving the return trip. An older man named Lonnie Craw-ford climbed up into the box and took the reins. Crawford was nowhere near as close-mouthed as Silent Sam had been, but his red-rimmed eyes and the way he flinched at loud noises told me he was suffering the effects of a serious hangover. He whispered that he sure would appreciate it if I wouldn't talk to him for at least an hour or so. I told him it was a deal. Crawford took his foot off the brake, gave the leaders their head, and the coach rolled out of Deadwood, headed north.

The trip back to Miles was pretty much a repeat of the passage to Deadwood. We changed horses at the same stations, crossed the same rivers, and ate the same meals at the midday and overnight stops. Crawford talked but little that first day, which was all right with me. I used the quiet to think back over my time down on the Crow Reservation and to consider my future plans.

It seemed to me there was little reason to return to Medicine Lodge. Archie and his boys were no longer a problem. Jeff Brown seemed to have the marshal's office well in hand. The town had acquired a city attorney, and there was talk of a justice of the peace coming sometime in the fall.

Of course, I knew the DuFresnes still didn't cotton much to Jeff Brown. I supposed they never would. To their way of thinking, the man would always be the wrong color and a burr in their blanket. Until Jeff showed up, J. W. and his son Buck had pretty well had things their own way in that part of the country. They didn't like taking orders from anyone, not even the law. Still, I knew Jeff had earned their respect. That went a long way toward keeping the peace.

The Indians had come to admire him, too. Jeff had won Archie Young Bull's respect through his courage and his strength. He had proved he was impartial. He would enforce the law for Indians the same as for whites. We had done our best to bring Goes to the Water's killer to justice. In the end, we had failed because the DuFresnes twisted the law with their money and influence. We had not been able to bring Curly Bunton to trial, but the Crows knew we had tried. Our efforts had not gone unnoticed.

Why did I seem unable to stop thinking about Medicine Lodge? When I did so, I found no reason for worry. I had told Ridgeway the full story of my time there—or nearly so—and he, too, saw no cause for concern. Peace and order had been restored. A good man occupied the city marshal's office, respected by all. There was peace—albeit an uneasy one—between white men and red.

And yet, each time I thought about the town and its people a feeling came over me that something bad was coming. Sorrow and danger seemed to lie just ahead.

I shook my head, to clear it. I tried to concentrate on the road ahead, the fast-moving team, and the free, open country leading back to Miles City, but the feeling of foreboding remained. I had never been much of a hand for hunches and such, and right then I wished the feeling that troubled me would either go away or make its meaning clear.

Ridgeway was waiting at the stage office when we pulled in. I had been gone just over a week, and it was good to see him again. I grinned, stepping down from the coach.

"No trouble," I said, "and nothing to fear—road agents know Fearless Fanshaw is here!"

It was then I saw the expression on the marshal's face. There was no humor there, no trace of that twinkle in his eye I'd come to know. Instead, there was tension in the set of his jaw and in the stiff way he held himself. He nodded, a curt bob of the head, as a man sometimes does when he has bad news to tell.

"There's no way to say this but straight out, son," he said. "Buck DuFresne is dead, and Jeff Brown has been arrested for his murder."

I do not recall entering the Rosebud Café, but I must have. Next thing I knew, Ridgeway and me were at a table inside, drinking coffee. They served good coffee at the Rosebud, but I don't know if mine was good that day or not. I was too busy trying to get my mind around Ridgeway's words.

"I was at the sheriff's office when the telegram came," Ridgeway said. "Tom Burke, city attorney at Medicine Lodge, sent it. Telegram said Buck DuFresne is dead. Said the sheriff was needed down there right away. It also said City Marshal Jeff Brown has been accused of Buck's murder."

"That can't be," I said. "I know Jeff. Whatever happened down there, Jeff Brown didn't murder anyone."

"Loyalty is a fine thing, son," Ridgeway said, "but over the years I've known of at least a dozen murders that were committed by people whose friends swore couldn't murder anyone."

"I don't care, Chance. Tell me Jeff killed someone in the line of duty or in self-defense and I'll say yes, sure, maybe so. But tell me he's a murderer, and I have to say you don't know what you're talkin' about. Respectfully."

Ridgeway frowned. His eyes narrowed. "Your opinion is noted," he said. "Do you want to hear the rest of it, or not?"

"Sure I do."

"The telegram came the day after you left on the stage for Deadwood. There was no way I could reach you. The sheriff wasn't here. He's testifying at a trial over in Billings. Bodie Winters, that big deputy you met, figured he should look into the case. He left for Medicine Lodge the same day.

"Now I'd like to believe he volunteered because he's a hard-worker and a dedicated lawman, but I have my doubts. Heaviest thing I've seen him pick up is a beer glass. As for dedication, I'd have to say Bodie Winters is more dedicated to his ambition than to the law. Bodie dreams of beating out his boss the sheriff in the next election. Bringing in Buck DuFresne's killer could go a long way toward making that dream come true."

I had a bad taste in my mouth, and it wasn't the coffee. "Yes," I said. "A feller with that kind of ambition might even bring in the wrong man. What makes him think Jeff Brown is his murderer?"

"Couple of things, according to the telegram he sent yesterday. He says Jeff once threatened to kill Buck if he showed his face back in Medicine Lodge."

"I told you about that, Chance. Buck pushed a fight on Jeff, and lost. Jeff posted him out of town, and one of the DuFresne riders said Buck would come in anyway. Jeff said, 'Tell him to come shootin' if he does.' What else?"

"Buck was killed by a shotgun blast, at close range. Jeff's scattergun was found at the scene."

"That doesn't mean he fired it. Or if he did, maybe he had to."

"Buck wasn't armed. Bodie couldn't find a weapon."

"Still, that doesn't mean—"

"There was a witness. Didn't see the shooting, but saw Jeff enter the scene."

"This 'scene' you keep talkin' about—where *did* the killing take place?"

"Bonnie Jo Hutchins's house. Somebody beat the woman so bad she's still in a coma. They found Buck in the parlor, dead as ashes."

For what seemed a long time, neither of us spoke. When Ridgeway finally broke the silence, his voice was soft. "You're goin' to Medicine Lodge whether I send you or not, ain't you, son?"

"Yes, sir," I said. "I figure I have to."

"I know," Ridgeway said. "So I'm sending you. Come daybreak, your horse will be saddled and waiting. Get the job done, Deputy."

As always, Ridgeway was as good as his word. The eastern sky was turning dusty rose as I walked up the boardwalk to Ringer and Johnson's. The young hostler I'd met my first day in Miles led my horse Rutherford out from the back of the barn. The boy smiled a greeting.

"Marshal Ridgeway said you'd be on time," he said. "Good morning, Deputy."

"Morning," I said. "Did I hear the marshal call you 'Elroy' the other day?"

"Yes, sir," the boy said. "Elroy Biggs. I hope to be a lawman myself some day."

I had packed my saddlebags and a blanket roll the night before. I tied them behind the saddle's cantle and grinned.

"You're going to the right school," I said, taking in the whole barn with my glance. "I was working in a livery stable in Dry Creek when I met Marshal Ridgeway. Became his deputy last summer."

I eased my hand between the latigo and the buckskin's withers to test the tightness of the saddle girth. I was pleased. Elroy had not drawn the cinch too tight. I told him so.

"Good job on the cinch, Elroy," I said.

Elroy beamed. "I like to let the ponies have a little slack when they're startin' out," he said. "You can always draw him up tighter after an hour or so."

I handed Elroy a four-bit piece. Rutherford rubbed his head against me until I took the hint and scratched his favorite spot behind his ears.

"We'll be riding the train as far as Junction," I said. "Then Rutherford will get to earn those oats you've been feedin' him."

"He's a good horse, mister," Elroy said.

"Yes," I said. "He is."

For just a moment I felt better than I had since I'd heard of Buck's murder and Jeff's arrest. Rutherford and me would ride the train west to Junction, then ford the Bighorn and head south to Medicine Lodge. I had no idea what I'd find there, but Ridgeway believed I could deal with whatever I had to. Because he did, I tended to believe I could, too.

At Junction, Rutherford came down the ramp from the stock car, slipping, snorting, and trembling like a hog on ice. Up ahead, the locomotive belched black smoke and steam. When the buckskin had all four feet on solid ground, he gave me a look that seemed to say if he never saw another iron horse it would be too soon.

I grinned, and swung into the saddle. "We've got nearly forty miles to cover today," I told him. "By the time we get to Medicine Lodge you may wish you were still riding the rails."

The season was late summer, the day sultry and hot. The snow pack had long since left the mountains, and the river was low and muddy. Wading and swimming, Rutherford carried me across the river. Dripping water, hooves clattering on the gravel, he carried me up onto the bank. I stepped down, to let him catch his breath. The saddle cinch had grown slack, and I snugged up the latigo before mounting again. Under the August sun, my boots and shaps were already drying. The ride to Medicine Lodge would be a hot one, I knew. I touched Rutherford with my spurs.

"There's no way to get there but to go there," I told him. The buckskin tossed his head and struck out at a fast walk.

Darkness had long since fallen by the time I turned Rutherford off the main road and into Medicine Lodge. Beneath a starry sky, the town slept in the coolness, its buildings black shapes in the gloom. I drew rein at the livery barn and stepped down. The doors were open to the night air, and the smoky lantern inside cast a dull glow out onto the street.

Arnie Moss came out of the stable's office, shading his eyes as he peered into the dark. "Can I help you, mister?" he asked.

I smiled. "If your name is Arnie Moss, you can," I said, stepping into the light. "I'm a poor, weary traveler, seeking lodging for this Republican horse."

His sudden grin made me feel welcome. "Merlin!" Arnie said. "Bring that buckskin plug inside! I had no idea he was interested in politics."

I shook Arnie's hand. "Well," I said, "he was named after Rutherford B. Hayes, so I guess he didn't have much choice. How have you been, Arnie?"

"I'm doin' all right," Arnie said, "but I can't say as much for the town. I expect you heard the news."

"I heard Jeff killed Buck DuFresne. Was that the way of it?"

"Somebody sure as hell did. Gave him both barrels of a shotgun—over at Bonnie Jo's."

I knew the answer, but I asked anyway. "Where's Jeff now?"

Arnie frowned. "Locked up, over at the jail. That big deputy sheriff arrested him for murder."

"Bodie Winters. I met him up in Miles."

"Cocky som'bitch. Never seen a man so full of himself. Struts around town like the head rooster at a chicken farm."

"Rumor has it he's running for sheriff. Has he talked to you?"

"About the killin'? Hell, no. He says he's workin' on the case, but he spends most of his time drinkin' with DuFresne's cowboys over at the Legal Tender."

"How about Jeff? How is he doing?"

"Damned if I know. Winters won't let him have visitors."

"He's about to make an exception to that rule."

I took my blanket roll and saddlebags from my saddle. "All right if I bunk in the loft tonight? I'll find a place to stay tomorrow."

"Hell, Merlin," Arnie said, "you don't have to ask. Stay as long as you like."

I climbed the ladder to the hayloft and rolled out my blankets. Down below, Arnie led the buckskin to a ration of oats and a stall. I lay back and closed my eyes. I breathed in the earthy smells of hay, horses, and sun-dried wood. Across town, Marshal Jeff Brown was a prisoner in his own jail. Did he lie awake tonight, I wondered, there in the darkness? Did he feel abandoned by the people he'd served and guarded? I sent him my thoughts. *You're not alone, Jeff. I'm back in Medicine Lodge. I'll see you in the morning.*

It was sunlight that woke me. The roof of Arnie's livery barn was missing more than a few shingles, and through a gap on the east side a sunbeam found my closed eyes and told me good morning. I was not really ready to be up and doing, but my pa's old silver watch said the hour was past seven o'clock. I saw that I had overslept.

Sometimes it seems my whole life has been spent getting up in the morning before I wanted to. One of my earliest memories was of Pa shaking me awake in the darkness, saying it was "daylight in the canyon" and time to rise and shine. I remembered the whiskey on his breath, and how it was that I got up and dressed, not because I wanted to, but because I wanted to please him.

I recalled my pardner, Orville, who had always woke up alert and ready to take on the day while my mind was still thick with sleep. During the time we rode together I was ever the victim of his japes and jingles until later in the morning when I was finally awake enough to hold my own against his banter.

And I remembered old Doughbelly Pierce, roundup cook for the M Cross, beating on a dishpan and calling us snoozing punchers to roll out. "Come and get your bloody wolf bait," he'd holler, "or I'll throw it out!"

He never did, of course, but I was always hungry in those days and I got up fast, just in case.

I washed up in the cold water of a horse trough and looked in on Rutherford to be sure he was all right. Arnie had wiped the animal down, had put him in a stall, and had left him a healthy portion of oats and hay.

Nevertheless, the little horse looked tired and trail-worn. I leaned across the gate and scratched him behind his ears. "Take the day off, old son," I said. "I won't be needing you for a while."

I crossed the street, moved up Main, and turned the corner. Passing Bonnie Jo's house and barbershop brought back a flood of memories, good and bad. I recalled the afternoon at the shop when Bonnie Jo had drawn the blinds and locked the door, shutting the world out and shutting us in.

I remembered the day she told me Buck DuFresne had beat and raped her. I felt again my hot anger and remembered the way I'd confronted Buck at the jail. I recalled his laughter as he told me the truth about him and Bonnie Jo. His words had stung like a lash: *Sometimes I get a little rough, but that's the way she likes it.*

Smarting and heartsick, I had gone to her. My pride had been hurt. I spoke to her in anger. I behaved like a lovesick schoolboy. I accused her of lying. Bonnie Jo had come to me. She had knelt before me. She said her heart was mine. She called me her "sweet cavalier." She turned my anger aside and persuaded me that she cared, because that's what I wanted to believe.

Now Bonnie Jo had been beaten again. She was in a coma, Ridgeway said, not able to tell what happened the night Buck was killed. Had Buck beaten her again that night? His body had been found in her parlor, riddled with buckshot. Who had killed him? Was it Bonnie Jo, defending herself? And if it was, how did Jeff's shotgun come to be in that room? I had questions aplenty, it seemed. I was determined to get myself some answers.

CHAPTER 16

▼

When I reached the raised walkway in front of the city marshal's office, I paused for a moment and looked up at the open door. I had spent much of my time in the office that summer, with Jeff and alone. Somehow, I expected the place to feel familiar, to hold a welcome feeling after my time away, but it did not. I knew that beyond the office, in a cell at the rear, Jefferson Brown, marshal of Medicine Lodge, was a prisoner charged with murder. There was no familiar feeling, no spirit of welcome there for me. I took a deep breath and stepped through the doorway.

I was prepared to see Bodie Winters behind Jeff's desk, looking pompous and important. That's not what I found. Jeff's chair was occupied, not by Winters but by a red-haired young cowboy called Pistol Wilson.

Wilson had been Buck DuFresne's chief bootlicker and flunky, and I had disliked the kid on sight. He had been with Buck the day the cowman fought Jeff there in front of the office. He had drawn his pistol when the fight went against Buck, and I had backed him off with a warning shot from my Winchester. Wilson had been especially prone to strut and run his mouth when in Buck's company, and he seemed to like nothing better than to push bartenders, waiters, and kids around.

Somehow, Wilson had convinced himself he was some kind of gunfighter. He took to wearing his gun low and tied down, and when he checked his weapon at the Legal Tender, he always had to twirl and spin it a time or two before handing it over.

Anyway, it was Pistol Wilson I saw when I stepped through the office door. He was asleep in Jeff's chair, his feet atop the desk. He wore a pair of California spurs, the rowels of which had cut ragged scratches in the desktop. Even though it was not yet eight o'clock, a half-filled whiskey bottle stood next to the scratches. I was already on the prod at the thought of Jeff Brown being locked in a cell and accused of murder. The sight of this red-haired sleeping beauty did nothing to improve my mood.

Even so, I probably would have remained calm if I hadn't noticed one small detail. Pinned to Wilson's shirt was Jeff's city marshal badge! All of a sudden, my sweet disposition turned sour as vinegar. I put my foot against the chair, and pushed. The chair—and its occupant—toppled backward with a crash. Wilson came awake with a start, his eyes big as saucers. I put a foot on his chest and let him look up the bore of my .44.

"Take that badge off," I said. "It belongs to a man worth ten of your kind."

Wilson's face had gone white. "But—I'm acting marshal now. I'm in charge—"

"Don't tell me that," I said. "That just irritates me. Where's Bodie Winters?"

"He—he's over at the Legal Tender! What—what do you want?"

"You know me, Pistol. I'm Merlin Fanshaw, deputy United States marshal. I'm here to talk to Jeff Brown."

"But—you can't! Bodie—deputy sheriff Winters—gave strict orders! The prisoner ain't to have any visitors!"

I bent over and plucked his pistol from the leather. "Then you'd better go find the deputy and tell him I'm changing his orders. I'll be in the back, talking to my friend."

Wilson rolled over and got to his feet. He stumbled and fell at the doorway, rose again, and scurried down the street as if his shirttail was on fire. I turned to the door that led to the cells and opened it. Jeff's smile was like a beacon, even in the dim light of the cage. He stood, facing me, his hands grasping the bars.

"Merlin!" he said. "I thought I heard your voice! Lord, but I am glad to see you."

I grinned. "Maybe it's none of my business, Marshal," I said, "but aren't you on the wrong side of those bars?"

"Some people think so," Jeff said. "Me, and maybe you."

Close up, it was clear that Jeff had recently taken a beating. His right eye was swollen and nearly closed. His lip was split, his left cheekbone bruised and puffy.

"I don't know what I'm going to do about you," I scolded. "I leave you alone for a day or two, and the first thing you do is get yourself in trouble."

I couldn't hold my grin. I looked again at his battered face, and asked, "Who worked you over, Jeff? Bodie Winters?"

Jeff nodded. "Took three of DuFresne's cowboys to hold me," he said. "I guess Bodie done it just because he could."

In the dim light, Jeff's eyes met mine and held them. "I didn't murder Buck DuFresne," he said.

"Hell, I know that," I said. "However it happened, I know you shot him because you had to."

"Didn't shoot him at all. I was making my rounds that night when I heard sounds of a scuffle, and screams coming from Bonnie Jo's house. I had just reached her front door when I heard a shotgun go off inside—two shots, one after the other. I rushed in, and found Buck lying in a pool of blood in the parlor. He wasn't armed. His clothes were scattered around, but there was no gun. The man was riddled with buckshot, and dying.

"Just beyond, in her sleeping room, I found Bonnie Jo sprawled on the floor in her nightdress. Somebody had beat the poor thing half to death. I held her and asked her what had happened, but she was unconscious and barely breathing. She made no answer. I don't reckon she even heard me.

"The bedroom window was open, and the screen was gone. I crossed the room and looked outside. I saw—or thought I saw—someone running away from the house, but it was pretty dark. I'm not sure.

"I heard people coming—turned out to be mostly DuFresne cowboys from up the street at the Legal Tender. I met them at the door and told them what I'd found. I said Buck had been shot, that he was dead. I told them about Bonnie Jo, too, and sent one of the boys to fetch Doc Westby.

"I let the boys come into the parlor to see for themselves. They looked at Buck's body. They saw, as I had, that he wasn't armed. Then one of the cowhands—Dobie Jackson, it was—found the shotgun. Whoever used it on Buck had fired both barrels and had thrown it aside. It was on the floor, behind a chair, half hidden by the drapery. Dobie picked it up and looked at me. I couldn't believe what I saw. The shotgun was *my* gun, Merlin—my 'just in case' gun!

"Hardy Randall was with the boys. He's that older hand who was with Buck the day we fought. Hardy took a long look at the shotgun, and then at me. He'd heard me tell Buck if he came to town again, he'd better come shootin'. Hardy put two and two together and came up with five. He said, 'Appears this nigger has murdered Buck, boys.'

"I told them Hardy was wrong. I said I hadn't killed Buck, but they weren't of a mind to listen. They jumped me and took my six-gun. Some of the boys wanted to hang me then and there, but Hardy said no, they would turn me over to the law. Somebody went for Tom Burke. Doc Westby came and pronounced Buck dead. Then he took Bonnie Jo away to his place.

"Burke came, and heard the boys accuse me. He looked at Buck's body. He listened to my account of what had happened. It all came back to the shotgun. Buck had been unarmed. He was dead, killed by my gun. I don't blame Tom; I know he had no choice. The boys brought me here to the jail and locked me up, and Tom telegraphed the sheriff's office in Miles City. A day later, Bodie Winters showed up and filed formal charges. Says he's planning to take me up to Miles this week."

"I'd have been here sooner if I'd known," I said. "I was on the stage to Deadwood when the telegram arrived."

Jeff nodded, but I'm not sure he heard me. He seemed distracted, baffled. He began to pace to and fro in his cell. I was some baffled myself. Somewhere in the events Jeff had recounted lay a key to the truth. I ran his words over in my mind, but found no answers, only more questions.

"How do you reckon your shotgun got over to Bonnie Jo's?" I asked.

Jeff shrugged. He shook his head. "Damned if I know, Merlin—mostly, I don't lock the office when I leave. I suppose anybody could have come in and taken it."

"Didn't you miss it?"

"No. I'd stopped carrying it on rounds. Most times I just wore my six-gun."

Jeff stopped his pacing. He sat down on the cell's narrow bunk. For the first time since I'd met him, the man seemed confused and uncertain.

"All right," I said, "we know you didn't kill Buck. Any idea who did?"

He raised his eyes to mine. "I've thought about it plenty, Merlin, but no, I have no idea."

"What about Bonnie Jo? Maybe she finally got tired of being abused, and struck back."

Jeff shrugged. "Maybe—anything's possible. But how would she get my shotgun?"

Just then, I heard the clomping of booted feet entering the office and coming fast. I knew my time with Jeff was at an end. I turned to face the door.

"Don't worry, pard," I said. "I won't rest until I get you cleared. Keep your chin up."

The door burst open with a bang. Bodie Winters filled the doorway, his gun in his hand. His eyes were wild.

"Damn you, Fanshaw!" he blustered. "What are you doing here?"

I grinned. "Questioning the prisoner," I said, "or I was, until you busted in. Marshal Ridgeway sent me."

"What the hell for? This is a matter for the sheriff's office."

"Ridgeway figures the case may have some federal aspects. I'm here to conduct my own investigation."

Bodie's face turned a deep purple. He looked as if he might explode. Behind him, Pistol Wilson had gone bug-eyed.

I pointed to the gun in Bodie's hand. "Unless you're fixin' to shoot me, I wish you'd put that hogleg up," I said, "or do you aim to arrest me, too?"

Reluctantly, Bodie eased the hammer down and slid his gun back into the leather. "I'd like to, by god," he muttered.

He pointed to Pistol Wilson, who cowered in the doorway behind him. "Didn't acting marshal Wilson here tell you no one was allowed to visit the prisoner?"

I grinned. "He did. I figured that order didn't apply to a deputy U.S. marshal."

Bodie scowled. His words came hard, through clenched teeth. "Well, I hope you've finished questioning the murderin' sonofabitch. I'm takin' him to Miles City in the morning."

I didn't figure to back down to the likes of Bodie Winters. "I'm finished for now," I said, "but Jeff Brown is no murderer. You go ahead and do what you need to, Bodie. I'll spend my time looking for the real killer."

Bodie and Pistol glared at me like I was a skunk who'd wandered into a tea party. I took a quick glance at Jeff as I left the room, and felt my spirits lift. His smile was bright enough to light the darkness.

The morning had turned cold and overcast by the time I stepped out of the marshal's office, and the smell of rain was in the air. A sharp wind swept up Main Street, stirring the dust and stinging my face with grit. I squinted against the wind and tugged my hat down tighter. Ahead, the hotel loomed up in the blowing dust, and I turned off Main and stepped inside. The lobby was mostly deserted at that hour. Only Ralph Moore, the desk clerk, and an old-timer asleep in an overstuffed chair, occupied the room.

Ralph smiled as I walked up to the counter. "Deputy Fanshaw," he said. "I heard you left town."

"I did," I said, "but I'm back now. I need a room for a couple of days."

Ralph turned the hotel register around and handed me a pen. "Sure thing," he said. "Terrible thing about Buck DuFresne. I guess you heard."

"I did. Heard about Bonnie Jo Hutchins, too. Any word on how she's doing?"

Ralph took a key off the wall and handed it to me. "Last I heard, she still hadn't come to. Doc Westby hired Bertha Haley to care for her."

I signed the register, and gave the pen back.

"Room's a dollar a day," Ralph said, glancing at my badge. His face assumed a pained expression. "Aw—you ain't gonna make me bill the government, are you?"

"No, I'll pay cash when I check out."

Outside, the wind had picked up, blowing harder. Big raindrops began to spatter on the windows facing the street.

"I'll fetch my gear, and be back in a bit," I said.

I had nearly reached the door when I heard Ralph say, "Too bad about Marshal Brown, ain't it?"

"Yeah," I said. "Too bad."

I found City Attorney Tom Burke in his small office on the second floor of the Cattlemen's Bank. The door was open, so there was no need for me to knock. I said, "Morning, Tom."

Recognizing me, he brightened. Behind his gold-rimmed eyeglasses, his clear blue eyes went serious as a grave, and a shadow seemed to fall across his face. The lawyer got up from his chair, his lanky form all elbows and knees, and walked around his desk to greet me. "Good morning, Merlin," he said. "I'm glad you're back."

"Are you, Tom?"

"I am," he said. "It's been a difficult week."

A large armchair stood facing his desk. He gestured toward it. "Have a seat," he said. "I'll tell you what I know."

I eased into the chair and pushed my hat back. "That's what I'm here for," I said. "I just talked to Jeff."

Tom's eyebrows rose. "I thought Jeff wasn't allowed visitors."

"He wasn't. Isn't. I didn't let that stop me."

"How can I help?"

"I don't believe Jeff had anything to do with Buck DuFresne's death," I said. "Why has he been arrested?"

"Circumstantial evidence," Tom said, counting on his fingers. "The murder weapon is Jeff's shotgun. Jeff was found inside Bonnie Jo's house with the victim. There had been bad blood between him and Buck. They fought, the day Buck's trial ended. Threats made. Motive. Opportunity. I authorized his arrest that night largely to prevent a lynching."

"Do you believe he killed Buck?"

Tom frowned. "The law doesn't care what I believe. The evidence points to Jeff. As city attorney, I have to act on the evidence. You know that."

"Yeah," I said, "but if the evidence is all circumstantial—"

Tom looked somber. "I didn't say the evidence is all circumstantial," he said slowly. "There is—a witness."

"You mean Bonnie Jo? But I understood she was still unconscious."

"No, not Bonnie Jo. Doc Westby tells me she has regained consciousness, but seems to have no memory of the night of the murder, or of anything else."

"Then who—"

"Leo LeBreche, cook for the DuFresne outfit. He was on the street that night. He says he saw Jeff cross over and enter the house."

"I didn't know LeBreche was back in the country. Well, there's nothing new in his testimony—Jeff already said he'd gone into the house."

"You don't understand, Merlin. LeBreche has signed a sworn deposition saying he saw Jeff cross the street and enter Bonnie Jo's house—carrying his double-barreled shotgun!"

I told Tom I'd keep in touch and made my way down the narrow staircase to the street below. The rain continued—it had become a steady drizzle that showed no sign of stopping anytime soon. I stood beneath the board awning, listening to the drumming overhead and watched the water form puddles out in the rutted street. A cowhand in a yellow slicker rode past at a trot, turned the corner and splashed up Trail Street. From the direction of the livery barn a townsman in a top buggy drove his carriage horse toward Front Street through the downpour. For some time I stood, watching the street, my thoughts on Jeff and the legal noose that seemed to be closing on him.

Jeff had told me he carried no shotgun the night of the murder, that he wore only his revolver. Leo LeBreche had sworn he'd seen Jeff enter Bonnie Jo's house, carrying a shotgun. Both could not be right; one must either be mistaken or deliberately lying. I believed Jeff. I had worked with him; I had come to know him as well as one man ever really knows another. I was convinced he was telling the truth. Someone had killed Buck DuFresne, but it hadn't been Jeff. I had to prove what I knew in my heart. And I had to do it soon.

The rumbling in my belly reminded me I hadn't eaten since early the day before. Just realizing the fact brought on a craving so strong I could think of nothing else. Suddenly, I was hungry as a wolf pup; my mind turned from Jeff's problems to feeding my craving. I turned, and made a beeline for the City Café.

Once inside, I shook the water off my hat and looked the place over. Good smells from the kitchen set my inner wolf to howling even louder, and I waited impatiently while the sad-eyed waiter I called Shuffles ambled toward me. The café was warm and dry after the chill rain outside. I asked my slow-footed guide to show me to a table near the stove, which he did.

The bill of fare said the daily special was beef stew and biscuits. I asked for a double order and coffee, to be delivered pronto. I think my desperate condition had an effect on the man—it seemed to me he headed back to the kitchen at a slightly faster snail's pace than usual.

There were only a few customers in the café that morning. My hunger had caught me between the breakfast hour and the noon rush. Ivan Friendly, from the express office, sat drinking coffee with Elwood Potts from the lumberyard. A pasty-faced gambler with hollow eyes sat alone, eating graveyard stew and hard-boiled eggs. At a corner table in back, a calico queen from Allie Watson's place dined on oatmeal and green tea. None of them seemed to take my notice, and that was fine with me. I had thinking to do, and plans to make.

Bodie Winters said he'd be taking Jeff to Miles City the next day. I figured he'd lock him in the county jail, and spend most of his time bragging to the bar-flies that he'd arrested the murderer of Buck DuFresne. Old J. W. DuFresne had made his dislike for Jeff clear from the beginning. Now, believing Jeff had murdered his only son, I figured the old man would do everything in his power to bring Jeff's trial to a speedy, and fatal, conclusion. I needed to buy Jeff some time, and I needed to get him a lawyer.

I came out of my reverie when I saw Shuffles coming with my order. He made his way across the room like a glacier with the brake on. I couldn't help but wish that he was in charge of Jeff's trial. At length, he arrived at my table and slowly set a heaping bowl of stew and a basket of hot biscuits before me. Then he poured me a cup of coffee and stepped back.

"Will you be wantin' anythin' else?" he asked.

"Just elbow room," I said.

I had pretty well gone through the biscuits and was closing in on the last of the stew when Shuffles came back. I was huddled over my bowl like a miser with his gold when Shuffles asked, "That stew any good?"

"I ate it so fast I'm not sure," I said. "Why? Haven't you tried it?"

Shuffles cackled. "Hell, no," he said. "I don't eat here. I take my meals at Ben's Hash House over on Front Street."

"Kind of a poor advertisement for the man who pays your wages," I told him. I went to finish my stew, then noticed he hadn't gone, but was still watching me. "Anyone ever tell you it's not polite to stare?" I asked.

"Sorry," he said. "It's just that you put me in mind of a feller I seen last week down at Ben's. Stranger, he was—mean lookin' and pale as a ghost. He was hunkered over his plate like a stray dog over a soup bone, afeared some other cur might come along and take it."

"That's a mighty interesting story," I said, sopping up the last of the stew with a biscuit, "but I came in here to eat, not to be entertained. Now go bring me a big piece of pie, more coffee, and the check, if you please."

"Sure thing," he said, and away he dashed, like a stampede of turtles.

The rain had stopped by the time I left the café. The sun had broken through, and patches of blue sky showed behind the ragged clouds. I crossed the muddy thoroughfare and walked north on Trail Street to Doc Westby's place. Doc had a boot scraper on the front porch of his house, and I was trying to clean the mud off my boots when he opened the door.

"Merlin," he said. "You here on business or pleasure?"

"A little of both, Doc," I said. "Have you got a minute?"

I could see I wasn't going to get my boots clean anytime soon, so I pulled them off and stood there in my socks.

"Come in," Doc said. "I'll pour you a little medicinal brandy."

Doc's kitchen was clean and tidy. After the rain, the sunshine that slanted in through its windows seemed especially bright. Doc opened one of the cabinets, reached up, and brought down a bottle. He placed it on the kitchen table, produced two glasses, and urged me to sit down. He seated himself across from me, uncorked the bottle, and poured three fingers of brandy into each glass.

"You said business and pleasure," he said. "Your business, or mine?"

I raised my glass and breathed in the brandy's strong fumes. "Sometimes," I said, "your business is my business."

Doc said nothing, but touched his glass to mine and sipped.

"Jeff Brown is accused of murdering Buck DuFresne," I began. "No matter how things look, and no matter what some people say, I don't believe he did.

"The trouble is Bodie Winters is hell-bent on bringing Jeff to trial. Far as I can tell, Bodie never even considered anyone else. J. W. DuFresne and the boys who ride for him decided Jeff is guilty, and Bodie seems more than willing to go along with them."

I sipped the brandy and swallowed. I felt its heat all the way down. "Bodie Winters has reasons of his own to want a quick trial and conviction. Word has it he's planning to run against his boss for sheriff in the next election."

Doc nodded. "And being known as the man who brought Buck's killer to justice would go a long way toward insuring his election."

"That's what he thinks, and he's right. The DuFresnes have a lot of friends."

Doc Westby swirled the brandy in his glass and drank. "For what it's worth," he said, "I don't believe Jeff is guilty, either. However, there is a great deal of circumstantial evidence against him."

"I know. I just heard this morning that one of DuFresne's men says he saw Jeff go into Bonnie Jo's house that night, carrying a shotgun."

We were both silent for a time. Then I asked, "Do you think Bonnie Jo could have shot Buck? I mean, maybe he beat her up just one time too many, and—"

Doc shook his head. "Could have shot him? Maybe. Should have shot him? Yes, some time ago. But from what I know of Bonnie Jo, I don't believe she did. There are women who seem to put up with beatings and abuse from a man forever. They may even be attracted to that kind. Sometimes, they break off with their abuser for a time, but they always seem to go back. I'm afraid Bonnie Jo is that type."

"How is she doing? I understand she's regained consciousness now."

"She has. Physically, she's improving. She's able to take a little nourishment, and she seems relatively free of pain. But she remembers nothing of that evening—not the beating, not the shooting. She doesn't even recall her own name."

"I was hoping I could talk to her," I said.

"Definitely not. And before you ask the question, I have no idea when—or if—she ever will remember."

There was nothing more to say. I nodded. "Well—I'd best be going. Much obliged for the brandy, Doc."

"Any time. I wish I could do more."

"I appreciate your time. It's hard to see a good man in trouble, and not be able to help."

Doc's voice was gentle. "Doctors feel like that all the time, Merlin."

CHAPTER 17

▼

Kyle Haddon lounged in the open doorway of the Legal Tender as I picked my way across the muddy street. The saloonkeeper wore his gray suit over a brocade vest, and he looked, as usual, well groomed as a show horse. "Welcome back, Deputy," he said. "You missed all the excitement."

I stepped up onto the boardwalk and stomped mud off my boots. "Not all, Kyle," I said. "It seems there is still plenty to go around."

Haddon smiled. "Yes," he said. "Are you on duty, or can I buy you a beer?"

"The answer to both questions is yes," I said, and followed him inside.

The Legal Tender was fairly quiet at that hour of the afternoon. A bored chippy with impossible red hair sat alone toward the back, dealing solitaire. A foursome of local merchants played pinochle at one of the tables. Thumbs Carlyle, the piano player, fumbled out a tune with his customary disregard for melody and rhythm. Two farmers nursed their beers and listened. Barkeep Jerry Paddock's replacement, a walleyed mixologist with the face of a pug, polished a beer stein and watched as we approached the bar.

"Two beers," Haddon said.

The bartender drew the beers with a practiced hand, and placed them before us. Haddon took his and led the way to a table. We clicked steins and took a sip.

I don't know if Haddon read my mind or if the killing was simply the principal topic of conversation at the time, but he raised his eyes and said, "Have you seen Jeff yet?"

I nodded. "First thing. I was up in Miles City when I heard about the killing. I came here as fast as I could."

Haddon was silent for a time. At the piano, Thumbs played five good notes in a row, and I guessed he was trying to play *Beautiful Dreamer*.

"You ought to fire that piano player," I said.

"I would," Haddon said, "but he's turned into quite an attraction. Customers can't believe how bad he is. They keep coming back to see if he has improved."

It was my turn to fall silent. Finally, I said, "I'm looking into the killing, Kyle. Anything you can tell me?"

"Not much. I saw Buck earlier that night. I remember thinking there would be trouble. I knew he was in town against the marshal's orders."

"Yeah. Jeff posted him out of town after the Paddock trial."

"He was already pretty drunk when he came in here. Said 'that uppity nigger' wasn't going to tell him when he could come to town. I told him I didn't want any trouble, and Buck said he didn't want to cause me any. There were several Rimfire cowboys in here at the time—Hardy Randall, Dobie Jackson, Pistol Wilson, that bunch. I think Buck was showing off some for the boys.

"Then he left. Gave me a wink, and said he'd be back later. I remember I was worried about him some—whiskey made him crazy."

"Whiskey's been blamed for lots of things it didn't do," I said. "Buck had a mean streak, drunk or sober. Whiskey just helped turn it loose."

"Maybe so. Anyway, I tried to get him to check that fancy gun of his, but he wouldn't. Told me he thought he'd just keep it awhile. Said he might need it 'to tree a coon.' Then he left, and that's the last time I saw him alive."

Suddenly, Kyle Haddon had my full attention. "Are you sure? About the gun, I mean."

"I just told you—"

"If he was wearing his gun when he left here, what happened to it? It wasn't in the room when they found him."

Haddon frowned. "I don't know—maybe Jeff took it after he—"

"If so, where is it now? He didn't have it when they arrested him."

"Maybe Buck left it somewhere on his way to Bonnie Jo's—his saddle, or—"

I took another sip of my beer and pushed the stein away. "Maybe. The whereabouts of that gun is just one more question, calling for an answer."

Across the room, Thumbs was trying to make up for his lack of skill by playing louder.

I stood up. "Thanks for the beer, Kyle," I said. "You really ought to fire that piano player."

There was a new padlock on Bonnie Jo's front door, and I figured Bodie Winters or Pistol Wilson had locked the place up to keep the curious out. If they had, it didn't work—I found my way in through an unlocked bedroom window.

Inside, the sleeping room was cold and dreary. Bonnie Jo's bed was rumpled and unmade, sheets and blankets twisted, one pillow on the floor. Her dresser lay on its side, its German plate mirror shattered into shards across the carpet. The door to her wardrobe was ajar, and some of her clothing had fallen from its hangers and was strewn about.

Memories came unbidden. I recalled the lazy afternoons we had spent together in that room. I remembered the loving, and the hunger of the flesh that caused me to turn a blind eye to what I knew of right and wrong. I felt again the softness of her touch, recalled the sound of her breathing and the silky feel of her hair. The white cotton blouse she had worn the day we met lay on the floor. I picked it up and found it still bore her scent.

Now Bonnie Jo lay battered and lost in a room at Doc Westby's, robbed of her memories and her very identity. Who had done such a terrible thing, and why? Had it been Buck? He had beaten women before, including Bonnie Jo. Had there been an intruder in the house before he arrived, someone else who attacked Bonnie Jo? My questions were multiplying like rabbits, while answers were scarce as fur on a hog.

I walked into the parlor. The curtains had been drawn, and the room felt sad and melancholy in the gloom. I opened the drapes, squinting against the brightness. Dust motes danced in the sunbeams. Deep shadows hid from the light. Bonnie Jo's settee stood in its place, across from the overstuffed wing chair.

Blood had pooled at the edge of the carpet, marking the place where Buck DuFresne had breathed his last. I counted six places in the wall above the stain where shotgun pellets had missed their mark and buried themselves in the plaster. They had not been needed. The double-ought buckshot that struck the cattleman had been sufficient for the job, and then some.

I walked slowly through the rooms a second time, trying to imagine the events of that evening. I stopped from time to time to examine a boot print, a smudge, a fallen chip of plaster. I listened, letting the house speak to me, hoping somehow to form an impression of what had happened there. Nothing came. I turned back toward the bedroom, and left the way I'd come in.

Back in my room at the hotel, I lay awake late into the night, my thoughts on Jeff and the killing of Buck DuFresne. I thought about my brief talk with Jeff at the jail. I remembered my conversations with Tom Burke, Doc Westby, and Kyle

Haddon, recalling their words and opinions. I revisited Bonnie Jo's cheerless house in my mind, and tried to picture what had happened the night of the murder. I ran it all—facts, hearsay, and impressions—over in my mind, and found I was no closer to the truth than before. The questions remained.

How had Jeff's shotgun come to be at the house? Leo LeBreche said he saw Jeff carrying the weapon when he approached Bonnie Jo's house that night. Who had fired it—Jeff? Bonnie Jo? Someone else? And what about Buck's gun? Kyle Haddon said Buck was wearing it when he left the Legal Tender, but it wasn't at the house when Jeff arrived. Where was it? The revolver had apparently just disappeared. A shotgun Jeff swears he didn't have that night had been seen in his hands. Even when I finally did fall asleep I slept poorly, but it wasn't the hotel's bed that caused me to toss and turn.

I was awake before dawn, driven by the plans I had made the night before. I wanted to see Jeff once more before Bodie Winters took him to Miles City, and I wanted to telegraph Marshal Ridgeway about finding Jeff a lawyer. I washed up at the commode in my room, locked the door behind me, and headed downstairs to the lobby.

Outside, the eastern sky grew lighter. Coming daylight had already begun to chase the darkness away, but the morning star still shone bright overhead. The streets of Medicine Lodge were still at that hour, but I saw a light in the window behind the express office and knew Ivan Friendly was up. He answered my knock in his nightshirt, and he looked rumpled and grumpy when he saw me.

"Fanshaw!" he said. "What the hell—?"

"I need to send a telegram to Marshal Ridgeway at Miles. Open your key, if you please."

"You could give a man a chance to wake up first," he complained. "Do you always get up in the dark, or haven't you been to bed yet?"

"People die in bed," I said, grinning. "I don't care to risk my life unnecessarily."

"People rest in bed, too," Ivan said. "Leastways, normal people do."

He carried a lamp into the express office, and opened the key.

"Send this," I said. "Winters bringing Jeff Brown to Miles. Leaving today. Please obtain legal counsel for Jeff. Am continuing my investigation, but need time. Will send full report soon."

Ivan's hand rested on the telegraph key, then swiftly tapped out my message. After a brief pause, the key clattered and stopped.

"The operator at the N.P. depot in Miles acknowledges receipt," Ivan said. "Now go away and let me get dressed."

I paid him for the telegram, and thanked him. "Much obliged, until you're better paid," I said. "I'm doing what I can to make sure a good man doesn't get railroaded."

Ivan showed me to the door. "Well," he said, "you sure as hell seem to be workin' day and night on the case."

My next stop was Jeff's cabin, behind the jail. Jeff had never locked the place, and I simply walked across the vacant lot and opened the door. Inside, the cabin was as I remembered it, clean and tidy, if a bit sparse. Jeff's bedroll lay atop a painted iron bedstead at the rear of the cabin, his old army trunk at its foot. A packing box served as a side table, which held a cheap alarm clock and a coal-oil lamp. I found what I was looking for in Jeff's trunk, walked out, and latched the door behind me.

Bodie Winters looked surprised when I walked into the marshal's office. "Fanshaw!" he said. "What are you doin' here?"

"Heard you were takin' Jeff out today. Thought I'd stop by and tell him goodbye."

"We already had our run-in about that. Like Pistol—acting marshal Wilson—told you, the prisoner ain't allowed to have visitors."

"I'm no visitor. I'm a lawman, like you."

"Damn you, Fanshaw! Are you tryin' to rile me? I said—"

"I know. You said 'no visitors.' And I said I'm not a visitor, I'm a lawman. We're all lawmen around here, Bodie—you're a Custer County deputy, Pistol is acting city marshal, I'm a federal deputy, and Jeff in there is the lawful marshal of Medicine Lodge. It's like a durn convention."

Bodie frowned. He stared at me. His fingers drummed a tattoo on the desktop. "All right," he said, "I'll give you five minutes. Then I'm puttin' irons on him and takin' him to catch the stage to Miles City."

"Much obliged, Bodie. There is one other thing."

His frown turned into a scowl. "What?"

I reached in my vest pocket and took out Jeff's harmonica. "I want Jeff to have his mouth organ."

Suspicion narrowed Bodie's eyes to slits. "Let's see it," he said.

I handed the harmonica over. Bodie examined it with care, suspicion in every line of his face. "What are you tryin' to pull, Fanshaw?"

"That harp means the world to Jeff," I said, "and it can do no harm to let him have it. It's not like he could harmonica you to death or something."

Bodie gave the harp back. "All right. Tell Pistol I said you've got five minutes."

Pistol Wilson was sitting in a chair facing Jeff's cell when I came through the doorway. He wore two revolvers and held a shotgun at the ready.

"You figure you've got enough weapons there, Pistol?" I asked. "I believe there might be some dynamite in the shed out back."

Wilson jumped when he recognized me. His eyes narrowed. He glared at me with an expression I suppose was meant to be scary, except in his case it merely made him look simple.

"Bodie told me I could have five minutes with the prisoner," I said. That should give you time to go find yourself a howitzer or something."

Wilson got to his feet, threw out his chest, and pushed past me as he swaggered out of the room. I suppose all that was to let me know he wasn't afraid of me. I was impressed. It was one of the finest swaggers I'd seen in a while.

I turned to Jeff, and met his smile with my own.

"You are a caution," Jeff said. "You've got that boy thinkin' you're half crazy."

"He could be right about that. Something about that kid brings out the mischief in me. How are you doing, pardner?"

Jeff held a hand out level before him and waggled it from side to side. "So-so. They're takin' me to Miles City today."

"So I hear. I telegraphed Ridgeway. Asked him to get you a lawyer."

Jeff nodded. "Hope he finds me a good one. I figure the county will want to hold my trial as soon as possible."

"You can trust Ridgeway. And me."

Jeff's eyes shone, but his voice was firm. "I know that, Merlin," he said. "I surely do."

For a moment, silence hung awkward between us. I wanted to assure him, to bring him some cheer, but now that I was with him I could think of nothing to say.

"How's Bonnie Jo doing?" he asked.

"Doc wouldn't let me see her. He says she's doing better, but she still has no memory of that evening."

"I'm sorry, Merlin. I know you care for her."

I found myself listening for Bodie and Pistol. They would be coming for Jeff any minute. "I expect my time's about up," I said. I took Jeff's harmonica from my pocket and passed it through the bars. "I thought maybe you'd want to take this with you," I said. "I understand she's got sixteen double holes and thirty-two super-fine reeds."

Jeff cradled the harmonica in his two big hands. His eyes were shining again, but this time his voice was unsteady. "Thank you, Merlin," he said. "It was mighty fine of you to think of it. Sometimes, when I get the blues, I like to play a sad song."

"Yes, I said. "You told me." Behind me, I heard footsteps. I gripped Jeff's hand, and turned to go. "Soon, we'll be celebrating in Miles City—and you can play me a happy song."

As I left the marshal's office, it was my eyes that were shining.

Promptly at eight o'clock in the morning, Bodie and Pistol walked Jeff down to the express office. Jeff shuffled along the rutted street in leg-irons, his shackled hands cuffed to a belly chain. Seeing him that way was almost more than I could bear, but I caught his eye as he passed and gave him a smile and a thumb's-up. There was a good-size crowd on hand, maybe thirty-five or forty people, Indians as well as whites. Some folks were there because they liked Jeff, and some because they didn't.

There were townspeople, cowboys from DuFresne's, and farmers from up the creek. I saw Kyle Haddon, Thumbs Carlyle, and the new bartender from the Legal Tender. I saw Tom Burke, and Mayor Junius Drysdale. Arnie Moss was there, and Ralph Moore, desk clerk at the hotel. Clifford Bidwell was on hand, getting the story for his newspaper.

I couldn't help noticing that Bodie Winters walked a little taller when he passed Clifford. I suppose a man has to pay special heed to the press when he's running for public office. Bodie opened the door to the coach, waved to the crowd, and got in beside Jeff. The driver kicked off the brake, shook the reins, and the six-horse team took the coach out on the road that would deliver Jeff to a murder trial.

The crowd began to break up and drift away. Pistol Wilson, Medicine Lodge's new acting marshal, passed a politic word with the mayor and strutted on up the street. For a moment there, I seriously considered shooting the durn whelp as a public service, but the moment passed and he got away.

I had made my plans. I was just turning toward the livery barn to fetch my horse when I saw Archie Young Bull watching me. He had been part of the crowd, and he had remained after the others had gone. Somehow, Archie managed to look sad and angry and proud all at the same time. I walked over to where he stood and held up my hand in greeting.

"*Kahée, baaláax,*" I said, "Hello, brother."

Archie's eyes blazed. "Law Bringer calls me brother, but he let the white dogs take Black White Man away."

"Only the white man's law can free Jeff from the white man's law," I said. "They took him because they believe he killed Buck DuFresne."

"He did not," Archie said.

"My heart tells me he did not. How do you know?"

"I followed him that night. I did not go with him when he made his rounds. I wanted to, but he said some of the white people would not like it. But I followed."

I waited for the rest of it.

"When he came to the woman's house, there were sounds of fighting. I watched him run across to the house. That is when I heard the sound of the gun. *Hiisée!* Very loud! Two times, from the house!

"Black White Man goes inside, and there is no more sound. Then, from the window comes a small man! He runs fast! He jumps over the fence! He crosses the street to the dark shadows behind the bank! I turn to follow him, but he has a horse in the shadows. He mounts the horse and rides away!

"Now the men come from the saloon—cowboys, drunk men, talking big. They go inside the house. I hear their voices, talking much, arguing. For a long time I wait. One man comes out—he goes to the boarding house, and comes back with the *akiliihawassee*—the lawyer—Burke. They go back in the house.

"I wait. After a long time, the men come out. They have taken Black White Man prisoner! They take him to the jail! They beat him up! They lock him in the room with bars! I try to talk to them—I tell them I want to see Black White Man. They say no! Go away, Archie! They will not hear me. They will not let me talk to our brother.

"After many hours, I go to my grandmother's lodge, but I can't sleep. They say Black White Man killed the rancher, Buck DuFresne, but I know it is not true. I try again to tell them, but nobody will listen. I go away then to fast and to pray to the Above Person. Now, when I come back, you are here, but you let them take our brother away. Will you now let them hang him?"

"I will not," I said. "Tell me more about the man you saw."

"He is a small white man, a stranger. He rides a *hisshe*—a bay horse. He goes up Medicine Lodge Creek the night of the killing. Will you go now to find him?

"Yes, my brother," I said. "And so will you, if you'll come with me."

Archie lowered his eyes. "I have no horse," he said.

"I will lend you a horse. A good one, and a saddle."

"*Éeh!*" Archie said, "Yes! I will go."

I always liked Archie's smile, maybe because it was so rare.

We left town at a lope, headed west on the Medicine Lodge Creek road. Archie was mounted on a smooth-gaited gelding I rented from Arnie Moss, and I, of course, rode Rutherford. I had no idea how long we might be out, but I had packed provisions for Archie and me in our saddlebags, and we each carried a blanket roll, carbine, and slicker.

I glanced at Archie as we rode, thinking about how much had changed in a few short months. Ridgeway had sent me to Medicine Lodge to help Jeff keep the peace, and to find and arrest Archie Young Bull. Now Jeff was in custody himself and charged with the murder of a prominent rancher, while Archie, former outlaw and renegade, rode with me as a kind of posse of one.

Fifteen miles later, we turned off the road and reined up near a good spring in a stand of cottonwood trees. Archie had not asked me where we were going; he had simply allowed me to lead our little war party. I let him in on my plans.

"We ride to DuFresne's ranch," I said. "We will not be welcome."

Archie nodded. "I will be less welcome even than you," he said. "The old one hates my people."

"J. W. DuFresne hates much," I said. "He hates Jeff because he is black, but also because he believes Jeff killed his son. Now he wants Jeff to die, and he will not rest until that happens. I must tell him what we know, that Jeff is innocent."

"He will not believe you."

"Maybe not, but I have to try to convince him. Also, I want to talk to Leo LeBreche, who cooks for DuFresne. He told the lawyer he saw Jeff go into the house that night, carrying his shotgun. I think DuFresne paid him to lie."

"What about the small man I saw—the man who ran from the house?"

"I think he is the man who killed Buck DuFresne," I said. "When you saw him that night—was he carrying something in his hands? Did he have a weapon?"

"*Éeh!*" Archie said, "Yes! He carried a gun belt. Before he mounted the bay horse, he buckled it around his waist."

Another piece of the puzzle had fallen into place. After so many questions, it was good at last to have an answer. Other answers were coming together in my brain, not yet complete but forming. With luck, I would find more answers at DuFresne's. I would find them because, for Jeff's sake, I had to.

CHAPTER 18

▼

Archie and me followed the wagon road up a long slope through stands of pine and scrub cedar until we reached the crest of the hill overlooking DuFresne's home ranch. Below, in a sheltered bend of Medicine Lodge Creek, lay the ranch buildings—the main house, bunkhouse, cook shack, barn, and smithy. I smelled the wood smoke before I saw it—a thin wisp that rose from the main house's chimney into the still, morning air.

At the bunkhouse, a man stepped out and emptied water from a basin onto the ground, then went back inside. Outside the cook shack, another man split kindling for the stove. Over at the round corral near the barn, cowhands watched as a rough-string rider worked at breaking a rank blue roan. I touched Rutherford with my spurs, and we descended the hill.

As we approached the long, main house, the same two dogs that had welcomed me on my previous visit came out barking and troubling our horses' heels. Rutherford seemed not to pay the dogs any mind, but I noticed he kept his eye on them as best he could. Archie's horse, too, seemed to pay them little heed.

We drew rein at the rail fence that marked the boundary of the yard, and sat facing the house.

Moments later, the door opened and Hardy Randall stepped out onto the porch. He was wearing a gun. "What can I do for you boys?"

"Merlin Fanshaw, deputy U.S. marshal," I said. "Here to see Mr. DuFresne."

Hardy's eyes measured me, then went to Archie. I could tell he didn't much like what he saw. "Mr. DuFresne ain't interested in anything you have to say. Go on back where you came from."

I stayed peaceful. "No offense, but I need to hear that from Mr. DuFresne himself."

Hardy's hand moved closer to the gun on his hip. His voice rose. "I said he don't want to talk to you! He's still grievin' his son's death! The man your coon friend murdered with his damn shotgun! Is that plain enough for you?"

"I've no wish to cause trouble, but I'm here on the law's business. I need to talk to Mr. DuFresne."

Rage twisted Hardy's features. He set his feet, crouching slightly, his hand nearly touching the handle of his gun. "You'll talk to no one, you nigger-lovin' bastard! Get off DuFresne land!'

It was time for straight talk. "Pull that gun and I'll kill you," I said.

Hardy hesitated. Anger was still plain on his face, but something else was there, too—fear. Ever so slowly, his hand moved away from his revolver.

Behind him, another figure appeared. J. W. DuFresne himself stepped through the doorway. He touched Hardy on the shoulder.

"That'll do, Hardy," he said, the way a man might call off a dog.

J. W. walked to the edge of the porch and looked at Archie and me. "You say you're here on the law's business," he said. "What do you want of me?"

"A few minutes of your time, Mr. DuFresne," I said. "A few questions."

The cattleman stood ramrod straight, his head high. For several moments he said nothing. At last, he replied. "Step down and come inside," he said. His eyes went to Archie, then back to me. "Only you, if you please."

Archie gave no sign that he understood DuFresne's slight. He sat his horse, his expression stoic and unreadable. I glanced at him and nodded, then dismounted and followed J. W. into the house. Hardy remained on the porch.

Inside, DuFresne offered me a chair by the fireplace, and sat down. Up close, his weathered face showed the strain of the past week's events. He seemed to have aged ten years since last I saw him.

"First of all," I said, "I'd like to extend my sympathy on your loss. Your son's murder was a terrible thing."

"Ah'm obliged, Deputy," he said. "Ah take comfort in the knowledge that his murderer is in custody—and that he will soon be dead, and in Hell."

"I'm afraid he isn't," I said. "Not yet. Jeff Brown did not kill your son."

The cattleman's eyes glinted. "Why, Buck must still be alive then! We had his funeral for nothing. Ah wonder who it was we buried in the graveyard that day."

"I understand you want Buck's killer brought to justice," I said, "So do I. I'm here because I need your help."

"Ah believe you're here because that nigger marshal is your friend. He's about to stand trial and hang for what he did, and you're tryin' to save him."

"No, sir. I believe another man killed Buck, and that he's still at large."

J. W. made no reply. As before, he fell silent for a time. When next he spoke, I had the feeling he had forgotten I was there and was talking to himself. He lowered his eyes, speaking in a voice so soft I could hardly make out the words.

"Everything," he said, "everything Ah've built, Ah built with Buck in mind. From the day he was born, that boy was mah shinin' pride. Don't rightly know what happened to him—seems like he changed somehow as he growed up. Sort of went bad. Maybe it was the whiskey. Drinkin' made him mean, reckless. Beatin' up women. Cuttin' that bartender. Mah fault, maybe. Maybe Ah should have raised him different—raised him better, some way—"

J. W. stopped. He seemed to awake, as from a trance. "Another man killed Buck? No, sir! Jeff Brown killed him! Damn nigger jailed my son! Put his black hands on mah boy! Picked a fight when Buck was drunk—beat him in front of his men—killed him, by god, with a damn shotgun!"

I stood up. "I'm sorry about your loss, Mr. DuFresne, but you're wrong, sir—dead wrong. Jeff Brown didn't kill your son. I'm trying hard to find the man who did."

J. W. seemed to grow calm again. "What is it you want from me, Deputy?" he asked.

"Your cook, Leo LeBreche. Can you tell me where he is?"

"Leo? Why—he's up on the mountain. Took a pack string and supplies to our line camp at Red Springs."

"I'd like to talk to him. When will he be back?"

"Day after tomorrow. Maybe later. Hard to say."

"Well," I said. "Much obliged for talking to me, Mr. DuFresne. I won't trouble you any longer."

Again, J. W. seemed to drift off, back into his dialogue with himself. As I walked to the door, I heard him say, "Don't matter. Nothin' matters much. Ain't nothin' gonna bring mah boy back."

Hardy waited, just outside the door. He watched, his face tight with rage, as I passed him and stepped off the porch. Archie sat his horse as before, his expression impassive. The cowhands we'd seen at the corral had left their work and had drawn closer, watching Archie with hate-filled eyes. I ducked under the hitch rail, picked up the reins, and stepped up onto Rutherford. Together, Archie and me backed our horses away, turned them, and headed out.

Once we were beyond the crest of the hill, I drew rein and waited. Archie had fallen behind me, but now came riding out of the timber and pulled up at my side.

"Nobody follows," he said. "I waited to see."

"*Itche,*" I said. "Good."

I liked Archie's patience, and his trust. He had asked nothing about my talk with J. W. DuFresne, nor did he question me now. He seemed to simply trust that I would tell him what was needful when I chose to.

I said, "The old man grieves much. His heart is on the ground."

Archie nodded. "He also hates much."

I raised my eyes to the cool mass of the Bighorn Mountains, off to the west. Sacred to the Crow Indians, the range rises nine thousand feet above the Little Bighorn valley in a series of wide ridges. I hadn't seen the range at firsthand, but I'd heard it offered a varied terrain, from year-round snowfields and deep canyons to wooded slopes and grassy meadows. The northern part of the Bighorns, a day's ride away, was mostly flat.

I knew DuFresne ran cattle there in the summer, and that he maintained a camp for a line rider at Red Springs. The outfit's cook, Leo LeBreche, would be the star witness against Jeff at his trial. LeBreche had sworn he saw Jeff carry his shotgun into Bonnie Jo's house. Jeff had told me otherwise, and so had Archie. I was convinced that J. W. had paid LeBreche to give false testimony in order to make certain Jeff was convicted. Now I had been told LeBreche was—conveniently—away, somewhere on the mountain. I had to find the man and ask him a few questions of my own.

I said as much to Archie. "I think this man, LeBreche, lied. His words will be bad for Jeff in the white man's court, unless I can cause him to change them. The old one told me LeBreche tends the line camp at Red Springs. Do you know the way?"

"*Éeh*—yes," Archie said. "I know."

Nightfall found us camped beside a trail that led to a deep and shadowed ravine Archie called *shipíte xakúpe*—or "black canyon." We had seen no one all that day, and the land itself seemed as untouched as Eden. Sundown had painted the clouds with fire as we rode up from below, but the color faded quickly. Now clear skies hoarded the dying light, and Archie and me sat by our small fire, watching the stars come out. The horses were hobbled on good grass, a cool breeze stirred the aspen leaves, and somewhere in the distance a night bird cried.

It should have been a pleasant time, a time of peace and rest, but my thoughts wouldn't leave me alone.

I thought of Jeff, locked in a cell up in Miles City, charged with a murder he didn't commit, and waiting for the imperfect judgment of men. I thought of J. W. DuFresne, who had built a cattle empire for a son who squandered his life on whiskey and reckless living, infected by his father's prejudice. Buck had died a violent death, shocking and terrible, yet almost expected, somehow.

Who had killed him? Not Jeff. Not Bonnie Jo, for her weakness and her need had been love, or what passed for it. Violence was not in her nature, and she was far more likely to be its victim than its dispenser.

The embers of our campfire glowed dull red. Archie sat looking into the coals, thinking his own thoughts. I lay back on my blankets and watched the stars come out. Remembered snatches of conversation came to me. Incidents. Names. One by one, pieces of the puzzle fell into place. Then, suddenly, everything came together. In that moment I knew who had killed Buck DuFresne, and I knew why.

We found Leo LeBreche at about midmorning the next day. He was riding down a long slope, leading two packhorses, and he seemed lost in his thoughts. From a shaded spruce grove below the trail, Archie and me watched him draw near. He had nearly reached the trees when I rode out and blocked his path.

"Morning, Leo," I said.

LeBreche looked startled. He reined up abruptly, his hand jerking toward the gun at his waist. "Merlin Fanshaw, deputy U.S. marshal," I said. "I talked to you at the ranch this summer when Curly killed the Indian boy."

Behind me, Archie rode out of the trees, his Winchester across his saddle forks.

LeBreche had recovered from his surprise, but he still looked nervous. "Yeah," he said. "I remember."

"At the time, I said if you were concealing information, I might have to arrest you. You didn't seem to like that idea much. In fact, you said something like, 'I ain't goin' back to no prison. No, sir.' Do you recall that conversation?"

LeBreche nodded.

"I'm here for two reasons, Leo," I said. "First, you've filed a false deposition in a murder case. You said you saw Jeff Brown with a shotgun in his hands, crossing the street to Bonnie Jo's the night of the murder. Turns out another witness was there. He saw Jeff cross the street, but he didn't see any shotgun. And he didn't see you.

"I'm thinking you weren't on that street at that time, and that you didn't see Jeff cross the street at all. I think you made that story up later, maybe because J. W. asked you to. What do you think?"

LeBreche looked sullen. "I said what I said. You can't prove—"

I drew my .44 and covered Leo. Archie rode up and took the man's pistol from its holster.

"I think I can," I said. "If I'm wrong, you'll go on breathing this clean mountain air and living in the wide-open spaces. But if I'm right, you'll go back for a stretch behind bars, at your age maybe for life."

I stepped down off Rutherford, while Archie took LeBreche's bridle reins.

"Get down, Leo," I said. "Let's discuss your future."

LeBreche was sweating now. I led him back into the spruce grove, and bade him sit down. He couldn't seem to keep his eyes still.

"Uh—you said you were here for two reasons," he said. "What's the second?"

"Let me tell you about the second, Leo. Suppose while you were in prison you came to know a feller. By the way, what did they send you away for?"

LeBreche looked at the ground before him. "I—I stole a few horses."

"All right," I said. "There you are, doin' hard time in the crowbar hotel for rustling. And one day, you meet a feller named Ed Hutchins. He's a bad-tempered gent and a killer, but you and Ed get to know one another. Maybe you even become friends. Time passes. They unlock the door and turn you loose. You say adios, and that's an end to it, you think.

"You hire on with the DuFresne Land and Cattle Company. You put the past behind you. Your riding days are pretty much over, but someplace—maybe in prison—you learned to cook. J. W. DuFresne makes you the outfit's bean master. You've got a good job with a big spread, and all you have to do is feed the boys on time and be loyal to the outfit.

"Sometimes that means you have to lie to the law to keep a cowboy, or the boss's son, out of trouble. The DuFresnes come to know you can be counted on to do just about anything they tell you to.

"Somewhere along the line, you hear from Ed, your old prison friend. Seems he's broke out of the pen and he's comin' back to Medicine Lodge. It's a mistake for him to come back, but he has a wife in town and he's missed her some. Also, he's heard some things about her behavior, and he's a mite upset.

"Now Ed Hutchins is a mighty jealous man. Fact is, he got sent up in the first place because he killed a feller he caught with his wife. He finds out she's up to her old tricks, and he goes hog wild and snake crazy.

"He has himself a bite of supper down at Ben's Hash House, steals a shotgun from the marshal's office, and drops in on his wayward wife. He's been told about her and Buck DuFresne—maybe he suspects she's waiting for Buck that very night. He beats her up some, as a sort of homecoming present, and then he gets carried away and hurts her bad. About that time, Buck walks in looking for romance, but he gets buckshot instead. Ed has bagged another of his wife's friends. Only this time, the dead man is Buck DuFresne, your boss's son.

"Your convict pardner leaves the shotgun behind. He takes Buck's gun belt and six-shooter and rides out for the tall and uncut. Nobody—except maybe you—knows who killed Buck, but circumstances make things look bad for Jeff Brown, the town marshal. Turns out J. W., your boss, hates the marshal because he's not white, and because he can't be bought or bullied. J. W. asks you to lie about Jeff, and since you don't have no more morals than a goat, you agree. How am I doin' so far?"

LeBreche looked pale. Sweat beaded his upper lip. He looked at the ground again. "You're tellin' the story," he said.

"All right," I said, "now you're between a rock and a hard place. If J. W. finds out the man who killed his son is your old pal, you lose your job and maybe your life. So you decide to help Ed disappear. You need to keep him quiet. Maybe you find him a hideout somewhere, a place to hole up. You bring him food, news, and such—maybe at the same time you're bringin' supplies up the mountain to DuFresne's line camp.

"People think Jeff killed Buck, and that's fine with you. Besides, J. W. wants the killer to be Jeff. So when he asks you to lie about seeing Jeff with a shotgun, you're only too happy to oblige."

I stood up. "The trouble is, a good man may hang because of your lies. I need you to tell the truth, Leo. I need to know where Ed Hutchins is—right now!"

LeBreche couldn't meet my eyes. "You're askin' me to rat on a friend," he said. "I ain't sure I can do that."

"I'm askin' you to help me find a murderer—and free an innocent man. I'm askin' you to do what's right. It's your call—freedom and a clear conscience, or life in prison and regret for as long as you live."

LeBreche looked out over the rolling hills and hollows, the timbered slopes and mountain parks, to the valley of the Little Bighorn. Blue mountains rose at the edge of the world. Clouds drifted overhead, their shadows sliding across the land.

"I don't believe I'd want to live, locked up in a cage again," he said. "All right, Deputy. I'll take you to Ed."

CHAPTER 19

▼

Leaving the packhorses in the spruce grove, LeBreche turned his saddle horse around and led Archie and me up the slope he had only recently descended. At the top, the country opened onto a sagebrush-studded flat, and beyond, at its edge, into a forest of lodgepole pine. We followed a game trail across the flat and into the trees, weaving our way through the timber until at last we reached the other side. Below us lay a broad valley, consisting of open parks and thick stands of pine and fir. The way ahead dropped off abruptly in a series of switchbacks, and we eased our mounts down the trail with care.

At the bottom, LeBreche waited for us beside a fast-flowing stream. He pointed to a park, just beyond the tree line.

"Ed is holed up maybe a mile east of here in an old trapper's cabin. I found the place two years ago, while I was up here huntin' elk."

I looked in the direction he had indicated. "All right," I said. "Let's go pay him a visit."

Holding our horses tot a fast walk, we made our way upstream. Ten minutes later, we stopped again. Screened by an opening in the trees, we looked out at the open park.

"There," LeBreche said. "Just below that tangle of deadfall, at the base of the cliff. That's the cabin."

I took my field glasses from my saddlebag and raised them to my eyes. Across the meadow, the scene sprang suddenly into sharp focus. Low to the ground, its logs silver with age stood an ancient cabin. Part of its roof had collapsed under the weight of winter snows. A rude, stone chimney lay fallen in the high grass. I saw no sign of life, no movement of any kind. I lowered the glasses and turned to LeBreche.

"I don't see anything," I said. "You sure he's there?"

LeBreche shrugged. "He was yesterday. No place else much he could be. Ed don't know the country." Leo's mouth formed a bitter line. "Besides, the poor devil trusts me to take care of him."

I raised the glasses again. That's when I saw the smoke. Thin and faint, it drifted into the still morning air from the ruined chimney.

"The 'poor devil' beat his wife half to death and murdered a man with a shotgun," I said, "but you're right—he is there. See the smoke?"

I returned the field glasses to my saddlebag. "What about weapons?" I asked. "Does Ed have a rifle?"

LeBreche shook his head. "No rifle. He has Buck's six-shooter and cartridge belt."

I turned to Archie. "I need you to get around behind the cabin without being seen. Find a place in the trees and watch the back."

Archie nodded. Hidden from view of the cabin by the trees, he turned his horse and rode away at a trot.

I looked at LeBreche. "We'll give Archie time to get in place. Does Ed have a horse nearby?"

"The bay. Keeps it back in the trees."

I checked the loads in my .44. "All right. Anything else I should know?"

LeBreche shook his head. He looked across the meadow, remembering. "The second year I was at Deer Lodge, a bull queer with a knife tried to kill me in the yard. Ed saw him coming. Warned me. I figure he saved my life. I—I guess I'm askin' you not to kill him if you don't have to."

"I want him alive as much as you do."

"Sure, sure. No offense. I'm just sayin' maybe if I go in alone, talk to him—maybe he'll give himself up."

I looked at LeBreche. His face showed no expression, but his eyes pleaded for him.

"It's worth a try," I said, looking away. "We'll ride over together. When we get near the cabin, we'll pull up. I'll wait while you talk to him."

LeBreche sighed. When he spoke, his voice was unsteady. "I'm obliged, Deputy. I owe you."

I raised the field glasses again. In the shadow of the trees behind he cabin, Archie crouched within the deadfall, watching the cabin. I returned the glasses to my saddlebag.

"Archie's in place," I told LeBreche. "Let's go."

LeBreche and me rode out of the trees and onto the meadow, our eyes fixed on the cabin. There in that open park, the silence seemed almost unnatural. A soft breeze sighed through the treetops and rippled the grass. I heard the rattle of my bridle bit, the creak of saddle leather. I heard the soft swish-thud of the horses' hooves as they plodded toward the cabin. I heard the beating of my own heart.

Twenty yards from the cabin, we drew rein. Ahead, its open door revealed nothing but darkness. I dismounted, my eyes fixed on the doorway. LeBreche stepped down and handed me his reins.

Walking toward the cabin, he called out, "It's all right, Ed. It's me, Leo."

The voice that answered was high-pitched and nasal. "Who's that with you?"

"Deputy U. S. Marshal," I answered. "I'm here to take you in, Hutchins."

LeBreche took a step closer. "It's over, Ed," he said. "Lawman knows everything."

"I'll bet he does," the voice snarled. "You ratted me out, you sonofabitch!"

Red fire streaked from the doorway. LeBreche jackknifed with the impact of the bullet, then fell facedown. The sound of the shot struck me like a fist. White smoke exploded into the sunlight. Startled, Leo's horse bolted. The bridle reins burned through my hand.

Ed's second shot was loud. I felt the wind from the bullet brush my face. My .44 was in my hand.

"Give it up, Hutchins," I called out. "Don't make this any worse."

His laughter was a dry cackle. "Don't see how it could be a hell of a lot worse, do you?"

Gunsmoke filled the air. I strained to see through the haze. Then dimly, just inside the door, I saw movement—Hutchins was coming out!

The waiter back in Medicine Lodge had described him well. Ed Hutchins was indeed "mean looking, and pale as a ghost." He walked into the light, both hands held high—but Buck's fancy revolver was in his right hand!

"Drop it!" I said. "Drop the gun!"

Hutchins face turned sly. His cold eyes seemed to glow. "No," he said. "I don't believe I will." Suddenly, he tensed, brought his arm down, and pointed the revolver at me!

The .44 bucked in my hand. I saw the slug strike Hutchins in the chest. He staggered, recovered, brought his gun to bear on me again. I shot him a second time, saw my bullet knock him off his feet and send him spinning. Ed Hutchins sprawled in the tall grass, and the meadow was still once again.

Archie had come around from behind the cabin. He ran to where LeBreche had fallen and bent over him.

I knelt at Hutchins's side and took Buck's revolver from his hand. His eyes flickered and opened. "Better this way," he rasped. He closed his eyes again.

Something in his voice made me check Buck's revolver. I flipped the loading gate open and turned the cylinder—all six cartridge cases bore the mark of the firing pin on the primers—the gun had been empty!

"Damn you!" I said. "You knew you'd fired your last shot—you came at me with an unloaded gun!"

His eyes fluttered, opened again. "Tried to kill me a rabbit yesterday. Only had two bullets left afterward. Leo got one. Missed you with the other."

"Why didn't you give up? Why did you make me shoot you?"

"My—choice, lawdog. Ain't—goin' back—to that—damn prison."

Hutchins fell back and lay still. This time he didn't close his eyes. I did it for him.

I turned to LeBreche. He sat in the grass, his hands grasping his belly, leaning back against Archie. He had lost his hat, and his eyes were wild. He bared his teeth and shook his head.

"Gut-shot, by god!" he grunted. "Hurts—like hell."

He pulled his shirt up to reveal a bullet wound just above his left hip. There was little bleeding, and I saw no sign of a punctured intestine. "We need to get you to Doc Westby fast. Can you ride?"

"I sure as hell ain't going to walk," he said.

It took maybe thirty minutes to locate and saddle the bay, pack Ed's body, and head out for Medicine Lodge. We picked up the packhorses at the spruce grove, and Archie led the way down the mountain. White-knuckled and hurting, but determined to make it to Doc Westby's, LeBreche clung to his saddle horn. We were six horses, a deputy marshal, an Indian, a wounded cook, and a corpse. We made quite a procession.

We rode into Medicine Lodge just at sundown, and for a mercy Doc Westby was at home. He examined LeBreche and pronounced him lucky.

"The bullet punctured the peritoneum, but didn't cause serious damage to the intestines, as far as I can tell. I'll clean the area thoroughly, and then take a few stitches and treat him with opium and poultices. Should be good as new in a week or so."

"I'm glad you were here, Doc," I said. "For a while there, I was afraid I'd have two dead men on my hands before we hit town." Briefly, I told him what had happened on the mountain that morning.

"Fortunately, we'll have a bed here for Leo," Doc said. "The—widow—Mrs. Hutchins—is about ready to return to her home."

"Bonnie Jo? She's all right? Does she remember—"

"See for yourself. She's in the sitting room."

Bonnie Jo looked terrible. I found her seated in a rocking chair by the window, watching the sunset. Her face bore the marks of her beating, and her skin was discolored and puffy. There were bruise marks on her throat, and her left arm was suspended in a sling. She wore her hair down about her shoulders, and she looked up, alarmed, at the sound of a strange footfall. I took my hat off as I entered the room, and smiled.

"Hello, Bonnie Jo," I said.

"Merlin!" she said. "How good to see you!"

I pulled up a chair, and sat, facing her. "You've had a bad time," I said, "but you're going to be fine. Doc says you'll be going home soon."

A shadow seemed to pass over her face. I knew she was thinking about the night of the murder. "Ed was like a crazy man," she said. "He broke out of prison with some other men. He came here. He hurt me—"

"Yes," I said. "And he killed Buck." For what seemed a long time, neither of us spoke. Outside, the red and gold sunset had gone to gray. "I have to tell you something," I said. "I tracked Ed down today, in the mountains."

Bonnie Jo's eyes widened. Her lip began to tremble. "He won't hurt you again," I said. "I wanted to take him alive, but—"

How does a man tell a woman he just shot her husband? I wondered. Even if the man was a brute and a murderer? In the end, I guess, he simply tells her.

"Bonnie Jo," I said. "Ed came at me. I shot him, and he died."

She leaned back in the rocker, her eyes sad. She breathed a deep sigh. After a moment she said softly, "Poor Ed. He had such a shabby, unhappy life."

Bonnie Jo turned back to me. She reached out and touched my hand. "He and I were never good for each other, not even in the beginning," she said. "I'm afraid it's partly my fault. Please don't blame yourself—I know you only did what you had to."

I didn't know what to say, so I said nothing. In the silence that followed, I looked at Bonnie Jo and recalled our secret, stolen hours together. Somehow, those times seemed a long while ago. I thought of the killing, and considered the random ways of chance. If Ed Hutchins had come back on a different day, at a different hour, it might well have been me in a cold, lonesome grave instead of Buck DuFresne.

I slid my chair back and stood up. "Well," I said. "I'd better be going, Bonnie Jo. I have a lot to do."

Her eyes caught mine, and held them. "Will I be seeing you again?" she asked.

I looked away. "You never know," I said. "Be well, Bonnie Jo."

"You, too," she said. "Goodbye, my sweet cavalier."

Doc Westby examined Ed Hutchins's body and ruled that he sure was dead, all right. Further, the doctor decreed that Ed had come to be in that condition because of the two .44 caliber slugs I had fired into his chest. City Attorney Tom Burke interviewed Archie, Leo, and me at Doc's house regarding the shooting, after which he declared it justifiable homicide. He also commended me for my action, but I didn't let his words go to my head. It isn't all that hard to win a gun battle when the other man's gun isn't loaded.

I guess it doesn't make any sense to be angry with a dead man, but I found that I was. I couldn't get over the fact that Ed Hutchins had used me to help him end his life. I felt that I had in effect helped him commit suicide. It was not a good feeling.

Burke took depositions from Archie and Leo regarding the night of Buck's murder. Leo confessed to aiding and abetting the fugitive, and to falsely testifying against Jeff. Archie told Burke he had watched Jeff enter Bonnie Jo's house, but that the marshal had not been armed with a shotgun at that time. He told of seeing Ed run from the house, carrying Buck's gun and belt, mount a horse, and ride away.

Burke wanted to make sure Archie realized the gravity of making a sworn statement in a murder case. "Archie Young Bull," he asked, "Are you absolutely certain your testimony in this matter is the truth, the whole truth, and nothing but the truth?"

"My words are true," Archie replied. "I am not a white man."

It was nearly ten o'clock that night when I walked into the express office. Behind the counter, Ivan Friendly smiled when he saw me and turned up the lamp.

"Evenin', Merlin," he said. "I thought I'd just wait for you this time—save you the trouble of wakin' me up."

"You were expecting me?"

Ivan nodded. "I reckon everybody in town has heard about you bringin' Ed Hutchins and Leo LeBreche in. I figured you might want to send a telegram."

"You figured right. To U.S. Marshal Chance Ridgeway, at his office in Helena."

Ivan opened the telegraph key and waited. "Send this," I said. "Have proof Jeff Brown innocent. Bringing depositions. Expect arrival Miles City Monday morning."

Ivan tapped out the message and stopped, waiting. Moments later, the key clattered briefly and went silent. "The Helena agent acknowledges receipt," Ivan said. "You want to wait for an answer?"

"No," I said. "Ridgeway may not even be in Helena. Send that same wire to Miles City. I figure he'll get the message, one place or the other."

Moments later, the second wire had been sent. As before, Ivan waited until the response came, then closed his key.

Suddenly, I felt dog-tired and bone-weary. Getting the telegrams sent off to Ridgeway seemed to have taken the last of my energy. I paid Ivan, and turned to go.

"Much obliged," I said. "Reckon I'll get me some sleep, and let you do the same. It's been a long day."

"A long day, but a good one," Ivan said. "Good night, Merlin."

Dawn was still half an hour away when I saddled Rutherford and packed my bedroll on the bay at the livery barn. I paid my bill, and said goodbye to Arnie Moss.

"You run a fine horse hotel," I told him. "Rutherford says he's going to tell all his friends."

"I appreciate that," Arnie said. "He can come back any time. You, too."

I swung into the saddle and rode north on the road that would lead me to Miles City. Five minutes later, I turned my horses off the track and up the Wolf Mountain foothills until I reached a vantage point. Looking back on the sleeping town, I opened the gates of memory and let the past come in.

Below, in the half-light of morning, I could see the livery barn I'd just left where the body of Goes to the Water had lain the day his killer brought it in. A block west, on the corner, stood Ed's Barbershop and Bonnie Jo's house. Her small cottage had been a place of passion and pleasure, and later, of violence and death.

Up the street, beyond the bank, stood the office and jail where I'd first met Jeff Brown and come to call him friend. Off to the right, its false front just beginning to catch the sun's first rays, was Kyle Haddon's Legal Tender, where men drank, gambled, and fought, and where for one Wednesday in June a saloon had become a courtroom.

And there, at the town's north end, stood Doc Westby's house, where the hurting had found help and healing for body and soul. The buildings of Medicine Lodge and the mountains beyond were places in my mind, but it was the people I remembered.

Fall was in the air that Sunday morning. I set my horses out on the road, noticing as I traveled the signs of autumn's coming. Along the river, fog lay tangled in the bottoms like cotton wool, and bright vapor hovered above the water. Already, the trees that lined the river's banks had begun to change color. Deer appeared in the shadows beneath the bluffs, and sunlight began to burn away the mist.

Rutherford took to the road in his quick-footed trot, heading into the day with his customary eagerness. I gave him his head and turned my thoughts inward, back to the showdown in the mountains, and the killing of Ed Hutchins.

I had killed Ed in self-defense, and to enforce the law. Ed had shot Leo LeBreche and had tried to kill me. By all I knew I was justified in using deadly force to stop him. I could not have known his gun was empty, or that he was deliberately using me to help him end his life. No man could blame me for what I had done. Most would praise me. Still, somehow, that didn't help.

Jeff had told me a lawman's gun was not his own. "It belongs to the people we're paid to protect," he had said. "It belongs to the law." I knew he was right. I also knew I would never forget that day on the mountain. Ed Hutchins would live on in my memory if nowhere else.

I passed the agency at midmorning, and continued on down the valley. Somewhere among the tents and buildings, I knew Major Weede would be managing his kingdom and reigning over his subjects. For the sake of the Crow people I hoped he would be a wise and just ruler, but I have to admit I had my doubts.

By sundown, I had crossed the Bighorn River and had moved on to Junction City. As twilight fell, I made camp on a grassy slope above the railroad tracks. I ate a supper of cold beef and biscuits I'd brought from the City Café, hobbled my horses, and crawled into my bedroll.

I remember looking up at the stars for a time. I worried some that a guilty conscience regarding the late Ed Hutchins might keep me awake, but it turned out I was more depraved than I thought. Before I could work up a proper attack of remorse, I fell into a deep and dreamless sleep.

When the train came through the next morning, I was waiting with my horses at the siding. The engine squealed to a stop, belching clouds of smoke and blasts of steam, and my horse Rutherford laid his ears back and showed the whites of his eyes. As luck would have it, the same flagman I'd met on my first trip to Junction was working the run. He seemed as glad to see me as if I owed him money.

I showed him my papers. I said I needed to load my horses and take the train to Miles City. Rutherford did a little dance and made it clear he wanted nothing whatever to do with the Northern Pacific, but we ignored him. With the help of a brakeman and a section hand from the caboose, the railroad boys let down a ramp and we loaded the horses. Twenty minutes later, we were on our way to Miles.

Marshal Ridgeway met me at the Miles City depot. Ten minutes after the train rolled in, I had unloaded my horses and arranged for their care. Ridgeway had rented a horse and buggy, and as we drove across town to the courthouse I filled him in on the recent events at Medicine Lodge.

Judge Benjamin Blackwood had been assigned the DuFresne murder case. We met with the judge in his office, and he seemed happy to see me again.

"Deputy Fanshaw!" he said. "Come in!"

He turned to Ridgeway. "Fanshaw was my bailiff at the DuFresne trial in Medicine Lodge. Buck DuFresne was the defendant in that trial. Now he's the murder victim. Life does have its ups and downs."

Judge Blackwood sat down behind his desk and invited us to sit across from him. "I understand you have some depositions to show me," he said.

"I sure do," I said, and handed them over.

To make a long story short, the judge read the depositions from Archie and Leo, heard my testimony, and dismissed all charges against Jeff Brown.

"I thought the charges were damned nonsense from the start," the judge said. "Circumstantial evidence, and not even much of that."

He stood up. "I like Marshal Brown," he said. "Damned glad we don't have to hang him."

"I'll tell you what," he continued. "Let's go down to the jail and I'll let you give Jeff the good news. Then we'll go over to the Cottage Saloon and I'll buy you gents a drink. Never touch the stuff myself, but I enjoy buying it for others."

I smiled. "I remember, from this summer. You told me you really are sober as a judge."

"Guilty as charged. Hope you won't hold it against me."

At the county jail, we found Deputy Sheriff Bodie Winters seated in a chair at the door that led to the cells. As Judge Blackwood, Marshal Ridgeway, and me walked toward him, he looked up in surprise. "Fanshaw!" he said. "What the hell—?"

"Give Deputy Fanshaw the key to the cells, Bodie," the judge said. "I've told him he can release Jeff Brown."

Winters's jaw dropped. He stared at the judge in disbelief. He looked like a man on the verge of apoplexy. "Uh—the key to the cells? You—you're releasin' Jeff Brown?"

Judge Blackwood beamed. "Indeed, Bodie. Give Fanshaw the key, please."

Winters stared. His face turned red. He almost seemed to vibrate. Confusion stamped his features, but he obeyed the judge. He reached up to the peg beside the door, took down the key, and handed it to me.

"He—he's in the third cell on the left," he said.

"Much obliged," I said, and went inside.

As I entered the dimly lit corridor, I saw that Jeff was lying on a narrow cot inside his cell. He sat up as I drew near his door, peering at me through the gloom.

"Merlin? Is that you? What—?"

I put on my most stern expression. "Jefferson Brown," I said, "I'm here to evict you from these accommodations. You are charged with impersonating a murderer, and of occupying this handsome prison cell under false pretenses. By order of Judge Blackwood, you are to vacate the premises immediately."

Jeff's smile lit up the cellblock. His voice was unsteady when he spoke. "Then I expect I'd better go," he said. "I surely wouldn't want to disobey the judge."

Later, over drinks at the Cottage Saloon, I told Jeff how Leo LeBreche had recanted his false testimony. I told him how Leo had led Archie and me to Ed Hutchins's hideout, and of the way Hutchins had used me, and my gun, to end his life. Afterward, out in front of the saloon, we said our goodbyes with a handshake. There was plenty we might have said to each other, but we didn't. With Jeff and me, there was no need.

Marshal Ridgeway was so pleased with the way I'd performed my duties it was all he could do to keep from telling me so. He gave me two months back pay and sent me to Dry Creek to wait for my next assignment. He did say he was glad I hadn't been killed in the shootout at the cabin. It would have been an inconvenience to him, he said, to have to train another deputy.

At the depot, the station agent arranged to have my horses loaded on a special car and sold me a ticket on the train to Silver City. When I asked him if the train was on time, he said no, actually it was late. "But it's not as late as it was yesterday," he added, "so it's almost like it's early."

When the "early" late train pulled in, I climbed the iron steps of a parlor car and found myself a seat. The conductor punched my ticket, put the stub in the slot beside the window, and sauntered off to the next car. The hogger blew the whistle, the cars tightened up with a jolt and a rattle, and the westbound rocked away, bound for Billings and Silver City. I watched the buildings and streets of Miles slip past my window, leaned back, and closed my eyes. It had been quite a summer.

It was full dark by the time the train reached Silver City. I put my horses up at the Blue Dog Livery, treated myself to supper at an uptown café, and rolled out my bed in a vacant stall at the barn. Come morning, I saddled Rutherford, packed my bedroll on the bay, and set out for Dry Creek. It felt good to be heading back to my home range, but somehow not as good as I'd expected.

As I drew near to Dry Creek, my thoughts turned more and more to Pandora. I longed to see her, to be with her again. I recalled how fine she was, with her dark, deep eyes and jet-black hair. I remembered her smile, and the way she always seemed to understand me, even when I didn't myself. Would she be pleased to see me, I wondered, or had her feelings cooled during our time apart?

Then, like a cloud blocking out the sunlight, memories of Bonnie Jo Hutchins and our time together that summer crossed my mind. I tried to justify myself, to insist that those hours on the sly had nothing to do with Pandora and me, but I knew better. There are choices a man makes that change things forever. I had made such a choice.

Pandora would understand, I told myself. I would confess all, and she would forgive me. Yes, I thought, she might forgive me, but she would never forget. In the end, I realized that telling her was the coward's way. Relieving my guilt by confessing to Pandora would cause her pain, and I could not bear to hurt her.

When I reined up at the boarding house in Dry Creek and stepped down off Rutherford in the yard, Pandora was watching from the front window as if she was waiting for me. A moment later, she flew out the door and down the steps. Her smile was a bright flash as she rushed into my arms, and I felt her tears warm upon my cheek.

"I missed you so much," she said. "How are you?"

"Just about perfect," I said, but I wasn't.

EPILOGUE

▼

Everyone connected with the DuFresne case seemed happy about Judge Black-wood's decision to release Jeff Brown except Deputy Sheriff Bodie Winters, who took it personal. The judge's dismissal ruined the deputy's run for county sheriff before it even began. Bodie seemed downright annoyed at Jeff for not being guilty. As far as I know, Jeff never did apologize to Bodie for being innocent.

The Medicine Lodge Town Council had the good sense to rehire Jeff as marshal and even offered him a pay increase. Jeff accepted the offer, but asked the town fathers to fund a full-time deputy, as well. When they agreed, Jeff hired Archie Young Bull for the job, and Medicine Lodge became the only town in the territory with a "Black White Man" as marshal and a "Red Man" as deputy.

Last I heard, law enforcement in the town was working slicker than calf slob-bers. Even Archie's renegade friends were careful to walk the straight and narrow. They didn't want to get Archie in trouble, nor cause him to lose his job.

Pistol Wilson gave up his temporary job as acting marshal of Medicine Lodge because of health reasons. Pistol was practicing his fast draw out behind the jail one afternoon when he got previous on the trigger and put a .45 slug through the meaty part of his thigh. Last time I talked to Jeff, he told me Pistol had given up his gunfighter ambitions and no longer carried a revolver.

Leo LeBreche recovered from his belly wound and quit his job with the DuFresne Land and Cattle Company. Judge Blackwell issued a bench warrant for Leo and gave him a strong lecture concerning false testimony before dropping the charges against him. Last I heard, Leo had left the Crow Reservation and had hired on as cook with a cow outfit over on the Yellowstone.

Bonnie Jo stayed on in Medicine Lodge. It turned out her late husband had owned a substantial paid-up insurance policy on his life, and Bonnie Jo had been his sole beneficiary. According to a story by Clifford Bidwell in *The Medicine Lodge Star,* she opened the shop again and hired a good-looking young man to help her with the barbering. And, I suppose, with other things.

0-595-33666-3

Printed in the United States
26303LVS00003B/1-39